Eve gave her temporary landlord a smile.

"Let me thank you again, Mr. Dawson, for your generosity toward Leo and myself. I assure you we will try to impose on you as little as possible during our stay."

He made a dismissive gesture. "As I said, there's lots of room in the house, and I like company, so I'm sure that won't be a problem." He spread his hands. "And please, drop the Mr. Dawson nonsense and just call me Chance."

Eve felt the warmth rising in her cheeks. "That would be highly improper. I barely know you."

"Nothing improper about it. I assure you, folks around here are pretty informal about such things."

She struggled with her notions of propriety versus her desire to be polite. She didn't want to risk insulting him. "I don't know—"

He cut off her protest, adding a cajoling note to his voice. "Oh, come now. I would consider it a favor."

This seemed genuinely important to him. "Very well." She nodded.

The touch of triumph in his grin should have irritated her, but for some reason it didn't.

Books by Winnie Griggs

Love Inspired Historical

The Hand-Me-Down Family
The Christmas Journey
The Proper Wife
Second Chance Family
A Baby Between Them
*Handpicked Husband
*The Bride Next Door
*A Family for Christmas

Love Inspired

The Heart's Song

*Texas Grooms

WINNIE GRIGGS

is a city girl born and raised in southeast Louisiana's Cajun Country, who grew up to marry a country boy from the hills of northwest Louisiana. Though her Prince Charming (who often wears the guise of a cattle rancher) is more comfortable riding a tractor than a white steed, the two of them have been living their own happily-ever-after for thirty-plus years. During that time they raised four proud-to-call-them-mine children and a too-numerous-to-count assortment of dogs, cats, fish, hamsters, turtles and 4-H sheep.

Winnie retired from her "day job" and now, in addition to her reading and writing, happily spends her time doing the things she loves best—spending time with her family, cooking and exploring flea markets.

Readers can contact Winnie at P.O. Box 14, Plain Dealing, LA 71064, or email her at winnie@winniegriggs.com.

A Family for Christmas

WINNIE GRIGGS

HARLEQUIN® LOVE INSPIRED® HISTORICAL

Recycling programs
for this product may
not exist in your area.

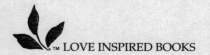 LOVE INSPIRED BOOKS

ISBN-13: 978-0-373-82983-5

A FAMILY FOR CHRISTMAS

Copyright © 2013 by Winnie Griggs

All rights reserved. Except for use in any review, the reproduction
or utilization of this work in whole or in part in any form by any
electronic, mechanical or other means, now known or hereafter
invented, including xerography, photocopying and recording, or in
any information storage or retrieval system, is forbidden without
the written permission of the editorial office, Love Inspired Books,
233 Broadway, New York, NY 10279 U.S.A.

This is a work of fiction. Names, characters, places and incidents are
either the product of the author's imagination or are used fictitiously, and
any resemblance to actual persons, living or dead, business establishments,
events or locales is entirely coincidental.

This edition published by arrangement with Love Inspired Books.

® and TM are trademarks of Love Inspired Books, used under license.
Trademarks indicated with ® are registered in the United States Patent
and Trademark Office, the Canadian Trade Marks Office and in other
countries.

www.LoveInspiredBooks.com

Printed in U.S.A.

Be hospitable to one another without grumbling. As each one has received a gift, minister it to one another, as good stewards of the manifold grace of God.
—*1 Peter* 4:9–10

For my wonderful agent Michelle
and talented, long-suffering editor Melissa
for their patience, encouragement and
understanding toward me throughout the
development and construction phases of this book.

Chapter One

Turnabout, Texas, November 1895

"Stop! You can't do this."

Eve's protests fell on deaf ears as the conductor continued to forcibly escort her young friend off the train without so much as a backward glance. She trotted to keep up with the long-legged official as he moved toward the exit, his fist firmly clutching Leo's collar.

"Please be careful!" she called out as she saw Leo stumble. "He's just a boy. Don't hurt him."

But the conductor still didn't slow down. Did the man have no feelings?

As soon as they were on the platform, Eve scooted around to face him, determined to halt his progress and make him listen to her.

"Mr. McIvers, you can't mean to just toss him from the train and leave him here." She tried to infuse her voice with as much authority and confidence as possible but was afraid there was a touch of pleading there, as well. How had she not realized before now that Leo was a stowaway?

She risked a glance Leo's way. The trapped, desperate look that had crossed the boy's face when the conductor pounced on him a moment ago was still there. It was enough to break her heart—no child should look so haunted.

"And what do you suggest I do with him?" The conductor, a beanpole of a man with bushy sideburns and an officious manner, looked down his nose at her as if she were no older than the ten-year-old in his grip.

She was used to such treatment. Even though she was a grown woman of twenty, with her slight build and standing barely five feet two inches with her hair up, folks often dismissed her as a child. But Eve drew herself up to her full height and tried to match his stern expression. "I'm certain there's been some kind of misunderstanding. If you'll just allow Leo to explain—"

Leo tried to shake himself free of the conductor's grasp, but the man tightened his hold. "The time to explain has come and gone," the man said sternly. "He's a stowaway, pure and simple. And he rides no farther on my train."

This situation was partly her fault. She should have guessed something was amiss when she first spotted the boy under the seat in front of her. She should have taken the time to figure out how to help him before it came to this. But she'd been so wrapped up in her own worries, so plagued by concerns of what the new life she was heading toward might be like, that she'd missed the signs. So instead, she'd merely assumed he was retrieving something that had fallen.

When she'd invited him to sit next to her and share her apple, it had been as much to distract herself from her own forebodings as to be kind to her new acquaintance. He'd fallen asleep with his head leaning against her and her heart had softened further toward him. But she'd become concerned about him being separated from his party and had quietly asked the conductor to let them know where the boy was. That was when the man had realized he had a stowaway on board.

Pulling her thoughts back to the present, Eve spread her hands, trying once more to appeal to the strict conductor's sympathies. "He's only a boy. What will become of him if you leave him here?"

But the man refused to bend. "Miss Pickering, I'm sure your concern does you credit, but don't let his age fool you. I've met his kind before and they'll smile innocently to your face while they pick your pocket. I imagine a scalawag like him will get on fine, or end up in jail one day."

Eve planted her fists on her hips. "You can't treat a child like a stray dog and dump him at your first opportunity."

She glanced around, looking for help of some sort, and her gaze snagged on that of a gentleman standing across the platform. Her eyes widened as she realized he was watching her. There was a note of curiosity and sympathy in his smoky blue eyes. And something else, something warm and compelling that made it impossible for her to look away, that made her certain she could trust him with her problems.

An older couple dressed for travel crossed between them, breaking the connection, and Eve abruptly came to her senses. She lifted her chin and turned back to Mr. McIvers. What in the world was she thinking? Such fanciful notions led to nothing but trouble. And asking a strange gentleman for assistance was not something a proper young lady did unless the circumstances were indeed dire.

Still feeling the impact of those eyes, she did her best to push that aside and deal with the more important issue at hand. "Where exactly are we?"

"Turnabout, Texas." The conductor didn't seem the least bit cowed by her earlier chastisements. "And it's a far piece from Tyler, which is where you were headed if I recollect rightly." He dug out his pocket watch and flipped it open. "I suggest you climb right back on the train unless you want to be left behind."

If he only knew how little desire she had to continue on to Tyler. It was for her a place of banishment, not a place for a pleasant visit. But that was neither here nor there. "You can't—"

The conductor didn't allow her to finish. "I *can,* and I *will.* Like I said, *nobody* rides for free on my train. He's lucky I waited for us to pull into the station and didn't throw him off as soon as I discovered him." He stared pointedly at her. "And if I were you, I'd check my belongings to make certain he hasn't pinched anything."

"I'd never take anything from her." The indignant declaration was the first thing Leo had said in his own defense since the conductor had grabbed him a few minutes earlier.

She gave the boy a reassuring smile. "I know you wouldn't, Leo."

The conductor shook his head in disgust. "I don't have any more time to waste on this." He finally released his hold, causing Leo to stumble a bit at the suddenness of it.

Then Mr. McIvers gave the bottom of his vest a sharp tug as he shot Leo a narrow-eyed look of contempt. "If I catch you stowing away on one of my trains again, I'll march you straight to the sheriff's office, even if I have to delay our departure to do it."

He glanced Eve's way and touched the bill of his cap in a perfunctory gesture. "We'll be leaving shortly. You'd be well advised to get back on board before this one sweet-talks you into doing something foolish." With that he turned and marched into the depot office without a backward glance.

She took the opportunity to look again at the blue-eyed stranger. But he was no longer there. Nor did a quick look around show him to be anywhere on the platform. So much for his being her white knight. She shook off that fanciful thought. They'd shared only a brief glance after all. Still, it was strange how she felt as though she had lost a friend.

She turned back to Leo, who was still glowering at the retreating form of his erstwhile captor. Then he glanced her way and his expression softened. "I appreciate you taking up for me, miss. You've been real nice." He puffed his chest out. "But don't you worry none. I'll get on fine. This town is as good a place as any for me to step off in."

Eve heard both the bravado and the underlying uncertainty in his voice. What was his story? Where were his parents? Was someone searching for him, worrying about him?

And what in the world was she going to do to fix this? She couldn't manage her own problems. Besides, even if her limited funds would cover his train fare, he didn't seem to have a particular destination in mind. Which meant he was running *from* something, not *to* something. The question was did he have good reason to do so?

She couldn't walk away until she learned more about his situation or found someone who could help him better than she could—and was willing to do so. Abandoning a child in need was the worst kind of callous betrayal.

Unfortunately, she didn't know a soul in this place. On the heel of that thought, her mind turned again to the man she'd exchanged glances with earlier. Had the sympathy in his eyes been real? *Would* he have helped if she hadn't turned away?

Well, no point dwelling on that now. Eve placed a hand on Leo's shoulder, mentally wincing at the thinness of it. "That's a very brave thing to say, Leo, but don't you worry, we'll figure something out."

She only hoped she could keep that promise. Thank the Good Lord she wouldn't have to do it on her own.

Heavenly Father, You must have let my and Leo's paths cross so I could help him. I'm not sure what good I'll be to him, but I won't abandon him and I know You won't abandon either of us. Just please, show me what it is I should do. I've never had anyone depending on me this way before and I couldn't bear it if I failed him.

One thing was for certain, neither she nor Leo would be on that train when it left the station today. Which meant she'd better retrieve her bag before it went on to Tyler without her.

She gave Leo an encouraging smile. "Give me a minute to collect my things, then you and I can decide what to do next. Okay?"

"You mean you're staying?"

If she hadn't already decided to stay, the flare of hope in his eyes would have cinched the deal. "Of course I'm staying. I told you we'd work things out, didn't I?" At his nod, she smiled. "Well, we can hardly do that if I'm on the train and you're still here."

Instructing Leo one last time to wait right where he was, she hurried back on board and made her way to her seat.

Everything had happened so quickly she'd barely had time to think of the ramifications of her actions, something her grandmother would say was typical of her. Her impulse to act first and think later was what had caused her current disgrace. Which had ultimately resulted in her being banished to Tyler.

And speaking of Tyler, what would her grandmother's friend, Mrs. O'Connell, think when Eve didn't get off the train at her appointed stop today as planned? Would she change her mind about taking Eve on as an apprentice?

And if so, would that actually be such a terrible thing?

After all, working in the back room of a millinery shop was not something she had ever aspired to.

Eve immediately took herself to task for that disrespectful and ungrateful thought. Her grandmother had gone to a lot of trouble to secure this position for her. It might not be what Eve wanted for herself, but she knew she should be thankful for the opportunity to make a fresh start. Of course, it would be easier to feel appreciative if her grandmother hadn't *also* made certain that the story of Eve's past followed her there.

What would it be like to *truly* have a fresh start, to go somewhere where no one knew her past, where no one was constantly watching her, waiting for her to stumble?

Well, at least now she had a short reprieve. No one here had any idea who she was or what her past was like. And what a freeing thought that was. Perhaps she'd even run into her blue-eyed knight again.

She gathered up her bag and shawl and hurried back out onto the platform with lighter steps than when she'd first started on this journey.

Chance Dawson stood inside the depot, leaning casually against the counter. He was here to check on a part he'd ordered for his current project. Hopefully it had arrived on the morning train.

From the looks of things, though, it was going to take Todd a while to sort through the mountain of mail and packages that had just come in. Not that Chance minded the wait. He wasn't in much of a hurry and besides, watching the folks around him was a hobby of his.

And there were plenty of folks to watch in here. Besides Lionel, the stationmaster, and Todd his helper, a number of others were in the depot office, waiting either to board the train or, like him, to check on arriving cargo.

But none was as interesting as the woman he'd seen out on the platform a few moments ago. The way that petite protector had faced down the conductor despite her obvious timidity had been impressive to watch. But when her gaze had locked with his, the overwhelming urge to come to her defense had rocked him. It was probably just as well she'd turned away from him.

Dotty Epps walked in just then, interrupting his thoughts. He and the elderly widow had formed an unlikely friendship this past year. She was one of the very few people who knew his secret and she not only kept it but didn't let it affect how she treated him.

"Not planning on leaving town on that train are you?" he said by way of greeting. "Turnabout just wouldn't be the same without you."

She gave him one of her cheery smiles. "You're not going to get rid of me so easily, Chance Dawson." She lifted the small parcel she was holding. "I'm just posting a package for my grandson. He has a birthday next week."

"Well, that's a relief." He turned serious. "How are things?" The recent loss of her home and most of her possessions to a fire had taken a toll, but it hadn't seemed to diminish her positive outlook on life.

Her smile acquired a wistful tone. "I miss my home, but the boardinghouse is comfortable. There's a whole lot less housework to be done, and more company, as well. My daughter keeps asking me to move to Jefferson to live with her and her family, but this is where my friends are."

"Well, you know if you need anything, you have only to ask."

She patted his hand. "Thank you, but I'm doing fine."

As she moved on to the counter, Chance returned to eavesdropping on the conductor. The man was energetically recounting a rather embellished version of how he'd expertly identified and dealt with the sly stowaway.

His story, which painted the kid as some sort of treacherous thief, differed significantly from what Chance had observed earlier. Of course, at the time he'd been more focused on the determined young woman who was so very staunchly defending the boy than on the conductor and the kid himself.

She had intrigued him, and it wasn't just that she'd taken up for the boy—though he did admire her for that. It was more the contradictions he'd sensed in her.

Her appearance—from her tightly coifed brown hair that not even a sudden gust of November wind could ruffle, to her high-collared, severe dress and stiff posture—proclaimed her to be a very prim and proper young lady, one who was a bit on the mousy side. She'd also seemed quite young. But when the petite defender had defiantly lifted her chin, he'd seen the flash of fire in her expressive brown eyes, a fire that made him think perhaps she wasn't quite so prim and proper after all—and definitely not mousy. The maturity he'd seen there surprised him, as well. She was much more than the child she'd looked at first sight.

Then she'd spotted him watching her. If she'd given him the least indication that she wanted his help with the conductor, he'd have immediately stepped forward. But instead she'd stiffened and very deliberately turned away. It wasn't at all the kind of reaction he was used to getting from the ladies of his acquaintance, especially one who was so obviously in a tight spot. He hadn't been sure what to make of it, so he'd shrugged it off and proceeded inside the depot.

But ever since then he'd had the nagging feeling he might have made the wrong call.

"I left him out there on the platform." The conductor's words to Lionel pulled Chance back to the present. "He's a shifty one. If I were you I'd keep a close eye on things around here until he moves on."

Dotty placed her hand on her heart. "Do you consider this man dangerous then? Should Sheriff Gleason be informed?"

Chance decided it was time to add his two cents. "This blackguard the conductor is describing happens to be a young boy, not a man."

Dotty wrinkled her nose. "Surely you don't mean that child I saw waiting on the platform a moment ago?" She stared at the conductor as if he'd had the bad manners to relate an off-color story. "Why, he can't be more than nine or ten years old and he certainly looked more forlorn than cunning."

Chance nodded. "Nevertheless, that's the accused."

The conductor, whose face had gained a reddish hue, gave them both a haughty look. "Just because he's young doesn't mean he ain't to be watched."

Chance raised a brow. "The young lady who stuck up for him earlier didn't seem to think he was a threat to anyone." In fact, she'd seemed ready to defend him against all comers.

The conductor tugged on his vest. "You know how young ladies are, too tenderhearted for their own good most times, especially when it comes to young'uns."

Tenderhearted? Maybe. But there seemed to be more backbone to the woman than that.

The conductor had apparently tired of the subject. He turned away, flipped open his pocket watch and informed the waiting passengers it was time to board.

Chance's thoughts were still on the stowaway's protectoress. He liked to puzzle out what made people act the way they did—and she offered an intriguing challenge. Too bad the woman wasn't sticking around.

He'd kept an eye on her peripherally through the depot window and had felt a small stab of disappointment when he saw her say goodbye to the boy and head back toward the train. He wasn't sure why, but a part of him had actually expected her to stay with the kid.

He supposed he shouldn't judge her, though—it would be foolhardy for her to strand herself overnight in a strange town, especially since she seemed to be traveling alone. And he had no idea if she was on a strict schedule of some sort—after all, Thanksgiving was just two days away.

Besides, he found it was always good practice to give a pretty girl the benefit of the doubt.

Chance glanced over as the conductor left the building, followed by the few last-minute passengers who hadn't yet boarded.

To his surprise the door had barely closed behind them when it was pushed open again and the woman and her young companion walked in.

Well, well, perhaps he'd have the opportunity to get to know her better after all.

Chapter Two

Eve ushered Leo into the depot and out of the blustery wind, still feeling as out of place as a turtle up a tree. She had no idea how to go about making certain Leo was taken care of. She didn't even know where the two of them would bed down tonight. But she knew she was doing the right thing and, for now, that was enough.

Of course, before she could figure out her next move, she really needed to get more information from Leo about his situation.

"Come on," she said with a nod toward the benches. "Let's sit down and talk."

Leo's expression turned wary, but he nodded.

Before crossing the room, Eve took quick stock of the other folks inside. The stationmaster, his scraggly mustache quivering as he scribbled in a ledger, stood behind the counter. A strapping adolescent was sorting through packages, stacking some against a wall and carrying others to another room.

The other two people present were a man and woman. The woman appeared to be about her grandmother's age, though she'd obviously not lived as harsh a life. Rather than hardness and a guarded demeanor, this woman had a kind face, graced with laugh lines and a soft smile.

But she took all of that in almost subconsciously. It was the gentleman who caught and held her attention. As soon as she realized that he was the same man she'd noticed watching her outside, her senses seemed to heighten in awareness.

There was something about him that both attracted her and put her on guard. With his light brown hair, boyish smile, and those blue eyes, he was handsome. And there seemed to be what she could only describe as a likeableness about him.

But it was coupled with an impish, amused air that gave her pause. All her instincts told her this was the sort of man her grandmother was forever warning her about—a man who dabbled in flirtations and enjoyed partaking in the occasional bit of mischief. The sort of man who'd led to her mother's downfall.

What was most strange about this whole situation was that she was getting all of these strong impressions of the man without ever having exchanged a word with him. Further proof, she supposed, that her grandmother was correct about her getting lost in her own flights of fancy.

"Can I help you with something, miss?"

The stationmaster's question brought Eve's attention back to herself and she reddened slightly as she realized the stranger had seen her staring at him. She quickly turned to the official with a smile. "No, thank you. We just wanted to get away from the wind for a few moments."

He gave a friendly wave toward the benches. "Make yourselves at home."

She nodded and continued on her way, but remained very aware of the blue-eyed stranger behind her.

The conductor's "All aboard" call came in from outside. There was no turning back now—she was well and truly committed to staying here for the time being. And she didn't regret that decision for a moment.

Eve sent up a silent prayer for help in finding just the right words, then took a deep breath. "Now we talk."

Leo perched on the very edge of the bench with his hands tightly gripping the seat on either side of him, as if ready to run any moment. "What about?"

Trying to put him more at ease, she infused as much warmth and encouragement in her smile as she could summon. "Why don't you start at the beginning and tell me how you came to be on that train?"

"I snuck on board when the train stopped at Texarkana." His tone indicated he wasn't going to volunteer any more information than he had to.

So, he really *was* a stowaway. She'd had some vague notion that he might have been abandoned by his guardian once he boarded. She didn't know whether to be relieved or worried that this was not the case, that he'd taken this step all on his own. But at least now she had a general idea of where he'd come from. "Why did you do such a thing? Don't you think your parents will be worried about you?"

His shoulders slumped. "My parents are dead. They passed on near about two years ago I think." His tone was flat, matter-of-fact. "No one else is gonna care one speck about what happens to me."

The idea that he could feel so very alone made her want to cry. She lightly touched his hand. "I'm so sorry." But surely he hadn't been on his own for two years. "Who's been looking out for you since then?"

He shifted evasively. "After my folks passed on, one of the neighbors took me in."

So he *did* have someone. That was a relief. Now, if she could just find out who that was and why he'd run away.

"Pardon me."

Eve gave a little start and jerked around to find the gentleman and lady she'd noticed earlier had approached. Both wore friendly smiles.

Her heartbeat slowed and she forced herself to return those smiles even though she was anxious to get back to her conversation with Leo. "Can I do something for you?"

"Actually, that was my question." The handsome stranger gave her a self-effacing smile. "I couldn't help but notice your little altercation with the conductor earlier. I get the impression Turnabout wasn't really your planned destination." He motioned to indicate he was including the woman standing beside him. "We just wanted to make certain you two were okay before we left the building."

So he *had* been watching her earlier. "That's very kind of you, Mr...."

"Dawson." He gave a short bow. "Chance Dawson, at your service. And this is Mrs. Epps."

"Well, Mr. Dawson, Mrs. Epps, I thank you kindly for your concern but we're fine." Truth to tell, she wasn't sure exactly what kind of help to ask for at this point. And she wouldn't know until she finished her conversation with Leo.

"No need to be bashful," Mrs. Epps said. "And please, call me Dotty. You'll find Turnabout is a friendly place where folks look out for each other."

Eve relaxed slightly and returned the woman's smile. "I'm sure this is a lovely town."

"Excuse me if this is a bit forward," Mr. Dawson said, "but do you need assistance finding accommodations for your time here? I can show you where the hotel is if you like."

Just then, rumbling sounds came from the vicinity of Leo's stomach. Eve mentally kicked herself for her thoughtlessness. If Leo was a runaway it had probably been quite some time since he'd had a decent meal. She should have thought of feeding him right away.

Before she could say anything, Mr. Dawson chimed in with a grin. "Sounds like someone's hungry. Why don't you let us at least show you where you can get a bite to eat?"

Deciding that, with Mrs. Epps present, there could be no impropriety in accepting his assistance, Eve nodded. "Thank you. That would be most welcome."

Mr. Dawson offered a hand to help her rise. "I don't think I caught your names."

His hand was warm and supportive. And just a little too comfortable.

She reluctantly released it as soon as she was on her feet. "I'm Eve Pickering, and my friend here is Leo."

He executed a slight bow. "Pleased to meet you and welcome to Turnabout." He reached for her carpet bag. "Allow me."

She wasn't certain how she felt about letting someone else take her bag, especially since it contained the sum total of all her earthly possessions.

But before she could form a response, he extended an arm toward the exit. "Very well then. If you're ready, I'll show you to Daisy's Restaurant. Best food in town."

Eve nodded and placed a hand on Leo's back as she headed for the exit. They had just reached the door when the stationmaster hailed Mr. Dawson.

"Looks like you have a letter," he said, holding up an envelope.

Mr. Dawson retrieved the letter and Eve thought she saw his expression change from mild curiosity to something stronger as he studied the envelope. But he tucked it into his pocket without bothering to open it and by the time he rejoined them at the door his expression had resumed its casual neighborliness. A curious look passed between him and Dotty, but then it was gone and he was holding the door open for them.

She wondered at his restraint. She'd never received a letter herself, but she imagined if she *had* that she would tear it open immediately and read the contents.

But perhaps this was an everyday occurrence for him.

As they stepped out onto the platform, Mr. Dawson turned to her. "So where have you traveled from?"

"A small town in Arkansas called Iron Bluff." Would she ever see that place again?

"And are you traveling in order to spend Thanksgiving with friends?" Mrs. Epps asked with a smile.

That was so far from the truth as to be laughable.

Mrs. Epps must have noticed something in her expression because she grimaced. "Please forgive me for prying. You don't have to answer. It's just the idle curiosity of an old woman."

"No need to apologize," she reassured the woman. "It's just that the truth is so mundane. I'm going to Tyler to secure employment. The fact that Thanksgiving is in two days is merely coincidence."

"Employment?" Mr. Dawson eyed her speculatively.

This was beginning to feel like an interrogation, but she didn't want to be rude to these strangers who were being kind. "Yes. I'm going to apprentice with a milliner there." She tried to infuse some positive emotion in her tone. "I've never actually met Mrs. O'Connell, but I understand she is very well respected for her craft."

Mrs. Epps's expression turned to dismay. "You can't mean to say you don't know anyone there. Oh, no, that won't do. My dear, Thanksgiving is meant to be spent with family and friends."

Eve wasn't quite certain how to respond. The thought that her new acquaintances might be feeling pity for her was mortifying.

Then Mrs. Epps surprised her by patting her arm. "I'm sorry. I'm sure you have compelling reasons. But if you decide to stay here for another few days, which I hope you will, you can participate in our Thanksgiving Festival. The whole town gets together for it and I assure you, you and Leo will be made quite welcome." She glanced over to Mr. Dawson. "Don't you agree, Chance?"

"I would never disagree with anything you said," Mr. Dawson replied gallantly. Then he grinned at Eve. "The Thanksgiving Festival is quite an event. Why, an opportunity to sample Dotty's orange spice carrots alone would make it worth extending your stay."

For a moment Eve was sorely tempted. After all, once she arrived in Tyler her chance to do as she pleased would be severely curtailed. But then reason reasserted itself. "I thank you both for the kind invitation, but my plans are a bit uncertain at the moment."

"Of course." Mrs. Epps smiled in understanding. "If your plans change, though, just keep in mind that we would be happy to include you in our gathering."

As they reached a street leading away from the tracks, Mrs. Epps paused. "I'm afraid this is where I must leave you. It was very nice making your acquaintance, Eve, and you, too, Leo. I hope to see you again before you leave town."

That brought Eve up short. "Aren't you going to join us for lunch?" Going to lunch with the two of them was one thing. Going to lunch alone with a strange man was something else altogether.

"I'm afraid not." She smiled. "Miss Daniels is away visiting her son and I promised to take her place in the weekly bridge game over at the boardinghouse."

Mr. Dawson's expression drooped melodramatically. "I suppose their good fortune in having your company is our loss."

The woman flapped her hand at him with a chiding expression. "Chance Dawson, get on with you now. You need to turn that sweet talk of yours where it'll do you more good—in other words on someone your own age instead of a matron like me."

"Dotty, how can you say such a thing? You *know* you're the light of my life."

Rolling her eyes, she turned to Eve. "Don't pay any mind to his foolishness, he's quite harmless really." Then she eyed Mr. Dawson. "And *you,* make sure you behave yourself."

Now, what did that mean?

But Mr. Dawson was holding his hands up, palms forward, a wounded expression on his face. "Dotty, my dear, you said it yourself, I'm harmless."

Mrs. Epps shook her head but there was a smile in her eyes. Then she gave them a wave. "Enjoy your lunch. And tell Daisy hello for me." With a friendly nod, she stepped off the sidewalk to cross the street.

Eve watched her go, feeling as if she'd lost a much-needed buffer. But she certainly couldn't back out now—that would be not only rude but extremely awkward. So she gave Mr. Dawson a smile and indicated she was ready to proceed.

They turned at the next corner and Mr. Dawson pointed out businesses and landmarks along the way. Eve made appropriate responses, but her thoughts were on her current situation. She needed to continue her discussion with Leo as soon as possible so she could decide what to do next.

Why had he run away? And what could someone as inept as she was do to help him?

A number of other folks on the sidewalk were going about their own business and quite a few of them greeted Mr. Dawson as they passed. Was it her imagination or were the smiles he received from the ladies, young and old alike, especially warm?

They'd gone about two blocks when a man hailed Chance and the three of them paused.

"Hi, Sheriff," Chance said, "what can I do for you?"

Eve sensed Leo stiffen beside her. Was he worried that the sheriff would find out he'd stowed away? She instinctively placed a protective hand on his shoulder.

"Are you by any chance coming from the train station?" the lawman asked Chance.

Though the man's smile was friendly enough and there was nothing threatening in his demeanor, something about the way he eyed her and Leo made Eve uncomfortable.

"Sure did." Mr. Dawson, apparently sharing none of her something's-wrong-here feeling, maintained an easy smile.

"I hear there was a bit of trouble over there. Something about a stowaway?"

Eve tried to draw Leo closer.

"That's right," Mr. Dawson answered, his face still relaxed. "But it's all over now and nothing to get you involved in."

Rather than commenting on that, the sheriff turned to her and Leo. "Care to introduce me to your friends, here?"

"Of course." Mr. Dawson's smile faded as he finally seemed to sense something was wrong. "Sheriff Gleason, this is Miss Eve Pickering and Leo. They just arrived on the morning train."

Eve nodded a greeting, not trusting herself to speak. Did

the lawman already know Leo was the stowaway? Surely he wouldn't arrest a little boy.

The sheriff tipped his hat Eve's direction. "Good day to you, ma'am." Then he turned to her companion. "Leo, is it? That wouldn't be short for Leonard Haskins would it?"

Not certain what was going on, Eve glanced down at Leo and was shocked to see most of the color had drained from his face. A heartbeat later Leo bolted, running down a side street like a cat with a hound on its tail. But Mr. Dawson was faster. Almost before Eve could react, the man had overtaken Leo and pulled him up short.

Mr. Dawson marched him back, his smoky blue eyes meeting hers sympathetically, almost apologetically.

But she couldn't deal with that right now. Instead she focused on Leo. "What's wrong? Why did you run?"

The boy didn't say anything, didn't even raise his head.

Still trying to make sense of what was going on, Eve turned to the sheriff. "Why are you looking for Leo?"

Sheriff Gleason gave her a steady look. "I think we'd all better head over to my office so we can straighten this out."

Chance kept a firm hold on Leo's arm as the four of them marched to Sheriff Gleason's office in silence. This was obviously about more than just the kid being a stowaway. Was it merely a matter of his parents, or whoever was responsible for him, having tracked him down? Or was the boy in more serious trouble?

And just how much deeper did he want to get personally involved in this? Being intrigued by Miss Pickering was one thing, but getting embroiled in the problems of a runaway kid he knew nothing about was something else altogether.

Besides, that letter he'd received earlier was starting to burn a hole in his pocket. He could feel the weight of it there, demanding his attention with the same no-refusal-tolerated attitude his father had always used.

He'd been caught completely off guard by the sight of that bold, flourishing handwriting that was unmistakably his father's. Why, after nearly a year and a half, was the man writing to him now? He'd figured the two of them had said everything they had to say to each other in that heated discussion just before he left Philadelphia. There'd been harsh, biting words on both sides. His father was not one to apologize, so that couldn't be it. And it wouldn't be in character for him to be inquiring after his youngest son's well-being. So what was it?

Then a sobering thought occurred to him.

Had something happened to one of his brothers? Perhaps he should go ahead and—

"Here we are."

The sheriff's words brought Chance back to the present. And logic told him that if the news was dire in nature his father would have sent a telegram, not a letter. If the news, whatever it was, had waited long enough to get here by mail, a little more time wouldn't make a difference. Even under normal circumstances he wouldn't attempt to read something under the scrutiny of anyone, friend or stranger. And this particular letter made that doubly true.

Chance escorted Leo inside and had just about decided to bow out and make his exit, when he made the mistake of glancing Miss Pickering's way. She looked so worried and confused.

Then she met his gaze and for just a moment he saw a plea there that tugged at all his protective instincts. But it was when she turned to face the sheriff and schooled her features, bracing herself, as if she were David preparing to face Goliath, that he was well and truly snagged.

How could he turn his back on such selfless courage?

He watched as she drew herself up to her limited height and turned back into that prim but fierce mouse he'd seen face down the conductor on the platform earlier.

"Sheriff Gleason," she said, "please explain to me what this is all about." There was no wavering in her tone, no indication of the dismay he'd seen on her face earlier.

The sheriff studied her a moment. "Are you this boy's guardian, Miss Pickering?"

Now that was an interesting question. Just how would the very proper Miss Pickering answer?

Chapter Three

The knots inside Eve tightened another turn. Surely he wouldn't dismiss her if she had no official relationship with Leo. If he did, who would stand up for the boy and look out for his interests? Mr. Dawson had been kind in a neighborly sort of way, but she wasn't at all certain she could count on him to go the extra mile for the boy.

She tilted her chin up a bit higher. "Not officially, but I consider myself his friend and temporary protector."

To her relief, the lawman nodded. "I see." He turned and picked up a piece of paper from his desk. "I received this telegram earlier today. Officials from Bent Oak sent similar ones to lawmen all along the train route asking us to be on the lookout for a boy named Leonard Haskins who stole a valuable pocket watch. There were indications he might have slipped on board the train at Texarkana."

He eyed Leo. "The boy's description is a pretty good match for your young friend here."

Just what kind of trouble was Leo in? "That doesn't mean Leo is the boy in question, or that the charges are true. He needs to have an opportunity to speak for himself."

The sheriff folded his arms with a nod. "I'm listening."

Eve turned to Leo, placing a hand on his shoulder. "It's time to tell us your side of the story." She put as much support and encouragement in her expression as she could, but Leo looked more angry and desperate than reassured.

She tried again, this time adding firmness to her tone. "It's always best to tell the truth. I promise I'm going to help you no matter what. But you need to do your part, as well."

"I *am* Leonard Haskins," he finally said.

"And the watch?" the sheriff pressed.

Leo reached into his pocket and slowly pulled out an ornate gold watch. He stared at the timepiece for a long moment, then held it out to the sheriff without a word.

The lawman took it and set it down on his desk.

Eve tried to maintain her composure. She was determined to stand by Leo, but would she be allowed to? Almost involuntarily, she glanced Mr. Dawson's way and found her spirits buoyed by the encouraging look he gave her.

As if he'd been waiting on a cue from her, Mr. Dawson turned to Sheriff Gleason. "What happens now?"

"I'll contact the sheriff responsible for Bent Oak and let him know we've recovered the watch and have the boy in custody. I imagine both Leo and the watch will be sent back to Bent Oak and—"

"No!" The exclamation exploded out of Leo as if from a gun. He would have darted out the door if Mr. Dawson hadn't grabbed him.

"Whoa now." Mr. Dawson stood solidly in place as Leo struggled frantically to get free.

It was all Eve could do not to rush over and try to still his struggles with an embrace.

When Leo finally gave up, he glared defiantly at the sheriff. "Lock me up for what I done if you have to, but don't send me back there. I won't go back to Mr. Belcher, I just won't." He was shaking with the intensity of his feelings.

"Leo, who is Mr. Belcher?"

Leo looked Eve's way but for a moment he didn't seem to really see her. After a heartbeat, though, his tension eased and his gaze met hers. "He's the neighbor who took me in when my folks died. Only he wasn't doing it 'cause he was feeling particularly kindly toward me." The bitter edge to his voice was jarring coming from one so young. "After the funeral he told me my pa owed him a lot of money and since he couldn't collect from him anymore, he aimed to see that I worked it off."

Eve's stomach clinched as she studied the boy's raggedy appearance and bony frame in light of what he'd just said. She resisted the urge to reach out to him, knowing instinctively he'd shy away from physical contact just now. "Leo, did he treat you badly?" she asked gently.

The boy shrugged, not meeting her gaze. "I found out he was a mean old coot, especially when he was drunk." He lifted his chin. "But I never let him see me cry."

Everything inside her cried out at that telling statement. Who would treat a child like this? She saw Mr. Dawson's jaw tighten, indicating he shared her outrage.

But Leo hadn't finished saying his piece. "I finally figured two years of my working sunup to sundown should have paid off any debt my pa owed him, if he actually owed him anything in the first place. So a few nights ago I just up and left while he was still sleeping." He gave them all a tight-jawed look. "And I don't aim to go back, no matter what."

"And the watch?" the sheriff asked.

Leo drew himself up. "I ain't no thief. I took it because it was rightfully mine."

"Yours?" The sheriff retrieved the timepiece and examined it. "This is a mighty expensive-looking item for a kid to own."

"It was my pa's. His great-granddad brought it over from England before he sailed here. He saved the life of some kind of nobleman and the man gave him that watch out of gratitude. My pa told me the story lots of times. He also said it would be mine someday." His face twisted into a dark glower. "But then Mr. Belcher took it from me—said it would serve as pay for my upkeep."

"That's a fine story, son, and I'm not saying I don't believe you, but can you prove it?" The lawman's tone was firm without being confrontational.

"Look inside," Leo answered. "Mr. Belcher tried to scratch them out, but there's the initials *CLH* and the year 1807 in there. That's my pa's great-granddad Charles Lewis Haskins and the year he received the watch." Then Leo shrugged. "If you still don't believe me there's likely someone back in Bent Oak who still remembers my pa carrying it when he went to church on Sunday."

Satisfied, Eve turned to the sheriff. "You can't arrest this boy for taking back what belongs to him. Especially after all he's been through."

The lawman raised a brow. "How do you know he's telling the truth?"

"I ain't no liar." Leo's tone reflected his indignation.

Mr. Dawson stepped in again. "Look, Ward, you must have some way of checking out his story. Until you do, we don't need to be in a hurry to send him back, do we?"

The sheriff rubbed his jaw. "I suppose I could make some inquiries. But until I hear back, I can't just let the kid run loose. I mean, there's no one to keep an eye on him while we wait."

"I'm old enough to take care of myself." The boy drew

his shoulders back and stood up straighter. "I been doing it the past two years anyway."

Sheriff Gleason shook his head. "Even so, I can't just let you out on your own until we get this matter straightened out."

Eve laid a hand on Leo's shoulder. "I'll take responsibility for him."

The lawman gave her a look that was both sympathetic and uncompromising. "No offense, Miss Pickering, but I don't know you. I don't know what kind of caretaker you'd make for a boy who might just get it in his head to run off again."

Eve turned to Leo. "Will you give me your solemn word that you won't run away again as long as you are in my care?"

The boy stared at her for several moments and she could see the internal struggle in his face. Finally he nodded. "Yes, ma'am, so long as I'm in *your* care, I won't run away." He glanced back at the sheriff. "But I ain't going back to Mr. Belcher's."

She turned back to the sheriff with satisfaction. "There. Leo won't be any trouble for me to take care of while you work on getting this whole disagreeable situation put to rights."

Sheriff Gleason, however, didn't appear to be convinced. "Miss Pickering, until we get to the bottom of this, we don't really know how good his word is, do we?"

She could understand the sheriff's attitude. After all, it was his job to be suspicious and cautious. But deep in her heart she believed every bit of Leo's story and she couldn't bear the thought of him having to spend time locked up in jail, especially given what he'd already been through.

How could she convince the man to see things as she did? *Dear Jesus, please help me find a way.*

Aware the sheriff was waiting for her to speak, Eve took a deep breath, still not certain what she would say. But she knew she had to—

"How about I help Miss Pickering keep an eye on the boy?"

Eve turned and stared at Mr. Dawson. Had he just volunteered to help her save Leo? Maybe she *had* misjudged him after all.

Chance was as surprised by his offer as the rest of the people in the room seemed to be. He'd uttered the words without thought, spurred entirely by the urge to wipe the worry lines from Miss Pickering's face.

He was always a pushover for a damsel in distress. This wasn't the first time that weakness had gotten him in trouble.

But now that he'd blurted out his rash offer, he couldn't very well take it back.

The distressed damsel and Sheriff Gleason spoke up at almost the same time.

"Mr. Dawson, that's very kind, but I assure you—"

"Are you offering to take responsibility for seeing the boy doesn't run off?"

Chance decided to ignore Miss Pickering's protest and respond to the sheriff's question instead. "Miss Pickering seems to think the boy's word can be trusted and I'm willing to bank on that." He gave Leo a pointed look. "At least until Leo gives me reason to think otherwise."

The sheriff eyed him doubtfully. "That's all well and good, but how do you plan to keep a close eye on him?"

That was a good question. But an idea was starting to form in the back of his mind. It was a bit unorthodox, but if he could pull it off, it would make him appear a hero with minimal effort on his part. And it might have the bonus of making for an interesting few days.

"I have an idea that might simplify matters for everyone. But I need to check on something before I explain." He turned to Miss Pickering. "Can you wait about thirty minutes before we eat?"

"Of course. But what—"

He didn't give her an opportunity to finish her question. "I'll explain when I return." He turned to the sheriff. "If it isn't an inconvenience, perhaps our visitors could wait here in your office? I won't be long."

Sheriff Gleason took his cue and gave Miss Pickering a short bow. "Of course. You and Leo are welcome to make yourselves at home."

But Miss Pickering was not to be denied her opportunity to protest. She had resumed her prim schoolmarm look and raised a hand. "Gentlemen, while I appreciate your attempt to assist Leo and me in this matter, don't you think I should have some say in whatever it is you're planning?"

Sheriff Gleason gave her a stern look. "Frankly, Miss Pickering, unless Chance here has a real good solution in mind, I don't see how I can keep from locking the boy up, at least for as long as it takes me to get to the bottom of this matter."

Chance tried one of his more persuasive smiles on her. "What do you say? Can you trust me to find a solution that'll make everyone happy? Or at least reserve judgment until you hear what I have in mind?"

She didn't seem particularly won over, but gave a slow nod. "I suppose that's a fair request."

So much for charming her. "Good girl."

He saw the startled look at his familiar address, but she didn't chide him again. Instead she turned to the sheriff. "Perhaps we can make good use of the time we'll spend waiting for Mr. Dawson to carry out his mysterious errand. We can get started on whatever inquiries need to be made to clear up this matter with Leo." She clasped her hands together. "After all, the sooner started, the sooner finished."

"Good idea." Sheriff Gleason moved around to the other side of his desk. "I'll draft a telegram and send it off today."

"Speaking of telegrams," Chance said to Eve, "isn't there someone in Tyler you need to notify about your postponed arrival?" He found it interesting that she seemed to have given so little thought to this sudden change in her own plans.

Miss Pickering's eyes widened and she placed a hand to her cheek. "Oh, my goodness. How could I have forgotten about Mrs. O'Connell? I imagine she'll be worried when I don't get off the train. I must send her a telegram immediately."

At least that had gotten her mind off quizzing him. "Well then, it looks like you folks won't have much time to miss me. I'll meet you back here in about a half hour."

Chance smiled as he exited the sheriff's office, headed for the boardinghouse. He'd succeeded in getting Miss Pickering to trust him, at least for the time being, and also in finding something to focus her attention on while he was gone. There was some hope that he could make a dent in her reserve yet. He grinned, relishing the thought of how much fun it would be to do that.

He'd have to get Dotty on board for his plan to work, but he didn't foresee any problem with that. Knowing she would be key to helping Turnabout's newest visitors be more comfortable would be all the incentive she needed.

Then his smile faded. Before talking to Dotty, there was one more thing he needed to do.

He'd put it off long enough. It was time to read the letter.

Chance turned his steps toward his own place. As soon

as he was inside, he tore the envelope open. Taking a deep breath, he focused all his concentration on deciphering the words on the paper in his hands. Some days he had more success than others.

Today was not one of those days.

He tried again, straining his eyes until they ached with the effort. But it was no use. His brain refused to translate the markings on the paper into anything that made sense.

Frustrated and shamed once again by his inability to do what most schoolchildren did with little effort, Chance refolded the letter and shoved it back into his pocket. Sharing the news in this letter—whatever it was—wasn't something he relished doing, but it seemed he had no choice.

Time to visit Dotty.

Ten minutes later he entered the parlor of the boardinghouse, where Dotty sat knitting.

"What, no bridge game?" he teased. "Did you just use that as an excuse not to have lunch with us?"

She set aside her needlework. "Not at all. Unfortunately Stanley wasn't feeling well so we didn't have enough folks to play." Then she leaned back, a puzzled expression on her face. "Surely you and our stranded visitors haven't had enough time to eat already?"

He took a seat across from her. "There's been a slight change of plans. But I've come to ask you a favor."

"Of course. The letter?"

Dotty knew of his affliction and had told him it was one her brother had shared. He'd hired her to take care of his account books, and she came over to his place twice a week, coincidentally on the days the newspaper was delivered. She not only handled his accounts, but she also took care of any paperwork he needed assistance with and read the newspaper to him.

Her matter-of-fact handling of the situation was a great balm to his wobbly self-esteem.

Now he pulled the letter from his pocket but didn't hand it over immediately. "There's that, of course. But there's something else."

"You've piqued my curiosity. But why don't we get the letter out of the way first?"

Chance nodded as he handed it over. "It's from my father."

She tilted her head, giving him a considering look. "You don't sound happy at the prospect of hearing from him."

He grimaced. "My father is not one to write unless there is something he wants."

Without further comment, she opened the letter and began reading.

Chauncey,

Dotty eyed him in amused surprise.

He shrugged, trying to hide his irritation. "It's my given name. I'm not overly fond of it, but Father insists on using it."

"I see." She turned back to the letter.

When you left Philadelphia and headed for that back-water town in Texas, I told you that you would be welcome to return home when and if you gained some maturity and restraint, and were ready to accept both the responsibilities and privileges that come with being a member of this family. Since you have not yet taken advantage of this invitation in the year and a half that has passed since that day, it leaves me to wonder if you have learned anything at all from the experience.

Dotty was doing a good job of keeping her voice and expression neutral but she had to be wondering about the letter's tone. That was his father, though, ready to get right to the heart of the matter without wasting time worrying about trivial matters such as how one was getting on.

Dotty continued:

Therefore I have decided that I will come to visit you to see what kind of life you've managed to build for yourself. And while I'm there, we can use some of that time to discuss your future.

I imagine you are thinking that there is nothing for us to discuss, but in that you would be mistaken. As it happens, it recently came to my attention that you have mortgaged your place to invest in a new venture. It may interest you to know that I now own that note, so yes, I do have some stake in your future.

You can expect me to arrive by mid-December and I will plan to spend Christmas with you before returning to Philadelphia.

Dotty looked back up as she refolded the letter. "And he signs it *Your father, Woodrow Dawson.*"

Everything inside Chance had tensed as Dotty read his father's words, drawing tighter and tighter, like a clockwork spring that would soon explode out of its case.

A moment later he took a deep breath and forced his fists to unclench. It wouldn't do to let Dotty see just how strongly the letter had affected him.

"I thank you for taking the time to read that for me."

She handed him the letter. "It sounds like you will have family with you for Christmas this year."

That was Dotty, always looking for the silver lining.

He attempted a grin. "As you can no doubt tell, my father and I did not part on the best of terms."

"Perhaps his upcoming visit will be an opportunity for the two of you to remedy that."

Not a chance. But he merely smiled and changed the subject. "Now, if I can impose on you to discuss the other favor I came here to ask."

"Of course."

Ten minutes later, Chance was out the door and headed back to the sheriff's office. Dotty had, of course, readily agreed to his scheme. But his pleasure in that was marred by the knowledge of his father's upcoming visit and what had prompted it.

When he left Philadelphia, he'd thought he was out from under his father's thumb for good. He should have known the despot wouldn't let it go. That thinly veiled threat in the letter was typical of the way his father handled disagreements.

And now the man held the note to his business. What a wretched situation. If he'd known this would be the outcome he'd never have risked borrowing the money in the first place. His excitement over the work he was doing to improve the stationary engine was quickly turning to ashes. But most of the money had been spent now and there was no going back.

Having his autocratic father arrive on his doorstep in a matter of weeks spelled nothing but trouble. For the man to decide to dedicate so much of his valuable time to the planned visit was certainly out of character. Which also signaled that something important was afoot.

No matter what leverage his father thought he held over him, if he expected Chance to be any more willing to bow to his strictures now than he had in the past, he would be in for a major disappointment.

Which was how their interactions usually left his father.

How in the world had the man managed to insinuate himself into his black-sheep-of-a-son's life again? How had he even learned about the loan?

Chance intended to get answers to those questions before he faced his father again.

And this time there would be one key difference in their confrontation. His father would be coming to *him,* a guest in *his* town, in *his* home—not the other way around.

And that was a strategic advantage Chance planned to make the most of.

Chapter Four

Eve waited impatiently for Mr. Dawson to return from his errand. She and the sheriff had sent their telegrams and the three of them had returned to his office several minutes ago. The sheriff was now doing some paperwork and Leo was gloomily staring out the window.

Eve chided herself for her self-absorption. As hard as this wait was for her, it must be ten times worse for him. At least she'd had her grandmother to care for her when she'd been abandoned. Leo had had *no one* when his parents passed away.

Heavenly Father, help me to remember that no matter how bad I may think my lot is, there is always someone struggling with something far worse.

The door swung open and Eve was relieved to see Mr. Dawson step through. About time! She popped up and met his gaze. "Well?"

His grin had an impudent quality to it. "Glad to see you missed me."

She waved a hand impatiently—a poor substitute for stomping her foot. Didn't he realize how anxious she was feeling? "I'm pleased to see you find some amusement in this situation, sir, but I assure you I do not. Are you ready to share your plan?"

"I am. And I'm happy to say I think this will be the answer to the sheriff's concerns. Not to mention, to some of your problems, as well."

Sheriff Gleason stood and came around to lean a hip on his desk. "Let's hear it then."

"My idea is to have Miss Pickering and Leo move into my place until we've settled the matter of Leo's culpability to everyone's satisfaction. I've got plenty of room over there and it'll be good to have a bit of company for a change."

Eve stiffened. How *dare* he? What kind of woman did he think she was? "Mr. Dawson, this is not only unacceptable but highly insulting. I—"

He stopped her by raising his palm and rudely speaking over her objections. "Please, hear me out. I assure you, I've taken the proprieties into account. I spoke to Dotty and she's agreed to move in as well, so there will be no fodder for the gossip mills or hint of scandal associated with the situation."

Eve took a deep breath and her face heated as she realized she'd jumped to the wrong conclusion. "My apologies."

He gave a short bow. "You're forgiven."

His good humor only made her feel worse. After all, his offer was generous. It not only provided a solution to the sheriff's concerns but also solved the problem of where she and Leo would sleep tonight.

On the other hand it still didn't sound quite proper. She couldn't help wondering what her grandmother and aunts would think if they heard. They would undoubtedly be horrified. And they'd say it was typical of her ability to embarrass them with her thoughtless ways.

Then she lifted her chin again. They had sent her into exile, so her behavior was no longer their concern.

The sheriff eyed Mr. Dawson as he rubbed his chin. "If you're willing to keep an eye on the boy and take responsibility for him sticking around, then I guess I'm okay with releasing him to your custody."

To *his* custody? "Just a minute, gentlemen. I thought everyone here understood that, while Mr. Dawson has generously agreed to assist, *I* am taking responsibility for Leo's care."

"Of course," Mr. Dawson said quickly. "You would undeniably have the final word in the matter of Leo's care. I'm just going to be close by if needed. Trust me. I plan to leave all the guardianship duties to you."

His assurance mollified her concerns, but contrarily, she was also a tad disappointed at his ready capitulation. It seemed he wanted to step in and save the day but not take any real responsibility. What kind of white knight was that?

Nevertheless, thanks to him they'd have a roof over their heads and warm beds to sleep in tonight.

Eve took a deep breath and formed a quick, silent prayer. *Thank You, Jesus. You have provided for our immediate needs, and used this stranger to do so. Help me to remember Your promise that we are never alone when we put our faith in You.*

"Now," Mr. Dawson said, "why don't we go have that bite to eat we were discussing earlier?"

When they stepped back out on the sidewalk, Eve gave her temporary landlord a smile. "Let me thank you, Mr. Dawson, for your generosity toward Leo and myself. I assure you we will try to impose on you as little as possible during our stay."

He made a dismissive gesture. "As I said, there's lots

of room and I like company, so I'm sure that won't be a problem." He spread his hands. "And please, I'd take it as a favor if you'd drop that fusty-sounding Mr. Dawson nonsense and just call me Chance."

Eve stiffened and felt the warmth rising in her cheeks. "That would be highly improper. I barely know you."

"Nothing improper about it. We're now members of the same household, at least for the next few days. And I assure you, folks around here are pretty informal about such things."

She mentally struggled with her notions of propriety versus her desire to be polite. She didn't want to risk insulting him after all he'd done. "I don't know—"

He cut off her protest, adding a cajoling note to his voice. "Oh, come now. I would consider it a favor."

This seemed genuinely important to him. And she could avoid using his name for the most part. She nodded with a conciliatory smile. "Very well."

"Thank you."

The touch of triumph in the grin that accompanied his words should have irritated her, but for some reason it didn't.

Then he swept an arm to his left. "Shall we? Daisy's Restaurant is just a couple of blocks in this direction."

Mr. Dawson—she still couldn't think of him by his first name—set a sedate pace for them, giving Eve time to study the town as they strolled. Since this was to be her home for the next couple of days, she wanted to learn as much about it as she could. And it gave her something to focus on other than the distracting man walking beside her.

The rumbling from Leo's stomach was getting more insistent.

Chance smiled down at the boy. "Don't worry. We'll be there in just a few minutes. I'm getting hungry myself."

Then he glanced her way. "You're going to like the food at Daisy's. She's one of the finest cooks around here."

Eve raised a brow at that. "That's quite a claim."

His brow arched. "You doubt me? I assure you, it's the absolute truth. Daisy's had the restaurant open for only a few months and already she has quite a contingent of regulars."

This kind of teasing banter was new to her and it flustered her a bit—but in a not unpleasant way. "Well, after such glowing praise, I am definitely looking forward to trying it out for myself."

He rewarded her with an appreciative grin. "You won't be disappointed." He waved to a two-story building they were approaching. "This is where our local newspaper, the *Turnabout Gazette*, gets printed. Daisy's husband, Everett, runs the place."

"How exciting to have such easy access to a newspaper."

"I don't know about exciting," he said dryly, "but it *is* handy. Everett prints the paper twice weekly and, don't tell him I said so, but he does a good job of mixing local and national news."

Then he nodded to the adjoining building. "Daisy's Restaurant is right next door." A moment later, he gave a flourishing wave. "And here we are."

Eve eyed the sign hanging above the door and smiled in delight. "Oh, how clever. And how welcoming." The Daisy's Restaurant sign was painted in colorful, cheery letters and the *i* had been dotted with a drawing of a daisy. This already felt like a friendly place.

Chance grinned. "Daisy painted that herself, and it really speaks to who she is."

When they stepped inside, he waved to the woman behind the counter. "Hello, Daisy. I've brought a couple of newcomers in to sample your cooking." He gave her a cheeky smile. "And I'll give you fair warning that I've been bragging on you, so you need to treat them to your best."

The woman lifted her chin and placed a hand on her hip. "Chance Dawson, you know good and well I give *all* my customers my best." While the words were said in a chiding tone, her smile indicated she hadn't really taken offense.

As she bustled out from behind the counter it became apparent that she was with child. And that she wasn't letting it slow her down.

Daisy turned to Eve and Leo. "Hello. I'm always glad to see new faces in here. I'm Daisy Fulton and I'm right pleased to welcome you to Turnabout and to my restaurant."

"Thank you. I'm Eve Pickering." Eve placed and hand on Leo's shoulder. "And this is Leo."

Daisy smiled down at the boy. "Pleased to meet you, too, Leo." Then she turned back to Eve. "Are you folks friends of Chance's?" She cast Mr. Dawson a teasing look. "He's always been a mite closemouthed about his life before he moved here."

Eve wasn't quite certain how to respond to that, but fortunately Mr. Dawson spoke up first.

"These two are recent acquaintances," he said. Then he assumed a haughty expression. "And as for my past, I *like* being a man of mystery."

Daisy rolled her eyes and cast a can-you-believe-him look Eve's way. "Some mystery." She turned back to Chance. "Chance Dawson, you are the *least* mysterious man I know."

Eve didn't bother to hide her grin. She was getting her first taste of what it felt like to be among folks who didn't know her history and she liked it. Very much.

Then Daisy waved them to the only unoccupied table.

"I shouldn't be chattering on like this when y'all came in here to eat. Just have a seat. The menu is posted on the board above the counter. Study it and then give me a wave when you're ready to order."

They moved to the table she'd indicated and Eve was startled when Chance held her chair for her. She wasn't used to such deference. As they took their seats, she studied the room with interest. The walls were painted the color of daffodils and the windows were flanked by cheery floral curtains hemmed with ruffles, tied back to let in the sunlight. Grandmother would disapprove of such frivolity, but Eve decided she liked it.

There were seven other tables in the place, and the occupants seemed to be enjoying their meals, lending weight to Mr. Dawson's earlier claims. She noticed the patrons were also trying to study her and Leo without being too obvious. But their curiosity seemed friendly enough and she found herself on the receiving end of more than one neighborly smile.

What really snagged and held Eve's attention, however, was the far wall, where three tall, sturdy bookcases stood behind a small table that obviously served as someone's desk. Both bookcases were crammed full of volumes of various sizes and colors. Such a wealth of reading material—it was all Eve could do not to cross over to read the titles.

Forcing herself to look away from the books, Eve turned back to read the menu, but not before she caught Mr. Dawson staring at her. He actually had the audacity to smile and lean back in his chair, continuing to study her.

She decided to ignore him and instead focus on the chalkboard. Unfortunately she remained uncomfortably aware of his gaze. As she read the menu, she studied the prices more than the food choices. She had to be careful with her funds—the pittance she had wouldn't last long.

"If you're having trouble deciding," Mr. Dawson said a moment later, "I'd recommend the rabbit stew. It's Daisy's Tuesday special and always delicious." His tone held no hint that he'd recognized her earlier discomfort.

Leo nodded enthusiastically. "That sounds good."

Mr. Dawson turned to her. "Shall I make that three orders?"

Eve studied the price and hesitated. Then she nodded. "Very well." A nice filling stew would hold her for the remainder of the day. And she did need to keep her strength up for the uncertainty ahead.

Mr. Dawson raised a hand to let Daisy know they were ready, and placed their order. Then he returned his attention to Eve. "I saw you studying Abigail's library a moment ago. I take it you enjoy reading."

Eve nodded, allowing a small smile to escape. "Very much." It was one of her guilty pleasures—one she hadn't had much opportunity to indulge in since she'd graduated from school.

"Perhaps you can get a closer look at the books once we've completed our meal and pick out something to read while you're in town."

"You mean they just let folks take them?" Did they value books so little here?

He shrugged. "It's a circulating library, which means the books are available to all subscribers. But Abigail always lets you have the first one free."

It was tempting, but she wouldn't really be here in town very long. And she didn't need to be beholden to yet another stranger. Rather than going into that with him, though, she settled for making a noncommittal sound.

Apparently taking that as agreement, he changed the

subject. "I believe you said you were headed to Tyler to find employment as a milliner's apprentice?"

"That's correct." Had Mrs. O'Connell received her telegram yet? What was she thinking about her truant would-be apprentice?

"Is becoming a milliner something you have a burning desire to do, if you don't mind my asking?"

What would he do if she said she *did* mind his asking? "A friend of my grandmother's runs a millinery shop in Tyler. Apparently she gets an increase in orders in the weeks between Thanksgiving and Christmas so she agreed to hire me on a trial basis for now. Once the New Year gets here, we are to both evaluate whether to continue the arrangement."

It wasn't really an answer to his specific question, and the look he gave her said he knew it. But he didn't press further. Instead, he turned to Leo. "And what about you?"

Leo shrugged. "The same." He traced a circle on the table. "I mean, I was looking for a big city, somewhere where I could find work and not stand out."

Mr. Dawson stroked his chin thoughtfully. "You know, if it's work you're looking for, Leo, you don't have to go all the way to Tyler. There's work to be had right here in Turnabout."

That caught Eve's interest. If she could find some temporary work here, it would give her an opportunity to replenish some of the funds she'd have to spend on meals and such before moving on. "What sort of work?"

He spread his hands. "I wasn't thinking of anything in particular, just that folks are always needing work done."

She swallowed her disappointment. Before she could make any sort of response, however, he turned to Leo. "In fact, things get pretty messy in my shop when I've got work piled up. I've been looking for someone to clean up around the place and help me keep things in order—you know sweep up, fetch things for me, run errands. That sort of thing."

Leo sat up straighter. "I could do that."

Mr. Dawson wrinkled his brow, as if the idea was something he hadn't yet considered, but Eve could tell it was what he'd been leading up to all along.

"Do you really think so?" the man asked. "I mean, it's hard work and I couldn't afford to pay much."

But Leo was leaning forward eagerly. "That's okay. I don't mind the work, and I'll need some money to get by on once the sheriff finds out I'm not lying."

Eve lightly touched his arm but kept her gaze on Chance. "Of course, since you are so generously opening your home to us, Leo and I will be happy to pitch in and help with the chores as much as we are able. And we wouldn't dream of taking payment." She withdrew her hand but gave Leo a pointed look. "Isn't that right?"

Leo's expression lost its eager edge, but he nodded. "Yes, ma'am."

She was pleased to have her faith in him proved true. But his comment about needing money to get by concerned her. Did the boy truly believe he would be allowed to go off on his own once matters were settled? He would need a guardian of some sort, whether he wanted one or not. But perhaps now was not the time to open that avenue of conversation.

However, it did bring up the question of just what *would* happen to him. And right now she didn't have an answer.

Their food arrived then, delivered by a younger girl with reddish-gold hair and a saucy smile.

"Hello, Abigail," Mr. Dawson greeted her. "Don't tell me Daisy let you into her kitchen."

"And just why would that come as a surprise to you?"

The girl gave him an indignant look. "You don't think Daisy is the only member of this family who can cook, do you?"

Mr. Dawson leaned back and raised his hands as if she'd attacked him. "Far be it from me to question your talents, in *any* arena."

The girl responded to his obvious teasing with a smile. "Actually, I'm in training. I'll be taking over for a few weeks after the baby comes."

Then she turned to Eve as she set a dish in front of her. "And since Chance here seems to have forgotten his manners, allow me to introduce myself. I'm Abigail Fulton. Daisy's husband is my brother."

They exchanged greetings as Abigail set out the food, then the girl disappeared back into the kitchen.

Eve noted the way Leo dug his spoon into his bowl, as if he hadn't eaten for days, which he well may not have. But there were other ways to nourish him, as well.

She briefly touched his arm. "Shall we say grace first?"

Leo set his spoon down, his cheeks turning red. "Sorry," he mumbled.

She smiled. "No need to apologize. We all forget sometimes." She turned to Mr. Dawson. "Would you care to lead us?"

As soon as the words were out of her mouth she wished them back. She'd put him on the spot! What if he wasn't comfortable with praying aloud?

Had her deplorable tendency to act first and think later caused her yet another misstep?

Chapter Five

Chance could tell from her expression that she wasn't certain he'd comply. Actually, while he didn't always remember to do so, he had no trouble at all offering up a prayer. His mother had taught him well before she passed. And while he'd had more than a few bouts of rebellion growing up, and still questioned why he'd been saddled with such a shameful affliction, he'd never really lost faith in the Almighty.

He nodded and folded his hands, elbows on the table. "Heavenly Father, bless this meal we are about to partake of, and watch over these visitors who have unexpectedly arrived in our community. Let them feel welcome here, for whatever time they may be with us. In Your Son's name we pray. Amen."

His companions echoed his amen, then they all picked up their spoons.

Chance had seen Eve's keen interest in the newspaper office when they'd passed by earlier. He'd also noticed the longing looks she'd sent toward Abigail's library when they first entered the restaurant. She obviously enjoyed reading—a pastime he envied but could never share.

He decided to circle back to the question she'd tried to

sidestep earlier. "So, Eve, *do* you have a burning desire to become a hat maker?"

He saw the walls go up in her expression and thought for a moment she'd ignore his question again. But he maintained an expression of innocent curiosity, and she finally responded politely, even if not altogether warmly.

"My taking a position as a milliner was actually my grandmother's idea," she said carefully. "The opportunities for employment in Iron Bluff are very limited so she contacted her friend Mrs. O'Connell, who graciously offered to take me in and train me."

Now, why was a sheltered young woman such as this worrying about employment in the first place—shouldn't she instead be finding a husband? Or was there a dearth of marriageable bachelors in Iron Bluff?

"I'm quite grateful for the opportunity," she added as she reached for her glass.

His questions had definitely brought back that stiff, schoolmarm demeanor in her. How much further would she let him press?

She set her glass down and faced him evenly. "As for your earlier question, I'm not so set on millinery work that I wouldn't be willing to do work of other kinds while I am here in Turnabout—housekeeper, cook, laundress—whatever might be available."

Did she truly want to find a job while she was here? Perhaps she didn't understand the arrangement he had offered her. "That's not necessary. I don't plan to charge you and Leo for the rooms. After all, they're just sitting empty right now and it won't cost me anything for you to stay there."

Her lips pursed primly. "That's very kind of you, but I'm not one to sit idle. Besides which, having a bit of pocket money would not go amiss."

Was she low on funds? He'd noticed the way she'd studied the menu with that furrow between her brows. He'd thought she was just trying to decide on a selection, but perhaps she'd been worrying about the prices. Finances could be a touchy subject, though, so he'd have to tread carefully. "I'll ask around and keep my ears open." He saw the quickly masked disappointment in her face. So she'd been serious about wanting to find work. He was curious to learn more. "Tell me, if you could have any job at all, what would you really like to do?"

He watched her swirl her spoon through the bowl of stew. "I've never really thought about that before."

That struck Chance as a very sad statement. Didn't she know how to dream? "Well, think about it now."

She was quiet for another moment. Then a slow, smile blossomed on her face. "I'd open a confectionery."

"What's a confectionery?" Leo asked.

She gave him an impish smile. "It's like a candy store."

The boy's eyes widened. "Oh, my goodness, wouldn't that be a grand place to work?"

Eve laughed and it totally transformed her face. She really was quite pretty when she allowed herself to relax. "That it would," she said.

"Why a confectionery?" Her answer had surprised him, but he was delighted by the unexpectedness of it.

She took on a faraway look. "When I was a schoolgirl, my Sunday school teacher would invite some of her students into her home at Christmastime. We would make all sorts of wondrous treats. She taught us to make fudge and caramels and pralines and all manner of sweet things—just bowls and platters full of them."

"What did you do with all that candy?" Leo asked. "Did you get to eat it?"

She gave him a conspiratorial smile. "Some. Because,

of course, we'd have to taste it along the way, just to make certain it had turned out okay, you understand."

"Sounds perfectly reasonable to me," Chance said. He found himself entranced by the softness in her now.

She cut a quick look his way, as if to make certain he wasn't making fun of her, then nodded and turned back to Leo.

"But we packed up the majority of those treats very carefully and sent the packages off to several orphanages as Christmas treats."

Chance was enjoying this sweet, playful side of her. But before he could comment, she seemed to realize that she'd revealed more of herself than she'd intended.

She straightened and dipped her spoon purposefully into her bowl. "Anyway, it turned out that I was very good at candy making. Miss Trosclair said I had a real knack for it."

Chance shook his head apologetically. "I'm afraid Turnabout doesn't have a confectionary shop so we can't offer you a job like that."

She nodded politely but that earlier softness was gone. "Having such a job would be nice, but as I said, I'll take whatever I can find." Then she gave him a pointed look. "I think it's my turn to ask a few questions."

Turning the tables on him was she? Good for her. "Ask away."

"Something Daisy said when we walked in makes me think you're not from here originally. So where are you from and how long have you lived in Turnabout?"

Easy enough questions to answer. "I was born and raised in Philadelphia, Pennsylvania. And I've been here about a year and a half."

Her brows went up. "You traveled a far piece to get here—much farther than either me or Leo."

If only she knew. "True. But I consider Turnabout home now."

"And you came all this way on your own?"

"Not exactly." How much should he share with her? Better stick with just the bare minimum. "There were four of us who traveled together," he continued. There was no point in mentioning that the catalyst had been an unorthodox marriage lottery they'd all participated in.

Her eyes widened in surprise. "Four city folk from Philadelphia decided to come to Turnabout, Texas?"

He grinned. "That we did."

"Why?"

Now her questions were getting a little more personal. "Business reasons." Technically true. "Not to say we planned to go into business together—just travel together. Daisy's husband, Everett, was one of my travel companions. Adam Barr, the town's banker and lawyer, and Mitch Parker, the schoolteacher, were the other two. We've all found our own reasons to stay." Though the four men had become friends after their arrival here, he'd never pried into what reasons they'd had for agreeing to the constraints that had been laid on them at the outset of their trip. Just as he'd never shared his own.

"So you've all stayed and become part of the town. That says a lot for the place. It must be special."

He nodded. "I've seen evidence that Turnabout lives up to its name. It's a good place for starting over and turning your life around." At least it had been for him and the others who'd traveled here with him.

But Chance had had enough of talking about himself. Figuring Eve probably needed time to think over the events of the day, he turned to Leo and kept up a steady stream of light, easy chatter with the boy through the rest of the meal. Leo seemed like a good kid. He also appeared to be more mature and guarded than most boys his age, but that was no doubt due to what he'd been through these past couple of years. If his story were true, this Belcher fellow deserved a flogging or worse.

Leo was the first to finish his bowl and Chance immediately ordered seconds for him with just a quick hand signal, barely missing a beat in the conversation.

When Eve finished her bowl he started to do the same, but she quickly let him know she'd had enough.

At one point, Abigail came around to check on them. "How was everything?"

"Delicious," Eve answered.

"I'll let Daisy know you enjoyed it."

"And just where is Daisy?" Chance asked. "I haven't seen her in a while."

Abigail began collecting their dishes. "Everett came by to check on her and insisted she get off her feet for a few minutes. Of course, Daisy rolled her eyes at him, but since the lunch rush is about over she agreed to let me see to things for a while." She grinned. "Everett convinced her I needed the practice."

Remembering Eve's earlier interest in the library, and guessing she wouldn't broach the subject on her own, Chance decided to make it easier for her.

"How's the library business these days?" he asked casually.

Abigail immediately became more animated. "Very good. I signed another subscriber yesterday and I'm planning to purchase several new titles right after Christmas." She sighed dramatically. "I miss having Constance partnering with me, but she absolutely loves her new job assisting Mr. Flaherty at the apothecary shop."

Chance nodded. "Mr. Flaherty seems pleased with the job she's doing." He glanced Eve's way, waiting for her to speak up. But when she didn't jump into the conversational opening, he decided to be more direct. "Speaking of your library, Miss Pickering here is interested in taking a look at your selection of books."

He sensed her stiffening without even looking her way. Didn't she know he was trying to help?

But Abigail apparently noticed nothing amiss. "Of course." The girl gave Eve a big smile. "I'd be glad to loan you a book, free of charge. Sort of a welcome-to-town gift, for you to read while you're here."

His companion shook her head, though this time there was nothing firm about the gesture. "That's very kind, but I don't want to take advantage—"

"Not at all." Abigail lowered her voice, as if sharing a secret. "Besides, it's good advertisement if folks see people borrowing my books." She waved toward the book-shelves. "Feel free to look over what's available while I clear these dishes."

Chance could see Eve's resolve wavering as she stared longingly at the bookshelves. Deciding she needed another nudge, he stood and pulled her chair out for her. Pitching his voice so only she could hear, he whispered, "It would be an insult for you to refuse Abigail's offer."

She gave him a doubtful look. "I certainly wouldn't want to offer her any insult." She glanced again toward the shelves. "Perhaps I'll go over and just take a look."

He watched her cross the room and then slowly, almost reverently, run her fingers along the rows of books, taking her time studying the various titles. What kind of book would she select? Would her prim and proper side win out and have her select a volume of dry essays or sermons? Or would her more daring side win out and point her to some more entertaining work of fiction?

She pulled out a book and smiled as she silently read

a passage. Suddenly, that familiar kick of jealousy tinged with shame twisted his gut and he turned away.

"Why is she so excited about a bunch of books?" Leo asked, wrinkling his nose.

Chance pushed his ugly emotions aside and smiled down at the boy. "You'd be surprised how many people enjoy reading," he answered. "There are a lot of adventures to be found between the pages of a good book." Some of his favorite memories were of his mother reading to him as a boy.

"Adventures?" That had obviously grabbed his attention.

Did the boy know how to read? If his story was true, he likely hadn't seen the inside of a schoolroom since he was eight years old, if at all. Maybe he should have a talk with Mitch about how to get Leo prepared for returning to the classroom eventually.

Then Chance pulled himself up short. He wasn't the kid's father and he certainly wasn't planning to make this little diversion a long-term commitment. He had too many problems of his own right now. Once the boy's guilt or innocence was determined, there would be decisions to be made about him, decisions that, one way or the other, would relieve Chance of any future responsibility.

With the unexpected visit from his father looming, he'd have plenty of other issues to deal with during the next few weeks.

Chance glanced toward Eve, who was still studying the bookshelves with single-minded focus. Did she realize she'd have to hand over Leo to someone else soon? Unless she intended to adopt the boy, which didn't seem likely given what little she'd revealed about her circumstances. Just how deep did her attachment go? Would she walk away gracefully and let the authorities do what must be done?

She finally plucked a book from the shelves and turned to rejoin them. Pausing at the desk, she dutifully wrote in the ledger, apparently following the directions the trusting Abigail had posted.

"What did you select?" he asked when she returned.

She held up a small book bound in leather with dark red lettering on the front. To his relief, she also described her selection. "It's a book of poetry."

Well now, wasn't that an unexpected and interesting choice?

So she *did* have a less straight-laced, more romantic side to her, even if it was buried a bit deep.

Yep, the next few days could prove interesting indeed.

Chapter Six

Eve clutched the borrowed book to her chest as they left the restaurant, feeling one part guilt and one part excitement. She shouldn't have taken advantage of Abigail's generosity the way she had, but the idea of having a book to read had been too irresistible a temptation.

They made a quick stop at the sheriff's office to retrieve her carpetbag and then headed for Mr. Dawson's place.

Eve still felt uncomfortable with the idea of moving into the home of an unmarried man, especially one she'd met only a few hours ago, but accepted that she had little choice in the matter. The fact that Dotty and the sheriff saw nothing amiss with the plan did reassure her. And she was selfishly glad Mr. Dawson had tapped Dotty to play the part of chaperone. She'd liked the woman almost on sight.

"Tell me," she asked Mr. Dawson, "what sort of business are you in?"

Was that a wince? Had she overstepped with her question?

But almost immediately he was flashing one of his carefree grins again. Perhaps she'd been mistaken, let her fancy run away with her as her grandmother often accused.

"I repair mechanical devices," he said.

"Mechanical?"

"Yes, I tinker around with all sorts of machinery—stationary engines, grandfather clocks, sewing machines—I repair and adjust them when they break down."

Leo's eyes lit up. "Are you working on anything right now?"

Mr. Dawson rubbed his jaw, but she saw a bit of a twinkle in his eyes. "Well, let's see. Mrs. Carlisle's sewing machine is giving her problems so I'm taking a look at it for her. And I've been spending a lot of my time lately tinkering with a stationary engine."

Leo nodded solemnly as if he knew exactly what Mr. Dawson was talking about.

"Of course, you might be more interested in the mechanical toys I've taken apart just to see how they work."

Leo's face brightened further. "Can I help with that?"

"We'll see. There's one other thing I work with that might interest you—I spend time making certain my motor carriage stays in good working order."

Leo stopped in his tracks, his eyes growing rounder. "You have a motor carriage?" He said it as if Mr. Dawson had just admitted to having a pirate's treasure hidden in his shop.

Even Eve was impressed with the announcement. She'd heard of motor carriages but had never actually seen such a thing.

"That I do," he answered proudly.

"Can I see it?" Leo was practically bouncing with excitement.

Mr. Dawson waved a hand to indicate they should move forward again. "You can not only see it, you can sit in it if you like." He turned to Eve. "Both of you."

Eve wasn't at all certain that was something either she or Leo should agree to. Was it safe? But she settled for smiling and giving him a noncommittal "We shall see" response.

As they turned the corner, Eve saw a building that had the unmistakable trappings of a saloon—most notably the swinging half doors and the faded but still legible sign proclaiming the name of the establishment to be The Blue Bottle.

She looked around at the neighboring buildings. Was Mr. Dawson's place nearby? She wasn't comfortable being in close proximity to such a place, but if that was the case she would do her best to make it work. She'd just have to keep a close eye on Leo to make certain he was shielded from any unsavory influences.

"From the frown on your face, I see you have some concerns about The Blue Bottle."

Eve gave him a direct look. "I'm not afraid to admit that I don't approve of such establishments."

He seemed amused by her words. "You can rest assured that the place no longer serves as a saloon."

Mollified by his words, she relaxed. "That *is* good news. Did the town close it?"

"No, I'm afraid providence did. It was shut down by a fire. It happened before I ever moved here."

"Oh." They were drawing closer now and she frowned as she studied the structure. "But it seems to be undamaged and still in use."

"The inside has been renovated, and yes, it's still in use. In fact I own it now."

Oh, my goodness. She stopped in her tracks just as they reached the corner of the building. That meant—

His grin had a mischievous edge. "That's right. I have my shop on the first floor and my living quarters on the second."

"You mean *this* is where we're going to be staying?"

He swept his hand forward with a flourish. "In all its glory."

A former saloon, of all things. Somehow it seemed very in character for this unorthodox gent to have set up shop in such an establishment. She slowly approached the entrance, feeling decidedly uncomfortable about what she might see inside. Just the idea of what all must have taken place in a former saloon was enough to send the warmth into her cheeks and her grandmother's scandalized voice resounding in her mind.

Which was foolish, she told herself firmly. It was merely a building and nothing more. Lifting her chin, she pushed through the swinging doors and stepped into a very large undivided room that took up most of the lower floor. She'd never been inside a saloon before, of course, so she'd had no idea what to expect.

To her relief, Mr. Dawson was as good as his word and there were very few traces remaining of the former den of iniquity. The most obvious remnant of the building's former purpose sat to her left—what had obviously been the counter where the drinks were dispensed. There was still a brass rail on the lower portion where she imagined men had propped their boots as they partook of the bar's offerings. Looking closer, though, there was something odd about the counter, as if part of it had been lopped off. A result of the fire perhaps?

As for the rest of the room, the section nearest the doors was bare except for two round tables that had been shoved together to the left of the entrance. Three unmatched wooden chairs, at least one of which bore scorch marks, flanked them. Is that where he entertained visitors? Assuming he ever *had* visitors.

Across the room, however, it was a different story. The area was as crowded and cluttered as this side was bare.

A pair of long worktables along with three smaller round ones were arranged in a seemingly random manner, all cluttered with an odd assortment of unidentifiable metal parts. There were also tools, jars, canisters, rags and crates scattered here and there. That was it. The walls were bare and there weren't any domestic touches to speak of. Nor was it what one would call neat and tidy.

This place was definitely more of a workshop than a home. "You have done a good job of erasing the signs of a fire."

"Thanks. I had to replace the staircase and a large portion of the floor. There was some damage to the far end of the counter but it's such a fine piece of workmanship that I couldn't bear to scrap the whole thing. And that east wall needed extensive repairs."

He pointed to the opposite wall, where she could see doors. "Thankfully the other rooms down here—the kitchen, office and storage room—suffered very little damage."

"So the building is now sound structurally?"

"Definitely." Then Mr. Dawson smiled without visible embarrassment. "Sorry for the mess. I like to take things apart in order to figure out how they work—or at least try to. Sometimes I don't get them put back together right away."

While her host talked, Eve kept an eye on Leo, who was already halfway across the room. "Don't touch anything," she warned him. She was as concerned for the boy's safety amid Mr. Dawson's mishmash of metal parts and wires as she was for the items themselves. Then she eyed the cluttered tables again. How did the man keep up with where everything was? "Do you work alone?"

"That I do. There's barely enough paying work here to

keep one man busy. But it's slowly picking up. And I have some plans for diversifying and expanding my business."

Something about his tone seemed odd. But before Eve could push further, Leo spoke up from across the room.

"You know how to fix *all* of this stuff?" There was a touch of awe in his tone.

Chance shrugged. "Most of it. And I haven't given up on the rest. I like trying to solve puzzles."

Eve smiled. She rather liked puzzles herself, but she had a feeling the two of them had entirely different activities in mind.

"Do you think I could learn, too?" Leo asked wistfully.

"I don't see why not—so long as you're willing to really work at it."

Eve was torn between being glad he hadn't squashed Leo's enthusiasm, and worrying that he was giving the boy false hope. After all, depending on what the sheriff's inquiries revealed, Leo might not be in Turnabout for very long.

Mr. Dawson raised a brow. "But you can start by learning how to keep this place neat and clean."

Eve swallowed a retort. Clean was one thing, but it would take hours, perhaps days, of effort to get this place neat and organized.

Leo changed the subject. "Where's your motor carriage?" He looked around as if expecting to see it lurking in some corner.

"There's a shed out behind the place where I store it." Mr. Dawson waved to a door on the far end of the room. "Come on, I'll show you."

Eve fought the urge to roll her eyes. He seemed as much a kid as Leo—easily distracted and always ready to play. "Before you do that," she said firmly, "why don't you show us to our rooms so we can get settled in."

Mr. Dawson gave her an apologetic grimace. "Of

course. First things first I suppose." He changed direction and moved toward the stairs.

Leo started to protest, but before Eve could say anything, Mr. Dawson's brow drew down in a warning look. "Miss Pickering is right—we should take care of business first." Then he winked. "But don't worry, there'll be time enough for play later."

Then he turned back to her and motioned toward the stairs. "It's right up this way. There are four rooms up here and they're all pretty much the same—only the view from the windows is different. My room is the last one on the right—you can have your pick of the other three. I'll leave it to you to make the assignments."

Eve looked around as they topped the stairs. The second floor was configured with a U-shaped landing over the far side of the building. There were two doors at the head of the stairs and one on either side facing each other.

"We'll reserve that one for Mrs. Epps," she said, pointing to the room next to Mr. Dawson's, "and, Leo, you can take the one next to her. I'll take the one on the end."

She followed Leo into the room she'd designated as his and saw that it was not overly large but still of a comfortable size and plainly furnished. She wasn't certain exactly what she'd expected in rooms above what had been a saloon, but it certainly wasn't this modest appointment.

She turned to her host. "This will do quite nicely. Thank you."

Mr. Dawson's smile gave her the impression he knew what she'd been expecting. "The upstairs was barely affected by the fire, only smoke damage and minor scorching on the landing. But I got rid of most of the gaudier furnishings."

"I see." Perhaps he wasn't as unmindful as she'd assumed.

He looked around, rubbing the back of his neck absently. "They're rather sparsely furnished I'm afraid. Like this room, each has a bed, a chest and a small vanity and that's about it. They've remained unused in the time I've been here so they'll probably need a good airing and a cleaning."

"The furnishings are more than adequate and the cleaning and airing are something Leo and I are quite capable of handling." Putting words to action, Eve crossed the room and opened the window, letting in the sunshine and crisp November air.

Then she turned back to Mr. Dawson. "I assume you have a broom and some dust rags we can use? Oh, and a line outside to hang the sheets on for an airing."

He gave a short bow. "Of course. Let me set your bag in your room and I'll fetch them for you."

"That's not necessary. I don't want you to feel as if you have to wait on us while we're here. Just point me in the right direction." She looked toward Leo. "In the meantime, would you strip the sheets from all three beds and carry them downstairs, please?"

Leo didn't look happy about postponing his opportunity to examine the motor carriage, but he nodded and started to work on the beds.

Eve followed Mr. Dawson from the room and paused with him in the hallway.

"I keep the broom and mop in the storeroom downstairs," he said. "Along with a lot of other odds and ends. You'll find it just to the right of the stairway. Feel free to help yourself to whatever you need."

"Thank you. I'm sure I'll find everything just fine."

"If you're certain you and Leo will be all right for a bit, I need to run a few errands and then see to moving Dotty."

Assuring him that they would be fine, Eve headed toward the room she'd reserved for Dotty. She wanted to have it aired out before the woman arrived.

How would Dotty feel about moving into what had once been a saloon? Then Eve gave herself a mental shake. Better not to think about the use the rooms might have been put to in times past. Collectively she and Leo would give this place new life and purpose over the next few days, and that was what mattered.

New life and purpose. She liked the sound of that.

Chance was still smiling as he stepped onto the sidewalk. Yep, the next few days were going to be mighty interesting. And mighty entertaining, as well. Just how far could he make the very proper Miss Pickering bend?

Then his smile faded. Before he fetched Dotty and her things, he had another errand to run. He needed answers about his father's claims and there was one person in town who might be able to give them to him. Adam Barr.

He walked into the bank and headed straight for Adam's office. Giving a perfunctory knock on the open door, he entered without waiting for an invitation.

Adam leaned back in his seat with a friendly smile. "Hello. Looking for another loan to diversify further? I hear you're giving Eunice Ortolon some competition."

Chance grimaced. Eunice was the owner of the town's one and only boardinghouse. "I see the local gossip mill is as efficient as ever."

Adam spread his hands, his grin widening. "Something like one of the town's most eligible bachelors taking in boarders, one of whom is an unmarried young woman new to town, is big news. You can't expect it to go unnoticed." He seemed to be enjoying Chance's discomfiture. "I'd love to hear the story behind it."

"Another time." Chance crossed his arms. "I actually wanted to talk to you about my loan."

Adam immediately became all business. "Of course. Should I close the door?"

"No." Chance gripped the back of the chair facing Adam's desk. "I just want to know if the bank still holds that loan?"

Adam's brow furrowed. "Of course. We don't make a practice of selling off our notes. Why would you ask?"

The knot in Chance's gut loosened slightly. But it wasn't like his father to lie. He moved around and flopped into the chair. "Because I received a letter from my father this morning stating that *he* held the note."

Adam straightened. "That's not possible."

"He claims it is. And my father may be a great many things, but a liar he is not."

Adam leaned back in his chair his expression puzzled. "I don't understand. I—" Suddenly his demeanor changed—his eyes widened a moment and then his lips thinned. "Oh."

"I assume you figured it out," Chance said dryly. He had a feeling he wasn't going to like whatever was coming. "Don't keep me in suspense."

"There *is* a new partner in the bank ownership."

"You took on a new partner? And it just happens to be my father?"

"Not exactly. I don't actually own any portion of the bank, remember? Jack's father and Thomas Pierce started up this business as equal partners."

Jack was Adam's adopted son.

"When Jack's father died," Adam continued, "Jack inherited his portion, and when I married Reggie I took responsibility for managing his interests. Then, when Pierce…*died* his wife inherited his portion."

Chance understood Adam's hesitation. Pierce had done the unthinkable—committed suicide when it became inevitable that his theft of bank funds would be discovered.

"What you may or may not know," Adam continued, "is that a large part of what was left of Thomas's estate went toward paying off his debt. Mrs. Pierce has been having a hard time of it financially this past year and a half."

Chance wasn't surprised. Eileen Pierce was known for her extravagant ways and had likely not taken well to the idea of living frugally. In fact, a lot of folks blamed her excesses for driving Thomas to steal in the first place.

Adam rubbed his jaw. "She told me about a week ago that a firm from back East had offered to buy out her portion, including the debts she still owed."

"And the name of the firm?"

"Arminda May Holdings."

Chance groaned. Arminda May had been the name of his father's mother.

"Does that mean your father is involved in the company?"

"My father *owns* the company."

Adam studied him carefully. "And I take it that that is not a good thing where you're concerned."

Now *there* was an understatement. "Let's just say my father and I have rarely seen eye to eye on anything."

"So it's not a coincidence that he decided to invest here in Turnabout."

Chance's smile held no humor. "Oh, no. In fact it was a very strategic move on his part."

"Anything I can do?"

Chance shook his head. "Thanks, but no. This is between him and me."

Adam nodded. "Let me know if that changes." Then he

grinned. "Now, do you want to tell me about your house-guests?"

Chance returned the grin, welcoming the change of subject. "Quite an interesting pair. Leo is a runaway who slipped aboard the train at Texarkana. He got caught and booted off here. Miss Pickering is a Good Samaritan who came to his rescue and is now stranded here in town because of it."

"And you took them in out of the goodness of your heart." Adam's tone held a there's-more-to-this-than-you're-saying air.

But Chance didn't rise to the bait. "It was one of those right place, right time things. I had lots of unused rooms and they needed a place to stay. And Ward, in his role as sheriff, insists on having someone he knows take responsibility for the boy until he can get the kid's story checked out. It'll only be for a couple of days."

"A sensible approach. I hear Dotty's moving in, as well."

"She had the advantage of having met them at the depot this morning and I could tell she took a fancy to them. And you know Dotty. I'd barely finished explaining the situation to her before she volunteered to help."

"Taking two lost lambs under her wing is going to perk Dotty right up."

Chance had thought as much himself. Dotty was happiest when she had had someone to fuss over. But he merely shrugged. "It's all temporary—one way or the other I expect those two will be gone before the week is out. In the meantime it'll be an interesting diversion—nothing more."

Adam raised a brow at that, as if he wasn't quite buying Chance's story. But Chance figured he'd already said enough—maybe too much. He stood and held out a hand. "I'd better be going. I need to stop at the blacksmith shop to talk to Wilbur, then I promised Dotty I'd go by the boardinghouse to help her move her things."

As Chance stepped out onto the sidewalk his thoughts turned back to his father. Adam had answered one of his questions. The other still remained. How in the world had his father known about the loan in the first place?

Was it possible the man had found a way to keep up with his affairs from afar? Chance wasn't sure if he was more surprised at his father's ability to do so or by the fact that he'd actually been interested enough in the son he considered a black sheep to go to the trouble.

But that was irrelevant now. The more important question was what was he going to do about it going forward? How was he going to counter his father's latest move to control him?

It was probably just as well Leo and Eve would be gone before his father arrived. The man would definitely not approve of him taking in two strangers, and he could make their stay very uncomfortable for them.

Then again, it might have been a fun meeting to watch. He had a feeling, beneath her meek exterior, Eve could give as good as she got.

Should he respond to his father's letter? Or just ignore it? No, ignoring it would send the wrong message.

When it came down to it, though, what could he really say? Telling his father not to come would serve no purpose. Once the man made his mind up about something nothing could dissuade him.

On the other hand, he couldn't tell his father he was looking forward to the visit—that would be an out and out lie.

He supposed he could just write and say that he'd received the letter and would be expecting him, then leave it at that. Direct and matter-of-fact with no hint of either confrontation or tractability. He'd get Dotty to write it up for him before he moved her into The Blue Bottle.

He only hoped he could maintain the same unflappable, businesslike demeanor when he and his father met together again face-to-face.

Chapter Seven

Eve found the storeroom Chance had mentioned without any problem. But when she opened the door she discovered much more than just cleaning supplies. The room was about half the size of one of the bedrooms upstairs and was crammed with chairs, tables and a mishmash of odds and ends, all in various stages of repair. Perhaps she would explore it a bit more when her immediate tasks were complete. After all, he *had* said to help herself to whatever she might need.

With Leo's assistance, she made quick work of the sweeping and dusting in all three rooms. As soon as those chores were done, she turned to Leo. "I have an idea of something we could do to surprise Mr. Dawson. Would you like to help me?"

His eyes brightened with interest. "Yes, ma'am."

She led him down to the storeroom and opened the door. "Let's see if we can find at least two additional tables in this group that are sturdy enough to set out. As for the chairs, we'll make use of as many as we can find that are still serviceable." She pushed up her sleeves. "Mr. Dawson isn't living here alone anymore. We need to have a proper sitting room, or as close to one as we can manage."

She spied a can of something near the door and peered inside. "Oh, good. This looks like furniture polish." She gave Leo a raised brow look. "Would you prefer to drag out the furniture and sort through it, or clean and polish the pieces?"

Leo didn't hesitate. "I'll sort through all this stuff."

She grinned. "I thought that might be your choice. Very well. I'll get started cleaning and polishing the pieces already out there while you begin on this. Most of the pieces appear to be damaged, but as you find something you think might work, drag it to the foot of the stairs."

Leo eventually found two tables and six chairs that seemed usable. Eve cleaned and polished them. When she had coaxed as much shine from the wooden surfaces as she could, she had Leo help her move things around until she was finally satisfied with the arrangement.

The four tables had been moved closer to the center of the open space and were arranged in pairs with a nice aisle between them. Each table had two chairs pulled up to it. And though there were still scorch marks visible on several of the pieces, they were clean and held a subtle gleam brought out by the polish.

"Do you think Mr. Dawson will like it?" Leo asked.

Eve rubbed her cheek thoughtfully. "I wish I had some tablecloths for them, but considering what we had to work with, I think we did quite well."

The words had barely crossed her lips when she heard the door swing open behind her. She turned to see Dotty and Mr. Dawson step inside. It seemed they were about to learn what Mr. Dawson thought of their efforts.

She set her cleaning rag down on one of the chairs and hurried to help Dotty with the load she was carrying.

"Mrs. Epps. It is so very good to see you again."

"Hello, my dear." Dotty wore a warm smile. "And none

of this Mrs. Epps business—it's Dotty, remember? Isn't it lovely how things have worked out for us to spend some time together?"

"Quite lovely." Eve held out a hand. "Here, let me take that for you." The item turned out to be a vining sort of potted plant with fuzzy green leaves that had a purple tinge to them. It was unusual-looking, but Eve decided she liked it.

She'd just set the plant down when Mr. Dawson cleared his throat. "Looks like you've been busy while I was gone."

She met his gaze diffidently. Did he think she'd been too presumptuous? "I hope you don't mind. I thought this arrangement might better accommodate your expanded household."

"It was indeed presumptuous." Then he smiled. "But I like the results so you're forgiven."

Eve relaxed. That warm glow she felt was from a job well done, she told herself, *not* from his infectious smile.

Dotty straightened. "If someone will show me which room is mine I'll start getting settled in."

Eve smiled. "Of course. We left you the room at the head of the stairs."

While Leo and Mr. Dawson carted Dotty's other belongings up the stairs, Eve helped her new friend unpack and set out her things.

"I want to thank you for agreeing to move out of your home and serve as chaperone for us these next few days," Eve said. "I know it must have been quite an imposition, but it has certainly simplified matters for Leo and me."

Dotty flipped her hand dismissively. "Not at all. And that boardinghouse might be where I live but it's not really my home."

Eve paused. "What do you mean?"

"My real home—the place where my Gregory brought me when we married, where my children were born and where my husband died, the place where we laughed and loved and grieved—that burned down six weeks ago."

"Oh, Dotty, I'm so very sorry." Eve immediately crossed the room and gave her an impulsive hug. Then she stepped back, mortified by her forwardness.

But Dotty seemed not to mind. "That's sweet of you to say, but please don't feel sorry for me. I had twenty-eight wonderful years with my Gregory and even more with my home. Everything happens for a reason and the Good Lord sees us through whatever comes our way."

Everything happens for a reason—did that include this day's events?

"Besides, I managed to save my family Bible and a necklace that belonged to my mother along with a few other personal items—that's all I really need."

Eve admired her positive attitude. But before Eve could respond, Mr. Dawson and Leo entered with another load of Dotty's things.

"That's the last of it," Mr. Dawson said. "Is there anything else we can do for you?"

"Oh dear me, no," Dotty said. "Thank you for all of your help." She turned to Eve. "You, too, my dear. Run along with you, I can finish up in here."

Eve nodded. "Very well. I'll bring in the sheets from the line. They should have had enough time to air out by now." She glanced Leo's way. "Want to help me?"

"Mr. Dawson brought her here in the motor carriage," Leo blurted out rather than answering her question.

Not that that was news to her. One would need to be deaf to have not heard their arrival earlier.

"You should see it—all big and shiny," he continued. Then he turned to Mr. Dawson. "Can I have a ride in it?"

"I do need to park it back in the shed," he said. "It's not

much of a ride but you're welcome to come along. That is, if Miss Pickering doesn't mind."

Leo shot her a pleading glance and she couldn't help but smile. She was quite pleased that Mr. Dawson had remembered to defer to her rather than make the decision himself. "I think I can manage to get the sheets in on my own."

She was rewarded with a brilliant smile from Leo.

Mr. Dawson straightened and gave Leo a wink. "Sounds like you're gonna get that ride you want." He turned to Eve and Dotty. "You two ladies are welcome to join us, if you like."

Dotty spoke up first. "I've just ridden in that fancy contraption of yours, Chance Dawson. I think I'll stay right where I am and finish getting settled in. I may even take myself a nap."

He turned to Eve. "And what about you?"

"Thank you, but as I said, I need to bring in the sheets and get the beds made up."

"Oh, I'm sure that can wait a bit," Dotty said. "You ought to go. A ride in that outlandish vehicle is worth experiencing at least once."

But Eve was determined not to let temptation take hold. "Those sheets won't take care of themselves. As my grandmother always said, if something needs doing, then it's better to do it sooner than later. I'm sure there will be other opportunities."

Dotty gave her a pointed look. "No offense to your grandmother, but *my* grandmother always said, 'A little play, every day, keeps the heart light and gay.'"

It seemed their grandmothers had been two very different women.

"I like that saying a *lot* better," Leo said.

"Me, too," Mr. Dawson added.

Eve ignored them both and gave Dotty a shake of her

head. "All the same, I'd prefer to take care of those sheets for now." Then she smiled at Leo and Mr. Dawson. "But I will accompany you as far as the bottom of the stairs."

Mr. Dawson shook his head, but he said nothing more on the subject, merely stood aside for her to precede him out the door.

She could tell he didn't understand her choice. Didn't he have any appreciation for a strong sense of responsibility? Perhaps she could show him by her example how industriousness was its own reward.

They were near the bottom of the stairs when something across the room caught her eye. Shoved up against one wall, almost hidden by the clutter, was a large object that looked very much like a piano.

She let Leo and Mr. Dawson go on ahead of her, lagging behind on the pretext of putting away the broom she'd set aside when Dotty arrived. Then she crossed the room, drawn to the instrument like a cat to cream. She traced a hand across the scratched and dusty surface, wincing at the obvious signs of neglect. Would it still play? Or had it been damaged by the fire?

Would Mr. Dawson mind if she tried it out? It had been quite a while since she'd had the opportunity to play.

Then she remembered that only moments ago she'd professed her belief in getting work done before play, and stepped back. Perhaps later this evening then.

She turned and determinedly headed outside without a backward look.

After parking the motor carriage, Chance spent some time letting Leo examine every aspect of it. The boy even climbed behind the wheel to pretend-drive the vehicle.

And all the while, he was thinking about the young woman busying herself with work that could have been easily put off. Was she doing it because she was truly so disciplined? Or was she trying to avoid spending time with him? Did she even know how to relax and have a bit of fun?

He had, in fact, turned down the boy's pleas for a longer ride in the motor carriage because he didn't think Eve would approve of the outing and he'd promised to let her decide matters concerning the boy. But he was going to need to find a way to get her to relax a bit or Leo would be caged tighter than a bear at the circus.

When they eventually went back inside, they found Eve vigorously polishing the counter. Did she plan to give his entire place a thorough cleaning?

"Hello there," he said, claiming her attention. "I'm headed over to the sawmill. Want to come along and get a look at the other end of town?"

She paused and he saw her flex her fingers. How long had she been at this?

"No, thank you. There are still a few things I'd like to get done here before supper."

Definitely much too serious and industrious. "Suit yourself."

"But speaking of supper," she said before he could turn away, "I was wondering—what time do you usually eat your evening meal?"

Was she already hungry? "Normally around five-thirty or so, but we can go early if you want to. I take most of my meals at Daisy's."

Eve shook her head. "Five-thirty is fine. But there'll be no need to go to Daisy's while I'm here. The least I can do to repay you for your generosity in giving us a place to stay is to cook your meals."

He grinned. Now there was a benefit he hadn't expected. "If you're waiting for me to refuse your offer, you're going to be disappointed."

She smiled at that. "Good. I'll warn you that I'm not as good a cook as Daisy, but I can prepare a meal that is both filling and satisfying."

"That's better than I can claim for my own attempts."

"It's settled then." She seemed genuinely pleased. "Just show me to your kitchen so I can take a look at how well your pantry is stocked and plan a menu."

Chance grimaced. "Since I don't do much cooking, I'm afraid you'll find it sadly lacking. Make me a list of what you'll need and I'll stop by the mercantile while I'm out." He could drop her list off and let Doug pull the items together while he took care of his other business, then pick up the order on his way back.

He led her into the kitchen and watched as she made a very thorough inventory, meticulously jotting down items as she went.

She finally turned and handed him her list. "You weren't exaggerating—the pantry is almost bare. I've listed what I consider staples."

Chance took a look at the list and whistled. He might not be able to read it, but he could tell it was *very* long. "Perhaps you'd better come with me after all."

She worried at her lower lip with her teeth, then reached to take the list back from him. "If it's too much I can try to eliminate some of the—"

He drew it back out of her reach. "No, no. You said these items were essentials, and I'm taking your word for that. But I insist that you accompany me in case Doug— the man who owns the mercantile—has questions about anything on the list."

She frowned uncertainly. "If you really think that's necessary..."

"I do."

"Can I go, too?" Leo looked at her hopefully.

Chance spoke up before she could. "If it's okay with Miss Pickering, it's okay with me."

"Of course you may." She moved to the stairs. "Just give me a minute to let Dotty know where we're going."

Chance smiled as he watched her climb the stairs. At least she hadn't asked for time to finish polishing the counter.

When they arrived at the mercantile they met Adam's wife, Reggie, and their adopted eight-year-old son, Jack, approaching from the other direction.

Chance quickly stepped forward. "Let me get that door for you."

Once inside Chance quickly made the introductions. "Eve, this is Regina Barr and her son, Jack. Reggie's one of the first people I met when I came here from Philadelphia. She's also a photographer extraordinaire."

Eve's eyes widened. "A photographer—how exciting."

Reggie grinned. "Not as exciting as it sounds, but I enjoy what I do."

Chance tilted his head in Eve's direction. "And Reggie, this is Eve Pickering, who just arrived in town on this morning's train, and her young friend Leo."

"Pleased to meet you," Reggie said. "And I'll admit that I'd already heard a little about Turnabout's most recent arrivals." She grinned. "In a town like Turnabout news gets around fast."

Chance was relieved to see Eve smile back at that. It was hard to tell just what sort of comment would get her back up.

"It would be the same in my hometown of Iron Bluff." Her expression softened further. "Everyone here has been very kind to a pair of stranded strangers. Especially Mr. Dawson."

The quick look of gratitude she shot his way caught

him by surprise. Perhaps his finer qualities hadn't been lost on her after all. But he noticed she still hadn't used his first name.

Reggie gave him an amused look. "So I've heard." Then she turned back to Eve. "I'm glad to hear you have a good first impression of our town." She cut Chance another amused look. "*And* its citizens."

Before Chance could respond, Jack stepped in and claimed Reggie's attention by tugging on her skirt. "Mr. Blakely said Posey and her pups are in the storeroom. Can I go look?"

Jack's mother glanced toward the mercantile owner. "If it's all right with Mr. Blakely, then I suppose so."

The man waved them toward the storeroom door. "It is. Just don't try to pick up any of the pups."

Eve nodded to Leo before he could ask the question they all knew was coming. "You can go along, too, if you like."

The two boys dashed off.

"I thought Mrs. Peavy normally did your shopping for you," Chance said.

Reggie nodded. "She's busy in the kitchen, getting started on her baking for the Thanksgiving Festival. She just needed a little extra cinnamon and some raisins." Then Reggie turned to Eve. "Has anyone told you about the festival yet?"

Eve nodded. "I've heard a mention or two."

Reggie touched her lightly on the arm. "You must come. I promise you'll be more than welcome there—you and Leo both."

"So I've been told. It sounds like a lovely tradition."

"Oh, it is." Reggie turned to Chance. "See that you explain it all to her and convince her to come."

"I'll do my best." But could he get his all-work-and-no-play houseguest to bend that far?

Chapter Eight

Eve allowed herself to bask for a moment in the obviously sincere invitation from Mr. Dawson's friend.

Then Mrs. Barr shifted the basket she held on her arm. "Well, I'll let you get on with your shopping. I need to finish mine and get back to the house. I left Patricia—that's my five-month-old—in Ira's care."

Eve smiled. "Of course. It was very nice meeting you, Mrs. Barr."

"Oh please, call me Reggie."

As they parted, Eve reflected on how friendly everyone here seemed. She was accustomed to being treated with more reserve, even by folks who'd known her all her life. Then again, these people didn't know her history the way those at home did. Would they treat her differently if they did?

While she and Mr. Dawson moved down the aisle of the mercantile collecting the items on her list, he explained to her that Ira Peavy and his wife were long-time members of the Barr household, more family than hired help. She was learning to appreciate how good he was at explaining things he knew she'd be curious about without her having to ask.

Eve went about her shopping in her usual methodical fashion, or at least she attempted to do so. Mr. Dawson stayed at her elbow and was constantly distracted by items not on the list—like canned peaches, walnuts and maple syrup. She tried to take him to task for it, but since he was quick to tell her that he was the one paying the bill, she finally gave up. By the time she'd checked off the last item on her list, the pile was quite high.

Then Eve had another thought. Telling Mr. Dawson she'd meet him at the counter in a moment, she headed to the corner where several bolts of fabric were shelved. A lovely blue print caught her eye. It was the color of a clear summer sky and had small, cream-colored dots sprinkled across it. Was it as soft as it looked?

Catching herself before her hand could reach out to test it, Eve resolutely turned to the more serviceable cloth next to it. She fingered a heavy cotton, wondering how much it would cost her to buy a few yards. Leo definitely needed new clothing, and she'd like to take care of that for him in the short time she had here. But try as she might, she couldn't figure out a way to make her money stretch far enough. She'd never had any money of her own—living off her grandmother's charity hadn't allowed her to earn anything. The meager funds she had with her had been given to her by her aunts with strict instructions that they be used wisely and hoarded as a hedge against emergencies since the money would be all she had to get by on for a while. For her first six months of being an apprentice for Mrs. O'Connell would earn only her room and board.

But Leo really needed something to wear that wasn't so raggedy-looking. Could she swallow her pride enough, for Leo's sake, to ask Mr. Dawson—

"If you're looking to make a new dress, I'd suggest

the blue rather than that brown." Mr. Dawson stood at her elbow.

She should have known he wouldn't wait patiently at the counter for her. She shook her head with a resolute smile. "It's not for me. All Leo has are the clothes on his back, such as they are. I would like to make him at least one spare change of clothing."

Chance nodded. "Good idea. So you're handy with a needle and thread, are you?"

She shrugged. "It's not something I excel at but I do well enough."

"I tell you what, let's make it a gift from both of us. If you're willing to put in the time to make it, I'll purchase the fabric."

She smiled in relief. "That sounds fair. If I get right on it this afternoon I think I can get him at least a new shirt by tomorrow. And perhaps by the festival I'll be able to get the pants done, as well. At least that will give him one decent change of clothes."

She'd have to sacrifice the time she'd planned to spend reading the book Abigail had loaned her, especially given that she'd likely be on her way to Tyler again in just a couple of days, but it would be worthwhile.

Chance rubbed his chin. "Of course, an active boy could use more than one change—you know, something for every day and then something for Sundays and special occasions. What do you think about taking one of my old suits and using the cloth to make an additional change of clothing for him? Assuming, of course, you have enough time before Leo's situation is resolved."

"I would be more than happy to. But don't you need your suit?"

He shrugged. "I have an older one that doesn't fit me very well anymore, but the fabric is still in good condition. I've been meaning to get rid of it, I just haven't gotten around to doing so."

Mr. Dawson was actually willing to discard a perfectly good suit as opposed to having it altered? Did he have so much money?

He rubbed his jaw thoughtfully. "It seems a shame to just throw it out, but if you prefer to use new cloth——"

"No, of course not," she said quickly. "I mean, if you truly don't want the suit any longer, it would be wasteful not to make use of it."

"Well then, let's see about getting this cloth cut for you and we'll be ready to go."

Eve said a silent prayer of gratitude. God was surely faithful to supply her needs. Even to the point of using someone else's castoffs to do so.

A few moments later, as Mr. Blakely added up their purchases, Eve glanced around for Leo.

"If you're looking for your boy," Mr. Blakely said, "he's still in the back with the pups."

With a thank-you, Eve headed for the storeroom. There she found Leo stooped over a crate.

He looked up when she came in. "Posey is feeding them."

"I see that."

"There's five puppies. What do you suppose Mr. Blakely's going to do with all of them?"

There was a world of longing in his tone and expression, but Eve didn't want to give him any false hope so she carefully worded her response. "I'm sure he'll either keep them or find really good homes for them."

"Oh."

She ignored the disappointment in his tone. "Time for us to go."

Leo stood and, casting one last lingering look at the dog and her pups, preceded her from the room.

By the time they were back in the mercantile proper, Mr. Dawson had settled the bill and made arrangements for delivery of the bulk of their purchases. During the walk back to his place, Leo talked nonstop about the dogs, especially one of the pups, a spotted one that seemed to have been the runt of the litter.

Finally, the boy turned to her. "Did you ever have a dog?"

She shook her head. "I'm afraid not." Her grandmother had considered animals that didn't contribute something to their livelihood to be a waste of time and food.

Leo turned to Mr. Dawson. "What about you?"

"A couple of them, actually. A spaniel we called Tolly and a setter we named Chet."

"We?" Eve asked as they reached The Blue Bottle.

"My brothers and I."

If she had to guess, she'd pick him as the youngest of the siblings. "How many brothers?"

"Three." He stepped forward to hold open the door.

"That must be nice—having a large family, I mean." She'd often thought having siblings would have made her childhood less lonely.

"It has both good points and bad."

She mulled that over as she stepped inside. "Do you see them often?"

"I haven't seen them since I left Philadelphia."

There was something in his tone that made her wonder if perhaps that had been his choice. Maybe she wasn't the only one who'd left home hoping to make a fresh start.

"Miss Pickering."

Eve turned to see the young man from the train depot standing just inside the doorway. "Yes. Can I help you?"

He held out a folded piece of paper. "This came for you a few minutes ago. It's a telegram."

It must be a response to the one I sent to Mrs. O'Connell. Not certain exactly what to expect, she thanked the young man and accepted the slip of paper. She stared at it a long moment before opening it. Finally she steeled herself and scanned the contents.

"Bad news?"

Apparently she hadn't been successful in masking her reaction to the message. Mr. Dawson was studying her with a slight worry—furrow on his brow.

"It's from Mrs. O'Connell, the milliner in Tyler I was supposed to meet. She's not happy that I stood her up."

"Didn't you explain the situation?"

"Only that there was a child in need that I had to assist."

"I see."

Eve couldn't tell what he was thinking. "She says that, in deference to my grandmother, she will hold the position for me until Monday. But this is a busy time of year for her and if I'm not there by then, I need not show up at all."

"That seems harsh."

"No. No, she's right. She made a special allowance to take me on and, from her perspective at least, I broke my word."

"So, what are you going to do?"

"Hopefully the sheriff will have confirmation of Leo's story before then and plans will be made for Leo's welfare. Once that's done, there really isn't any reason for me to remain here."

"I can take care of my own welfare." Leo's tone was defensive and defiant. Then he softened. "But I'll sure be sorry not to have you around here anymore."

"Don't worry, I won't leave until I'm certain you're surrounded by good and loving people."

She wasn't sure how reassured Leo was by her words, but she truly meant them.

She just hoped she could make that happen in the four and a half days between now and Monday.

As Chance carried the items he'd carted from the mercantile into the kitchen he found himself wondering about Eve's words. He absolutely believed she meant what she said about not leaving Leo until she was certain he would be properly cared for. It was amazing to him how much she'd already disrupted her own plans to aid this little boy she'd met only this morning.

But did she truly believe it could all be resolved in five days' time? Reading between the lines he could tell she wasn't eager to start her new life in Tyler. But it seemed just as obvious she was determined to do so anyway.

Which seemed a shame. If one was going to embark on a new adventure, a fresh start, one should look forward to it eagerly, just as he had when he left Philadelphia to come here.

Perhaps she hadn't had any say in the matter. If that was the case could he help change that?

That thought drew him up short. He'd taken responsibility for seeing that she had a roof over her head the next few days, not for solving her happiness issues. What was it about this petite mouse of a woman that had him wanting to slay all her dragons?

Eve looked around the supper table. Supper was over and from all appearances the others were happy with the dishes she'd managed to prepare.

Mr. Dawson pushed back from the table with a satisfied smile. "You were too modest earlier. That was a mighty fine meal."

Eve's chest warmed at his praise, but she knew he was being generous. "Thank you. I got a late start so I didn't have time to bake bread. But perhaps I can remedy that tomorrow."

"No need for apologies," he assured her. "I don't think any of us are leaving the table hungry."

Dotty stood and reached for an empty platter. "You cooked the meal, so you must let me do the cleanup."

Eve frowned. "I'll do no such thing. I—"

But Dotty shook her head. "No arguments—I insist. I haven't seen you stop for even a minute since I arrived. Run along with you and relax for a bit."

"I like to keep busy." Besides, she'd been taught the younger members of the household never sat down to rest before the older ones did.

But Dotty was apparently having none of it. "Then find something relaxing to keep busy with."

Not wanting to get into an argument, Eve decided on a compromise. "Well, if you insist on taking care of the kitchen, I do have some sewing to attend to."

The older woman gave her an exasperated look. "That wasn't exactly what I had in mind." She turned to Chance. "You try to talk some sense into her. If anyone knows how to relax and enjoy life, it's you."

Eve had no trouble believing that.

Mr. Dawson smiled. "I'll see what I can do." He turned to Eve. "I seem to recall your borrowing a book from Abigail this morning."

Dotty gave a satisfied nod. "Now that sounds like just the thing." She turned to Leo. "As for you young man, I will allow *you* to assist me." She nodded toward the table. "Why don't you fetch me a stack of those dirty dishes while I fill the basin with warm water?"

Leo didn't look very happy with the request but to his credit he answered politely enough. "Yes, ma'am."

Mr. Dawson gave Eve a short bow and swept his arm toward the door. "Shall we leave these two to their work?"

Eve nodded and preceded him from the room. Once they were in the main room, she turned to him with a businesslike smile. "I appreciate that you and Dotty are trying to be kind, but I think it best if I get to sewing those new clothes for Leo. He is in dire need of them."

"Well, I certainly won't try to force you to relax. You're free to do as you please."

Eve was caught off guard by his easy capitulation. But before she'd taken more than a couple of steps toward the stairs, he spoke again. "By the way, I saw you eyeing the piano earlier. Do you play?"

He'd seen that? She thought she'd waited until she was alone to examine it. But there was no point in denying her interest. "Mrs. Mulvaney, our church pianist, taught me to play so I could fill in for her when she couldn't be there. Though I'm not as good as she is I've always enjoyed playing." In fact, she found great joy in it.

But there was sewing to be done. She turned her steps resolutely toward the stairs.

Chance noticed Eve had a tendency to downplay her abilities. She'd done it with her cooking earlier, when talking about her sewing skills and now this. Was she merely modest or did she really not know her own talents?

But rather than pursuing that train of thought, he spoke up quickly before she could reach the stairway. "The instrument was here when I took ownership of the place and other than to move it out of my way, I haven't paid much attention to it since then. To tell you the truth, I'm not even sure if it still functions." He saw a hint of longing in her eyes as she turned back to study the piano.

So she *was* more tempted than she'd let on. "Before you collect your sewing, I'd consider it a favor if you'd play a tune or two so I can see if it still works." He pulled a chair from one of the workbenches and set it in front of the instrument. "I don't know what became of the original bench—this is the best I can do for now."

She hesitated and he saw her nibble at her lower lip as she glanced guiltily toward the stairs. Would her strict sense of duty win out over her desire to give the instrument a try?

Time to press a little harder. "It truly would be a help to me to have someone who knows what they're doing try it out. Then I'll know whether it's worth the effort to get it tuned or I should just chop it up for firewood."

She cast him a horrified glance. "Oh, surely you wouldn't do that? I mean, other than the scorch marks, it looks to be intact." She moved toward the instrument. "I suppose the sewing can wait just a few more minutes."

He managed to suppress a triumphant grin. "If you're sure it's not an imposition…"

A smile tugged at her lips and there was a flash of guilty anticipation in her eyes. It was the same expression she'd worn when studying the titles in Abigail's library. He liked her smile—it was the guilty part that bothered him. Why couldn't she just take pleasure in such harmless entertainments?

He swiped at the bench with a rag, then lifted the keyboard cover. "How's this?"

Eve settled onto the bench gracefully then smiled up at him. "Thank you, it will do nicely."

She placed her hands on the keyboard and he wondered what song she would select.

She tentatively played a few opening notes, then paused. There was no sheet music—had she forgotten the rest? Or was it his presence that inhibited her?

But then she straightened, lifted her head and started again. This time she played with more confidence, seeming to lose herself in the music. He recognized the melody from a hymn his mother used to sing while she was gardening. As Eve played on, she hit a few flat notes but overall it seemed the instrument was sound.

When the piece was ended, she rested her hands on her lap, and her mind seemed to be miles away.

"That was quite good."

She jumped, as if she'd forgotten he was standing there. Then she quickly stood and moved away from the instrument. "I… Thank you."

That protective urge he'd felt twice earlier, once on the platform at the depot and once in the sheriff's office, kicked in again.

Luckily, Dotty and Leo stepped out of the kitchen before he could respond. "Eve, you must be responsible for that lovely music," Dotty said.

Chance answered first, glad for a reason to shift his train of thought. "Of course. And any sour notes you heard were a result of the piano being out of tune. I'll see about getting that taken care of tomorrow—I've heard Daisy mention that her father has that skill."

Predictably, Eve protested. "Oh, no. That's not nec—"

He raised a brow. "Are you telling me I shouldn't get my own piano tuned?"

She reddened. "No, of course not. I only meant—"

"Good. Then it's settled."

He turned to Leo, letting her know he considered the subject closed. "Do you know how to play checkers?"

"Yes, sir."

"Then what do you say we see which one of us is the better strategist?"

Chance felt Eve watching as they set up the board and settled into their game, but he refrained from so much as glancing her way.

A moment later she headed upstairs and he watched her climb and turn to her room. She hadn't said her good-nights so he assumed she wasn't retiring for the evening. At least he sincerely hoped not.

For Leo's sake, of course.

A few minutes later she reappeared with her sewing basket in hand. So much for her relaxing with a book.

He watched peripherally as she crossed the room to the table where Dotty sat. Not that she seemed to be paying any attention to him. Instead she asked Dotty about the knitting project the widow was working on and admired her work.

Once she'd settled into her own needlework, Eve seemed in the mood to fill the conversational void.

"I've heard several mentions of the Thanksgiving Festival since I arrived," she said to Dotty. "Can you tell me more about it?"

Did that mean she'd decided to attend?

"Oh, it's a wonderful time of fellowship," Dotty said enthusiastically. "Everything is focused on celebrating God's bounty and enjoying each other's company. There's lots of food—supplied by the townsfolk themselves, of course."

Dotty resumed her knitting. "Just before lunch Reverend Harper will preside over a short prayer service. There are also games and competitions for both the adults and the children. And of course in the afternoon there's a dance."

"A dance?"

Chance heard a note of something more than idle curiosity in her voice. Was it surprise, nervousness or something else?

"Oh, yes," Dotty responded. "It's quite gay. I don't participate as I did when my Gregory was alive—these days I spend more time in the schoolhouse watching over the infants and toddlers so the young mothers can enjoy themselves."

"I like little ones."

There was a distinct note of relief in Eve's voice. Did she plan to hide out with the little children when the dancing started? He'd have to make sure that didn't happen. "Don't you enjoy going to dances?" he asked.

She turned to him, her cheeks pink. "I don't know. I've never attended one."

"Oh, my stars." Dotty sounded truly shocked. Then she reached over and patted Eve's hand. "Well, then it's high time you did. And I guarantee you'll have a fine time."

Eve fiddled with a button at her throat. "I understand the meal is truly a feast. I'd like to contribute something if I may."

Chance noticed she'd changed the subject without really agreeing to anything concerning the dance.

"There's no need for you to feel obliged," Dotty said. "You're a guest in our town. We don't expect you to provide any of the food."

"Nevertheless, I wouldn't feel right taking part without contributing something."

Was she always so serious about everything—even about something as celebratory and full of fellowship as the upcoming town festival?

"That's very admirable," Dotty was saying. "Of *course,* you may prepare something if you feel so strongly about it. Is there specific dish you had in mind?"

Leo spoke up before Eve could answer. "How about making some of that candy you were talking about?"

"Candy?" Dotty looked intrigued.

Eve waved a hand dismissively. "I mentioned earlier that I enjoy candy making. But this is probably not the right occasion for that. I can prepare some bread or a vegetable dish of some sort."

"Candy sounds a lot better." Leo's expression was hopeful.

"I'm with Leo," Chance chimed in as he made another move on the checkerboard. "There'll be vegetables and breads aplenty. Candy, on the other hand, would be something special." He gave her an innocent look. "Unless that's too much trouble."

"Oh, no, I actually enjoy making candy." Then she turned to Dotty. "What do you think? I mean, candy sounds like a frivolous offering for such a solemn occasion."

"Land sakes, no. It's not so much a solemn occasion as a celebration. I think candy would be a very popular offering. And as Chance mentioned, there will be lots of traditional dishes there already."

Her face lit up. "Very well then, candy it is."

For a woman with the courage to face down the conductor the way she had, she sure was timid when it came to other areas of her life. What had made her so afraid to pursue the things she enjoyed?

Eve smiled as Leo let out a whoop.

"What kind of candy are you going to make?" the boy asked eagerly.

A little bubble of excitement tickled her insides as she thought about his question. It would be such fun to try her hand at candy making again. "It depends on what sort of supplies I can get my hands on, but I think we'll definitely have sugared pecans and pumpkinseed brittle since there should be an abundance of both ingredients. I'd also like to make some pretty fondant candies and maybe some chocolates, but I'm not certain I'll have time to get it all done."

"Oh, boy." Leo leaned forward. "If you need someone to taste for you, I'll be glad to take care of that."

Mr. Dawson grinned. "I'm with Leo, those all sound like delicious treats. And I may just have to arm wrestle him for the chance at being your taster."

"I'm certain I can use two tasters when the time comes."

He glanced Leo's way. "And we can earn that treat by gathering some pecans. I know just the place—we can head out first thing tomorrow."

He glanced Dotty's way. "I hope you're bringing that carrot dish you fixed last year."

"I am." She glanced Eve's way. "Orange-spiced carrots—it was my Gregory's favorite. And, as it happens, I'd planned to make a couple of pumpkin pies, as well. The seeds are yours to use in your brittle if you like."

Later that evening, Eve escorted Leo up to his room. He professed himself to be too old to be tucked in like a baby, but she insisted on fussing over him anyway. The boy had been too long without any cosseting and she aimed to remedy that for the short time she would be in his life.

How long would that be? She couldn't imagine it would take more than a day or two for the sheriff to get a response to his inquiries. Perhaps a little longer since Thanksgiving was the day after tomorrow. But then what? If Leo was truly alone, what would become of him? And what role did she want to play in that? More to the point, what role would she be *allowed* to play in that?

Father above, I know that You are in charge and that things will work out according to Your perfect will. But

*please forgive me for continuing to worry over the matter.
I so want to do whatever I can to assist You, or at least
not get in Your way, to see that Leo is well taken care of.
He's seen so much harshness in his young life. He deserves
to find a home where he will be loved and well cared for.
Show me how to help him.*

   Amen.

Chapter Nine

The next morning, right after breakfast, Eve and Dotty went down to the mercantile to purchase supplies for the cooking they intended to do.

Eve shopped carefully. It was going to take a good portion of her funds to get what she needed, but it didn't feel right using Mr. Dawson's pantry items to prepare her treats. If her stay here lasted much longer she'd have to find some way to earn a bit of money. Of course, this could all be resolved soon and her little adventure would be over. She'd be free to resume her journey and take up her role as a milliner's apprentice.

However, she refused to dwell on that vision of her future at the moment. The here and now was much more exciting, and there would be time enough to think of that after Thanksgiving.

Eve found sharing the kitchen with Dotty was quite different from sharing it with her grandmother. Dotty loved to talk and was full of droll stories about the town and its people, about Thanksgiving Festivals past and about her own life. She tried to draw Eve out about her own life and plans, but Eve managed to deflect most of her questions.

She also showed great interest in Eve's candy-making

efforts, offering to assist without being intrusive, and praising the results.

True to his word, Chance had roused Leo early to go pecan picking and when they returned midmorning they had gathered up more than enough for Eve's candy making. He and Leo sat at the kitchen table cracking and cleaning the nuts while she and Dotty cooked and baked. The conversation was light and teasing and altogether a new experience for Eve.

By the time they halted for a quick lunch, Dotty had one pie cooling on the sill and another in the oven, and Eve had two trays of candies prepared.

Right after lunch, Mr. Johnson, Daisy's father, came by and worked on the piano, while Chance headed into his workshop to tinker with something mechanical that Eve didn't recognize.

When the piano tuner had finished his work, Chance insisted she sit down and play them a song to make certain the instrument was as it should be.

All in all, Eve couldn't remember when she'd spent a happier day.

Thanksgiving morning dawned clear and crisp, cool without being uncomfortably cold—perfect for the festivities, which were to be held outdoors for the most part.

Chance escorted Eve, Leo and Dotty to the school grounds, where already a large crowd gathered. Eve liked the look of this place. The building was painted a cheerful red with white trim, and the schoolyard was well kept and equipped with three teeter-totters and a couple of swings, which were already in use by groups of laughing children.

When they stepped inside the schoolhouse, the first person Eve saw was Reggie Barr, who bustled over to greet them. "Adam was looking for you earlier," she said to Chance.

He hefted the large basket that held Dotty's pies and a few other dishes. "Just tell me where to set this and I'll go track him down."

"Just put it here and we will take care of getting it to the proper spot on the tables." Then she turned to Leo. "Jack and some of the other boys are tossing horseshoes around back by the well if you'd care to join them."

Chance placed a hand on the boy's shoulder. "Come on, I'll show you where that is."

Eve thought both of them looked happy to have an excuse to leave what was obviously the women's domain.

"Where's that sweet little baby girl of yours?" Dotty asked.

"Mrs. Peavy has her for now. I volunteered to help organize the food as it arrives." She grinned. "One of the least demanding jobs the Ladies' Auxiliary had on the list."

There were over a dozen tables lining the walls and all of them held an abundance of food. Eve looked over the platters that weighed down the tables and inhaled appreciatively. "Oh, my, doesn't this all smell wonderful? If it tastes even half as good, then it appears we're in for quite a meal. I imagine there'll be folks tripping over themselves to get a taste."

Reggie laughed. "The ladies of the town outdo themselves every year. Truth to tell, I think there's a bit of a competitive streak involved."

Eve returned her smile. "I suppose there's nothing wrong with striving to do one's best."

Reggie looked inside the basket Chance had set down. "Now, let's have a peek at what goodies you've brought us." Then she grinned in delight. "I see your orange-spiced carrots in here. Thank goodness—it wouldn't be Thanksgiving without them."

"Eve here has a special treat also," Dotty said.

Reggie glanced up. "And what might that be?"

Eve smiled uncertainly. "I made some candies."

"Oooh, that sounds marvelous."

Eve was certain she was just being kind. "I'm afraid it's not much, especially compared to all these beautiful dishes spread out on the tables."

Dotty tsked. "She's just being modest. I tasted a few of these yesterday and I predict they'll go fast. You'd better grab one while you can."

Reggie grinned. "Thanks for the warning. That's one of the good things about this assignment—I get to do a bit of tasting before the meal actually starts." Then she straightened. "And speaking of my job, let's figure out where we're going to set out the yummy contributions you ladies brought."

Just as Eve set the last of the platters on the table, a second woman, one she hadn't met yet, came up to them. "Hello there. You must be Eve Pickering, Mr. Dawson's friend. I'm Eunice Ortolon and I run the boardinghouse here in town."

"Mrs. Ortolon, I'm very glad to meet you. I've passed by your establishment and it looks like a lovely place."

The woman preened. "Why thank you, dear. I do try to keep a tidy, respectable residence for my boarders." She looked at the platters Eve had just placed on the table. "And what have we here?"

Dotty spoke up before Eve could say anything. "Eve has made some candies for us. Don't they look delicious?"

"Candies, you say?" Mrs. Ortolon's tone implied she wasn't certain she approved. "Yes, very nice." Then she smiled at Eve. "Make certain you taste my apple pecan pie—it's right over there. But you'll have to be quick—it always goes fast."

"I'm sure it's quite delicious."

Dotty took Eve's elbow. "Oh, there's Reverend Harper and his wife. Allow me to introduce you." She smiled at Mrs. Ortolon. "Please excuse us, Eunice."

After that, Eve found herself being introduced to and greeted by what seemed to be the entire town. Everyone was friendly and welcoming—so much so that she almost felt like a fraud. Would they be so friendly if they knew her background?

The shifting groups of people seemed almost overwhelming. Except for school and church, she'd led a rather solitary life. The home she'd shared with her grandmother had been on the outskirts of town and not many folks had occasion to pass that way. But today, whenever she turned around, Dotty or Reggie or Daisy was at her elbow, pulling her into another group of friends, introducing her, making her feel warmly accepted. And she enjoyed just strolling around, watching the games. Chance and Leo participated in the three-legged race and took third place. When she gave Leo a congratulatory hug she was pleased to feel him lean into it for just a heartbeat before pulling away with little-boy disdain for such signs of affection.

At one point, Chance approached her with another man in tow. "Eve, this is Adam Barr, Reggie's husband. Adam, this is one of my new houseguests, Eve Pickering."

"Pleased to meet you." Mr. Barr gave her a short bow. "And might I say those candies of yours were a real treat. I barely got a taste before the platter was empty."

"Thank you."

Chance reclaimed her attention. "I discussed Leo's situation with Adam. He's a lawyer and I thought we might need his professional advice at some point."

Did he really think it would come to that? But it was interesting that he had said *we* instead of *you.* "No offense, Mr. Barr, but I hope we *won't* be needing your services."

"No offense taken. Just know that I am willing to help should the need arise." He gave another short bow. "Now if you'll excuse me, I see Reggie is signaling for me to join her."

When he'd gone, Eve turned to Chance. "Do you really think we might need a lawyer?"

Chance shrugged. "Since we don't know the full extent of Leo's problems, I figured it wouldn't hurt to have Adam at least aware of the situation should we discover the boy is in real trouble."

Her expression must have conveyed her worry because he quickly gave her arm a light touch. "Don't worry, whatever the situation, we'll see Leo is taken care of."

Eve nodded, reassured in spite of herself. What was it about this man that made her trust he could work it all out?

Around eleven-thirty, Reverend Harper presided over a short service of Thanksgiving out in the schoolyard. Then he gave thanks for the meal and everyone began to file through the schoolhouse, filling their plates from the oh-so-tempting bounty there.

Several tables with benches had been set up both inside the adjoining classrooms and out in the yard. By tacit agreement these were reserved for the elderly and less agile townsfolk. Everyone else found other accommodations such as the schoolhouse steps or makeshift benches that had been set up, and even blankets spread in the open sunshine.

Eve saw Dotty at one of the inside tables with a group of ladies who appeared close to her in age. Before she could decide whether or not to join her, Chance appeared at her elbow.

"There you are," he said. "I found us a spot to eat."

She hesitated a moment. "Have you seen Leo?"

"He's with Reggie's family. He and Jack have apparently become good friends." He swept a hand out. "Now, if you'll come this way." He steered her to a makeshift table, constructed from a couple of planks set atop two barrels, where Daisy's family was seated. Eve was introduced to the only member of the group she hadn't yet met, Daisy's husband, Everett. She was immediately charmed by his slight British accent and his dry wit. And also by his solicitation for his heavy-with-child wife.

As the meal progressed, Eve felt a yearning grow inside her that was almost a physical ache. The joy and bond these people shared, and that they seemed willing to extend to her, was something she was afraid to accept. Because she knew it couldn't last, and if she ever let it in, she wasn't sure she could stand it when it was ripped away.

After the meal, the activities picked up again. The youngsters indulged in games of tag, horseshoes and even marbles. Some of the girls found a jump rope to play with. Checkerboards and chessboards came out as did dominos and tiddledywinks.

Eve found herself drawn into a discussion of the best way to can fruit.

Abigail approached her at one point in the afternoon. "I understand you're the one who brought that tray of pumpkinseed brittle."

"I am."

"I've never had such a treat before. Who would have guessed that pumpkinseeds could be so scrumptious."

Eve warmed at the praise. "Thank you. I'm glad you enjoyed it."

"I have some friends back in Boston I'd like to send

gifts to for Christmas. I was wondering if you'd be willing to make another batch that I could purchase from you?
I mean if you're going to be here for a few more days and
it's not too much of an imposition."

She'd really liked it that much? "I'd be happy to, but
you don't have to pay me."

"Oh, but—"

"Consider it payment for that book you loaned me from
your library."

Abigail grinned. "Well, if you put it that way I suppose
I won't argue. But I insist on paying for the ingredients."
She smiled. "Which is not saying a lot because I can get
the seeds from Daisy—she's been baking a lot of pumpkin pies lately for the restaurant."

Eve returned her smile. "In that case you have a deal. I'll
prepare a batch for you as soon as you get me the seeds."

As Abigail walked away, Eve felt a small spark of pride.
Someone had actually wanted to *purchase* her candies. If
things didn't work out for her with Mrs. O'Connell, perhaps she could find a position at a candy store there in
Tyler.

Chance smiled. He'd overheard the exchange between
Abigail and Eve and had seen the way it had put that unfamiliar smile of self-satisfaction on Eve's face. Had she
finally started to come out of that timid shell she'd encased
herself in? Perhaps there was hope he could entice her to
participate in the dance after all.

And he was honest enough to admit his motives for
wanting that weren't entirely altruistic.

Chapter Ten

❧

By late afternoon, a large area had been cleared and two men with fiddles took their places on the edge of the circle. After some initial tuning, they began to play a lively tune. It wasn't long before young men began to draw ladies onto the makeshift dance floor. Like butterflies on the wind, twirling couples with tapping feet and swishing skirts soon filled the area.

After only a few minutes, Eve realized her toes were tapping, as well. She drew her shawl closer around her shoulders, feeling the chill of the day. When the second set started, she quietly turned away from the dancers and moved toward the schoolhouse. She glanced toward the children playing with a stick and ball on the other end of the schoolyard. Satisfied Leo was still among them, she stepped through the schoolhouse door. The music was still audible inside but much more muted.

The schoolroom itself was surprisingly full. This was where the babies were bedded down with some of the ladies taking shifts to watch over them. There were also others moving in and out to revisit the refreshment tables, which still contained quite a bit of food.

As she slowly crossed the room, Eve thought about the

merriment outside. Chance seemed to be in high demand as a dance partner. Abigail had quickly claimed him for the first dance, leaving several disappointed ladies in her wake. Almost before he'd escorted her back to the crowd of onlookers, another lady, one closer to his own age, claimed him for the next dance.

Eve herself hadn't been without petitioners. Daisy's husband had gallantly asked her to dance with him for the first set, but she'd managed to decline by responding she had a pebble in her shoe. She'd moved to one of the nearby benches to remove the offending pebble but still, the sight of the happy dancers and the beat of the music had momentarily entranced her, filling her with a yearning to take part that surprised her.

When she'd realized what was happening she immediately retreated inside.

Looking for a familiar face, she spotted Dotty gently holding the Barrs' little girl.

"Why, hello there," Dotty said as she approached. "Are you enjoying yourself?"

Eve smiled. "Very much so. Everyone is friendly and the festival itself is everything you said it would be."

"Good. And not to say I told you so, but those candies of yours were quite a popular offering today. They certainly disappeared quickly."

Eve had heard that over and over this afternoon. She'd never dreamed her candies would be so well received. "It was the least I could do. I appreciate everyone allowing Leo and me to participate in the festivities."

"That's what Thanksgiving is all about, isn't it?" Dotty patted the baby. "Leo seems to be enjoying himself, as well."

"It does my heart good to see him smiling so freely. I

think he's struck up a friendship with Reggie's son." She doubted he'd had many friends these past few years.

Then Dotty turned serious. "Pardon my asking, but what are you doing in here? You should be out there enjoying yourself with the young folk, not in here watching over the babies with us old folk. You can't tell me no one's asked you to dance."

"I've been asked, but I'm afraid I'm not one for dancing."

"Bless my soul, why ever not? Just because you've never danced before is no reason to be shy about it." Her expression softened. "I remember in my younger days how I did enjoy whirling around the dance floor on the arm of a handsome lad. Nothing like it to make a girl feel alive." She sighed like a young schoolgirl. "And my Gregory was the best of the lot. He made me feel graceful and beautiful."

Eve could still hear the music through the open door and felt her pulse respond to it. It was all she could do to keep her foot from tapping again. What would it be like to do as Dotty described, to surrender to the joy of the music? Her treacherous mind pictured it in vivid detail. It took her a moment to realize the partner she pictured herself dancing with was Chance.

Oh, dear. That will not do. Theirs was not that sort of relationship.

Reggie and Daisy approached arm in arm. "How is Patricia doing?" Reggie asked.

Dotty glanced down at the now-still bundle in her arms. "She's sleeping soundly, the little lamb. Don't you worry about her. I'll come fetch you if she gets hungry."

"I've come to relieve you," Daisy said.

"Oh, there's no need for that." Dotty waved her hand in a shooing motion. "Y'all just go on and enjoy the music while you can."

Daisy eased herself into a chair next to Dotty. "Actually, I've been ordered by my worrywart of a husband to get off of my feet for a while."

Reggie laughed. "Husbands can be such fussbudgets when their wives are expecting."

Daisy rolled her eyes. "Amen. Still, it doesn't hurt to indulge them occasionally." Then she reached over to take Patricia from Dotty. "And don't tell me you're not itching to get out there yourself."

Dotty handed over the baby. "I do enjoy a good spin on the dance floor." She grinned at her companions. "I imagine we more experienced folk can still show you young'uns a thing or two."

Reggie laughed. "I never doubted that for a minute. Let me just have a look at Patricia before I go back out."

Dotty tilted her head Eve's way. "You need to help me convince this one. She's never attended a dance before and I think she's a bit shy."

"Is that true?" Reggie's eyes widened and both she and Daisy looked at Eve as if she'd admitted to never having tasted water.

"Well, yes. I mean, dancing is such a frivolous activity and there were always more productive things to—" She halted abruptly as the heat climbed in her face. Had she just insulted her new friends?

But Daisy was shaking her head with a smile. "A person needs to find time to enjoy herself as well as work. Even the Bible tells us that there is a time for everything in life, including a time to weep and a time to laugh, a time to mourn and a time to *dance*."

Reggie nodded firmly. "Absolutely." She took both of Eve's hands and drew her toward the door. "Come along, we're going to fill that void in your education right now."

"Oh, no. I——" Eve felt a bubble of panic rise in her throat.

"I'm not taking no for an answer. And don't worry about learning the steps. There's nothing to it, especially if you have the right partner. And I know just the man for the job. Chance is wonderful when it comes to making his partner feel at ease. And I think he'd like to be rescued from the designs of a few matchmaking matrons."

"He didn't appear to be bothered by it earlier."

Reggie laughed. "So you *did* notice him." She gave Eve's hand another tug. "Stop dragging your feet. It sounds like the current set is winding down."

Eve tried to protest once more, but Reggie was having none of it. In less than a minute she found herself on the edge of the crowd of dancers.

The music had just stopped and Chance was escorting his current partner back to a group of other young people. Reggie hailed him and he excused himself from the group with a smile.

Chance was approached twice on his way to meet them and both times he extricated himself with a quick word and a smile.

"There you are," he said to Eve as he neared. "I wondered where you'd disappeared to."

Had he really noted her absence or was he just being polite? She tried to maintain a calm demeanor. "I stepped inside the schoolhouse for a few minutes."

"Ah, slipping back to the tables for seconds, were you?"

Reggie tapped his arm lightly. "Stop your teasing. I have an assignment for you."

Chance gave a short bow. "At your service, as always."

"Eve here has never participated in a dance before and I'm looking for someone who can guide her through the steps."

Chance gave her a gallant smile and offered her his arm. "It would be my pleasure to partner you in your first dance."

It was so wrong for Reggie to paint him into a corner this way. The poor man really had no choice but to comply. "Oh, please, that's not necessary." It was hard to put much conviction in her tone, though, when she was sorely tempted.

"Perhaps it's not necessary, but it *is* fun." He jiggled his elbow. "Shall we?"

"But I don't dance."

A small furrow appeared above his brow. "You mean you *haven't* danced."

"No, I mean yes—I mean I've never—"

"So we've already established. Don't worry, you'll get the hang of it in no time."

"You don't understand. I don't want—"

But, just as Reggie had earlier, he paid no attention whatsoever to her protests. "No need to be shy or embarrassed. This isn't some fancy drawing room. No one here worries about how well you do, so long as you're having fun."

His words served only to remind her that he had been to fancy drawing rooms and no doubt danced with ladies far more graceful than she.

Eve caught sight of Reverend Harper leading his wife out onto the dance floor and her resistance wavered once more. Surely, if the preacher participated, there could be nothing inherently wrong with the activity. And it would be only one dance, just to see how it felt.

"Besides," Chance continued with a hint of challenge in his tone, "if I can help make candy, then you can dance."

Why did he care so much? Was it because he was trying to please Reggie, who'd backed him into this corner?

But people were starting to notice their discussion and Eve decided it would be best to just dance with him and get it over with. After that she could disappear back into the schoolhouse.

And truth to tell, she was a bit curious as to what it would be like to give in to the music the way the other dancers were doing.

Before she quite realized that they had moved, she found herself on the edge of the dance floor, facing Chance.

"Rest your hands on my shoulders, like so," he said as he positioned her hands. "I'm going to place my hands lightly at your waist, like so."

The feel of his hands at her waist shocked her, sent a little shiver of surprise coursing through her.

But Chance's expression didn't change and she quickly got herself back under control. Of course it was nothing to him, he'd held any number of ladies thusly tonight. It was just the novelty of it that had caught her off guard.

"Now, keep your eyes on mine, relax and feel the rhythm of the music."

Feel the rhythm of the music—yes, she could do that. Relaxing might be a little more difficult.

"Ready?" When she nodded, he smiled approval. "Good girl. Just follow my lead."

He began leading her through the steps of the dance, patiently directing her.

At first Eve was self-conscious, stiff. She was still very aware of the way he held her and of the warmth radiating from him under her own hands. But his gaze held hers, full of encouragement, and challenging her to keep time with him. It didn't take her long to relax into the music and let all her worries slip away for a little while. It was as if she and Chance were encased in a bubble of sound and movement and glowing, swirling colors. For the moment that was all that existed—that and the feel of Chance's hands at her waist, connecting her to him, making her feel safe.

It was a lively tune and by the time it was over, her pulse was pounding with the exertion and exhilaration, and she was laughing. She understood now why everyone was enjoying themselves so much, why Dotty had spoken of dancing in such glowing terms.

Chance smiled down approvingly and it warmed her down to her toes. She couldn't remember feeling quite this happy before.

He turned to lead her out of the dance circle and abruptly the bubble burst. The real world came crashing back in and she saw herself as her grandmother would see her—as the embodiment of her wayward mother. The smile died on her lips and she stumbled slightly.

Chance's expression turned from pleasure to concern as he took a firmer hold of her elbow. "Are you all right? Do you need to sit down for a moment?"

She stepped away from him. "No, I—" She took a deep breath and attempted a polite, dismissive smile. "I thank you for the dance. You're an excellent teacher. But I think I'm just tired from all of the day's activities. If you'll excuse me, I believe I'll find Leo and head back to your place."

His concerned expression deepened. "You're much too pale. Why don't you sit a minute and let me get you a glass of punch?"

"No." Eve realized she'd said that a bit sharper than she'd intended. She took a breath and moderated her tone. "I mean, that's very kind, but I think it best if I just go back to my room and rest." She attempted a smile. "I'm okay, truly."

"Then at least let me escort you."

She took another step back, widening the distance between them. "That won't be necessary. I'm perfectly fine. Just a little tired is all." She glanced around, glad for a reason to drop her gaze from his. "Have you seen Leo?"

"He's over by that hickory tree with a bunch of other kids." His tone had lost most of its warmth. She felt a pang of regret, but perhaps it was best. It wasn't his fault she'd let her guard down. And that she suddenly couldn't seem to think straight

"It's early yet," he continued in that same formal tone, "and there's no point in cutting *his* fun short. I'll see that he gets back well before bedtime."

Eve hesitated. Her gut reaction was to hold tight to Leo, to keep him close. But she knew he needed some fun in his life right now, a chance to be carefree as a child should, as he hadn't been able to be since his parents passed away.

She finally nodded, then turned and walked away.

Chapter Eleven

Chance watched Eve leave the schoolyard, her back stiff, her steps determined. What had just happened? He was absolutely certain she'd been enjoying herself out on the dance floor. And that enjoyment had transformed her into graceful young woman.

And to be perfectly honest, he'd been enjoying himself. She was so small, so fragile seeming—it had made him feel protective. Holding her petite form had felt very right. And knowing he was her first dance partner added an extra fillip of pleasure. Watching her discover the delight of moving in time to the music, so completely losing herself to the rhythm of the piece, had been quite satisfying.

But then the music had ended and it was as if someone had dumped a bucket of cold water over her. As if she'd suddenly realized she was having fun and her prim nature had been shocked, had rebelled.

Well, she'd had a taste of it now, and he strongly suspected she'd savored that taste, in spite of herself. If that made her uncomfortable, wounded her sensibilities, then so be it. Her biggest problem was that she needed more practice at having fun—perhaps then it wouldn't frighten her.

At least she'd had the sense to not let her own crisis of conscience spoil Leo's fun.

Chance was momentarily distracted by the sight of Walter Hendricks, the carpenter, talking to his son Calvin. A moment later Walter gave Calvin a clap on the shoulder and a broad smile of approval.

The sharp stab of jealousy he felt took him completely by surprise. He couldn't remember a time when he'd had such a moment with his own father. He thought he'd long ago gotten past letting that affect him but apparently it could still catch him at unguarded moments.

He'd need to work on his control before his father arrived.

Eve walked through the nearly deserted streets of town, her mind a tangle of emotions. Her grandmother had always warned her against participating in the town dances or any such activity that included single young men. It was just such an event, after all, that had set the wheels in motion that led to her mother's downfall.

But surely an activity that the whole town, including the preacher, participated in couldn't be as sinful and fraught with temptation as her grandmother believed. And it had felt so wonderful, so joyous, so *fun*.

But maybe that was the problem. Maybe it wasn't the activity itself, but her response to it that was so dangerous. Maybe she was more like her mother than she had believed.

Because, if she were being totally honest with herself, it hadn't been just the music that she had enjoyed, but the experience of being held by Chance. Something in her had responded to his attention and the sensation of being safe and somehow valued while he held her. Is that how her mother had felt when she'd first danced with her father?

Oh, why had she given in? She should have stayed in the

schoolhouse with the babies and their caretakers. Things had been going so well—she'd made new friends and felt she was making a difference with Leo. And now, like so many times before, she'd failed to think things through.

Her grandmother had been right—when faced with the temptation, she had succumbed. It was a slippery slope and she needed to make very certain she didn't slide down it.

If only she'd held to her convictions she wouldn't have felt this need to retreat like a coward. Was she turning into her mother? *Please, God, don't let that happen. I want to be a good girl.*

She didn't foresee much chance of her facing that particular temptation again. Once she left Turnabout to start her new life, she'd probably not have another opportunity to dance, at least not with Chance.

Now, why didn't that thought bring her comfort?

Chapter Twelve

When Chance plopped down at his workbench the next morning it was barely light outside. Truth to tell he hadn't slept well the night before. He wasn't sure if it was the memory of that dance with Eve—of holding her, of the sweet smell of her hair, of the sight of her joyful smile— that had kept sleep at bay. Or if it was her abrupt transformation back into the stiff, guarded woman he'd thought had disappeared for good.

In either case, he found himself wanting to find ways to bring that smile back, just to see if it was as bewitching as he remembered.

He hadn't had much opportunity to speak to Eve when he, Leo and Dotty had returned from the festival yesterday. Predictably they'd found her in the kitchen, cleaning the stove. She'd immediately sent Leo to get cleaned up and ready for bed. Then, after some chitchat with Dotty, during which she'd never once looked his way, she'd excused herself, as well.

Oh, there'd been nothing he could fault her for. She'd been polite to him, in fact overly so. But there was a distance between them that hadn't been there since he'd first encountered her. Had that been only two days ago? Why did it feel as if he'd known her so much longer?

His current line of thought brought him up short again. What was happening? Eve was only going to be here for a few more days, and she certainly wasn't the kind of girl to enter into a casual flirtation with. Which was all he really wanted.

Wasn't it?

He looked up at the sound of someone on the stairs and found the subject of his thoughts descending. Which face would she show today?

"Good morning," he said. "Feeling better today?"

She smiled but didn't quite meet his gaze. "Yes, thank you. I'll have breakfast prepared in just a bit."

He saw the tentativeness in her, as if she wasn't certain of her reception. "No rush," he said casually. "I haven't seen Leo or Dotty come down yet."

Some of the tension in her demeanor eased and she seemed poised to say more. But a heartbeat later she nodded and turned toward the kitchen.

Disappointed that she hadn't engaged in more conversation, he watched her cross the room. She paused at the counter and it was his turn to stiffen as he realized what had caught her attention.

"Is this today's newspaper?" Her tone was much more animated than it had been earlier.

"Yes." He subscribed to the paper, but normally Dotty read it to him. He wasn't certain how he was going to handle that while Eve was here. "Feel free to borrow it if you like."

"Thank you." She seemed genuinely delighted. "Perhaps after breakfast then." And with another smile she disappeared into the kitchen.

Would she smile at him that way if she knew his secret?

* * *

Eve went through the motions of cooking breakfast, but her mind was elsewhere. The encounter with Chance this morning had gone better than she'd dared hope. There was none of the censure she'd expected. That was a relief, yes, but curiously it was also a bit of a letdown. It was as if her dancing with such abandon and then withdrawal from him hadn't affected him at all. And why should it? To him it had just been a dance, something he'd done hundreds of times before. She doubted she'd served as a very remarkable partner. Apparently she had, in fact, been quite forgettable.

Breakfast passed pleasantly enough, though she let the others carry most of the conversation. An easy thing since Leo wanted to excitedly recap everything he'd done at the festival.

Later, after she'd meticulously cleaned the kitchen, Eve stepped back out into the main room, feeling at a bit of a loss as to what she should do next. She found Dotty there, reading the paper to Leo. Chance had returned to his workbench and had his head down over whatever he was working on. He glanced up to smile a greeting her way, then went right back to work.

What now? She supposed she could start on lunch. Or perhaps get that old suit Chance had given her and begin to refashion it. But before she had taken two steps toward the stairs, her interest was snagged by the article Dotty was reading. Almost without thinking, she gave in to the temptation to join her and Leo.

Dotty looked up. "Ah, there you are. Would you mind taking over for me? I'd like to get back to work on this shawl I'm knitting—it's a Christmas gift for my daughter."

"Of course." Eve eagerly took the paper and scanned the front-page article on yesterday's festival until she found the spot where Dotty had left off.

Chapter Thirteen

Chance continued tinkering with the old clock Mrs. Northram had asked him to take a look at as he listened to Eve read the paper. And read it she did, all the way through, even the advertisements. She had a wonderful voice, feminine yet strong, alive with nuance and emotion. Her love for reading, which he'd merely suspected earlier, came shining through in her face. And in the way she paused occasionally to make astute or humorous comments on what she had just read.

And trust Dotty to handle the matter of reading to him with great tact and absolutely no prompting from him. As soon as they'd excused themselves from breakfast she'd insisted on reading it to Leo.

"Chance."

He glanced up at the sound of Eve's hail. It was the first time she'd used his first name and he decided he rather liked the sound of it on her lips. "Yes?"

"How often did you say the paper is printed?"

"Twice a week, Fridays and Tuesdays."

She nodded and he detected a note of disappointment in the gesture. But she dropped the subject and turned to Leo. "Tell me, do you know how to read or write?"

Leo shifted in his seat. "I used to be able to read a little. But I couldn't read nothing like that newspaper."

"*Anything* like that newspaper," she corrected. "The first thing we need to do, then, once we get your name cleared, is get you enrolled in school. Reading is a *very* important skill to have."

Chance mentally winced at that reminder of what he lacked.

"I've known other folks, grown-up folks, who can't read. Like the man who helped Pa plow his fields in the spring."

"The poor man probably never had the opportunity to learn. But we will see that you do." She leaned forward. "A man who can read is not only more respected and knowledgeable, but he is much harder to take advantage of. You don't want to be someone who must lean on others to do his reading for him, do you?"

Chance cast a quick glance Dotty's way to see how she was reacting to this. She met his gaze with a sympathetic one of her own. But Eve wasn't through. Was it because she felt so strongly about this, or was she just trying to convince Leo that he needed to go back to school?

"Not only is reading important," Eve was saying, "but it's fun, too. There are so many wonderful adventures you can go on, just by losing yourself in the pages of a book."

Leo glanced across the room. "That's what Mr. Dawson said when you were looking at the books in the restaurant."

"He did?" Eve glanced his way with approval shining from her eyes. "I'm glad to hear Mr. Dawson shares my love of books."

Chance made a noncommittal sound then focused back on his work. Or at least tried to.

But she wasn't going to let him off so easily. "Do you

have some favorite stories to recommend to a boy Leo's age?"

Chance remembered his mother reading to him as a young boy and dredged up the titles of his favorites. "*Robinson Crusoe* and anything by Jules Verne."

Eve gave him a smile of approval and turned back to Leo. Why did he feel as if he'd just lied to her? He'd never actually said a word about liking to read, just about liking books. Surely he wasn't responsible for any conclusions she might be jumping to.

Later that morning, when Eve and Dotty were in the kitchen, Chance looked up from his workbench to see he had visitors. Adam had pushed through the swinging doors and had Jack and Ira Peavy with him.

Chance stood and headed across the room. He noticed Jack and Leo made a beeline for each other.

Before they could do more than exchange greetings, the kitchen door opened and Eve and Dotty stepped out, curiosity on their faces.

As soon as Adam spotted them his face lit in a broad smile. "Good morning, ladies. Your presence sure does brighten up this old workroom of Chance's." He glanced around. "In fact, I see you've added quite a few softer touches since the last time I was in here. A definite improvement."

"Hey! Are you implying I didn't keep this place neat and comfortable before now?" Chance gave him a mock frown to go with his accusation.

Adam spread his hands. "Let's just say it's looking much better—especially the caliber of the residents."

Chance grinned in response. "Is there something we can do for you?" He studied his friend closely. Adam's manner seemed relaxed and unhurried, but something about him led Chance to believe this was more than a casual visit.

Adam nodded toward his son, who was exploring the workshop with Leo as his guide. "Mrs. Peavy is in the mood to make some persimmon jelly and Jack and Ira here are heading out to pick some of the fruit for her. We thought Leo might want to go along and maybe collect some for you, as well."

"How kind of you to think of him," Eve said. "Persimmons would make a welcome addition to our table."

"Does that mean I can go?" Leo asked hopefully.

She hesitated, then nodded. "Of course."

With an enthusiastic whoop, Leo and Jack crossed the room to join Mr. Peavy.

Once the boys and Ira were gone, Chance folded his arms across his chest and stared levelly at Adam. "I assume you have some news for us."

"News?" Eve echoed.

"Yes." Adam glanced from Chance to Eve. "There was a letter for Sheriff Gleason on this morning's train."

"A response to his inquiry about Leo you mean," Chance said matter-of-factly. He hoped there weren't any unpleasant surprises in the letter.

"Yes." Adam's expression and tone didn't give anything away. "But Ward should be the one to explain all this. He'll be here in just a moment."

Chance nodded, keeping his expression unconcerned for Eve's sake. But his mind was churning over the possibilities. Explain all what? It didn't sound as if it was going to be good news—why else would the sheriff send Adam on ahead to clear Leo out of here?

"Surely it's confirmation of Leo's story," Eve said, her voice attempting to strike a confident note.

Adam rubbed the back of his neck. "For the most part."

Now what did that mean?

But before he could say anything, Sheriff Gleason walked in.

"Right on cue," Adam said, a hint of relief in his tone.

Chance swept an arm toward the nearest table. "Let's all have a seat." Once they'd settled into their chairs he faced the sheriff. "Now, what's the news?"

"I guess Adam already told you I got a letter on this morning's train," the sheriff said. At their nod, he continued. "It was from the preacher in Leo's hometown. He's verified most of Leo's story for us."

"I knew it," Eve said, the relief on her face evident. "Leo is not bad, just desperate for a better life."

"According to the preacher," the lawman continued, "Leo's folks died of a fever about two years ago, just as he said. Melvin Belcher took him in."

"And nobody thought to check in on him when Leo didn't show up for school?"

"Apparently it happened right around the end of the school year. And since Belcher has a farm some distance from town, nobody saw Leo or missed him for the rest of the summer. The reverend admits that, by the time school started back up in the fall, the folks in town had pretty much forgotten about Leo."

"How awful." Eve's face held a touch of that defiant protector Chance had seen on the train platform.

He could understand her outrage, though. He shared it.

"I assure you the preacher seemed very contrite about the matter."

"As well he should be," Eve said firmly.

"So what about this Belcher character?" Chance didn't bother to hide the anger in his voice.

"Of course he's denying any charges of having mistreated the boy." The sheriff sounded as if he didn't believe this any more than Chance did. "And from what I gather, he's well respected in Bent Oak. Seems the story he's putting out is that Leo was such a handful after his parents' death—going into rages, mistreating the livestock, breaking things—that he kept him close to home for his own good and the good of others in the community."

Predictably Eve stiffened and her expression turned to one of determination. "I don't believe it!"

"Having met Leo, I can't say as I give it much credit, either."

"We can't let that man near Leo." Eve tilted her chin up defiantly. "I'll slip out of town with him in tow before I let that man get his hands on Leo again."

Chance smiled. For all her prim exterior, she could certainly be a bit of a tigress when something got her good and riled.

"Don't worry, that won't be necessary." Chance hadn't lent his protection to these two just to abandon them when things turned sticky. Anyone who wanted to send Leo back to that bully of a man would have to come through him.

The sheriff nodded reassuringly. "Don't worry, either of you. Belcher has no legal claim to the boy and Leo doesn't have to go back there, especially given our suspicions. But neither can he be left on his own."

"Of course not." Eve's schoolmarm demeanor was firmly back in place. "He needs a proper home."

Adam raised a brow. "You have any ideas on that front?"

"Why, no." She looked surprised. "You all know the people around here much better than I do. Surely you can find a family who would be willing to take him in."

Sheriff Gleason rubbed his chin. "We can ask around, of course. The trouble is, stories about his past, even if they're false, might give folks pause." He eyed them evenly. "Of course there's always the orphanage up Parsonville way."

"No!" Eve's exclamation was sharp and immediate. "I mean, I know orphanages are necessary institutions and that they do fine work, but Leo has been through so much already. He deserves to be part of a loving family." She looked at each of the men in turn. "Surely we won't let him be forgotten by an entire community yet again."

"*Every* child deserves a loving family," Chance said. He hadn't had the happiest of childhoods himself; he certainly didn't want others to share that misery.

"Unfortunately, that's not always possible." Sheriff Gleason spread his hands. "The challenge is going to be finding someone willing to take him in with his background."

Chance's fists curled in frustration. He knew exactly how it felt to be judged on something you had no control over. Leo deserved better.

"Does everyone have to know?" Eve's voice was tentative. "I'm not advocating we lie," she added quickly, "just that we don't offer up information if we don't have to."

The sheriff shrugged. "We don't have to advertise it, no. But most folks already know he's a runaway and that he stowed away on that train. They're going to want to know the full story before they take him in."

Eve's expression fell but she rallied enough to try another argument. "Since the full story includes our certainty of Leo's innocence, surely that won't be a problem."

"As I said, I'll do my best to find him a home." Then the sheriff gave Eve a pointed look. "I assume I can count on you to continue looking after him for now."

"Of course. In fact, I insist."

"We both will," Chance said firmly. "At least until Monday." Had she already forgotten her deadline?

The sheriff and Adam turned to Eve with a question in their expressions.

Eve shifted her weight, a soft flush climbing in her cheeks. It seemed she *had* momentarily forgotten.

"The job waiting for me in Tyler will only be held until then," she said apologetically. "If I tarry any longer it will go to someone else."

"I see. Well then, I'll begin making inquiries on Leo's behalf right away." Then the sheriff reached into his pocket. "I almost forgot. There's one other thing we need to take care of." He held the pocket watch out in his palm. "Belcher claims Leo's father gave this to him in payment of a debt."

Chance stiffened. "And you believe him?"

"Whether I believe him or not doesn't matter. It'll ultimately be for a judge to decide if they both want to press their claims." He grimaced. "However, Belcher states he'll let the boy keep it—for a price."

Eve looked as if she was ready to chew nails. "And that price is?"

"Fifteen dollars."

"Fifteen dollars!" Her voice actually rose a few notches.

"We can fight him on it in court," Adam said quickly. "And I'm certainly willing to help with that. But it's going to be Leo's word against Belcher's. And the fact that Leo ran away, and then slipped onto that train without paying his fare is not going to add to his credibility any."

"I'll pay it." The words were out of Chance's mouth before he'd even realized it. But he didn't regret them. He'd find the money.

Eve spun around and stared at him as if he'd spoken in a foreign language. "What?"

"I said I'll pay it. It'll be worth it just to make sure the blackguard is completely out of Leo's life. And a boy should have some keepsake of his home and family."

The warm admiration that crept into her eyes held him spellbound for a heartbeat.

Then the sheriff pushed back from the table and cleared his throat. "Well then, I think that will settle matters with this Belcher fellow. There won't be any need to deal with him further."

Chance gave a short nod as the men rose. *Amen to that.*

Eve stood more slowly, giving the sheriff a bright smile. "I want to thank you for handling this matter so quickly and so effectively. I know Leo will appreciate it, as well. And I'm sure he'll sleep better tonight than he has in a long while."

"Just doing my job, ma'am."

As Chance escorted his friends to the door, he relished again that admiring glance she'd sent his way. It was kind of nice to be noticed for something he'd done, rather than as part of a flirtation.

Chance assured Adam and Ward that he'd send the fifteen dollars today to Reverend Ferris to deliver to Belcher. He didn't trust Leo's former "caretaker" enough to send it directly to him—much better to have a witness to the fact that he did indeed receive it.

"For someone who just got good news, you don't look very happy."

Chance turned around at the sound of Dotty's voice. He'd all but forgotten she was in the room. Her comment, however, had been directed toward Eve.

"Oh, I *am* pleased," Eve replied. "Very pleased that Leo's been vindicated. I always believed he was innocent, but now everyone else will know it, as well. And he won't have to feel as if he has to keep running."

She fiddled with a button at her throat. "I was thinking about the fact that I'll have to leave here on Monday. Turnabout was just starting to feel like home."

For some reason, Chance's spirits lifted at her admission that she was enjoying her stay. Perhaps he was finally getting through to her.

She turned to him. "But of course this is not about me. I think the first thing I must do is have a talk with Leo when he returns."

"*We* must have a talk with him, you mean. And I agree. Do you want to take the lead or should I?"

To his surprise she didn't argue the point with him. In fact he thought he detected the merest hint of relief in her expression. "If you don't mind, I think it best if I do."

He executed a short bow, willing to concede that point to her. "Of course."

"If I might make a suggestion?" Dotty interjected.

"Absolutely."

"From what I've observed, that boy seems so set on striking out on his own that he might not react well initially to the idea of others determining where he's going to live."

Eve frowned. "But he's a smart boy. Surely he'll understand that we can't leave him to fend for himself."

"Still it might be a good idea to give him a reminder of how nice family life can be—if he had the right kind of family, I mean."

Chance had an idea where she was headed, but preferred to let her explain. "Do you have something specific in mind?"

"Perhaps the two of you could take him for a ride in that motor carriage of yours this afternoon," Dotty said. "It's a mild day—perhaps you could even have a little picnic or at least find a nice spot for a stroll. Really enjoy the afternoon. And then break the news to him before you return."

"An excellent idea," Chance said.

"That may not be such a good idea," Eve said at the same time.

"Why ever not?" Chance gave her an exasperated look. Was her objection to the plan the fact that it might involve some frivolous fun?

"I don't want to sound self-centered, but I'm afraid Leo may be forming something of an attachment to me," she said. "And while I share that affection, I don't want to encourage a stronger attachment. He's already been so hurt and disappointed by those who are supposed to be his caretakers—I don't want him to feel abandoned again when I leave on Monday."

"My dear," Dotty said with a wry smile, "I'm afraid that chain has already been forged. The attachment Leo feels for you is very real—you are, after all, the champion who stood up for him on multiple occasions. One more outing is not going to change things significantly."

Chance nodded. "Dotty's right. And I agree that an outing is a good idea." Then he gave her a challenging smile. "Unless you're afraid to ride in my motor carriage."

Eve straightened. "Of course not." She chewed at her lip and touched the button at her throat a moment, then nodded. "Very well. We'll take him for an outing and break the news then." She looked at Chance, her expression troubled. "How do you think he'll react?"

"Leo's a tough kid—he wouldn't want us to mollycoddle him. But he'll probably argue that he can fend for himself."

Eve grimaced. "Then, as Dotty has so wisely stated, we'll have to show him how much he'll miss if he doesn't let himself be part of a family again."

Chance envied the way she spoke so highly of family. Had her own life been such a happy one? If so, why had she left it all behind?

He suddenly realized he'd gone from wanting to change

her way of looking at fun, to wanting to learn much more about what was really driving this very hard-to-figure-out young lady.

As Eve moved toward the kitchen, she realized again what a truly good man Chance was. He'd stepped up to do that kind thing for Leo without any second thoughts. She and Leo had been truly blessed to cross paths with him when they arrived in town.

Thinking of Leo, she felt the uncertainty wash over her again. Could they really find a good home for Leo in so short a time? Could she leave on Monday if they hadn't?

Truth to tell, she would be sad to leave Turnabout even if they *did* find a family to take Leo in. She'd made so many friends in the short time she'd been here. And she'd gotten a glimpse of what life could be without the cloud of her past hanging over her.

But there was no changing that past. If she made a permanent home here, she couldn't keep her history secret forever, and when that changed so would the way folks looked at her. No, the important thing was to focus on what was best for Leo and then to move on as she'd originally intended.

But would it be so wrong to enjoy this freedom and relative anonymity while she had it?

Chapter Fourteen

Leo returned thirty minutes later with a pail full of persimmons.

Eve spent time carefully examining his pickings with fulsome admiration. She was pleased to see his chest puff out in a show of pride at the praise.

After several minutes of this Chance cleared his throat. "I thought I'd take the motor carriage out today for a little drive."

Eve smiled as Leo immediately set the persimmons aside. "Oh, boy! Can I come along?"

"Certainly."

Leo turned to Eve and Dotty. "Did y'all want to come, too?"

Dotty shook her head. "No, thank you. I want to get a little further along on my knitting project."

"I'll go," Eve said. "I'm ready for a bit of fresh air and according to Mrs. Epps, riding in that vehicle is something everyone should try." Truth to tell she was actually looking forward to the experience. It seemed such an adventurous thing to do, which appealed to her just now. "And since we haven't eaten lunch yet, why don't I fix a picnic basket to take along?"

Chance nodded. "Sounds good." Then he put a hand on Leo's shoulder. "But we'll take care of packing the basket. You need to fetch a shawl or wrap—it'll be breezy riding in Tizzie."

"Tizzie?"

Was that a touch of self-consciousness in his grin? "It's what I call the motor carriage." He made a shooing motion with his hand. "Now, while you're upstairs getting a wrap, I suggest you also find something you can use to tie your hat on securely."

Ten minutes later they were climbing into Tizzie. Eve insisted Leo sit in the front next to Chance and she settled into the backseat. She listened with interest as Chance explained in simple terms how one started the vehicle and then demonstrated each step. When at last the engine was puttering, she felt that she almost understood the process. Not for the first time she thought he'd make a remarkable teacher. Perhaps he could work with Leo on his reading and writing skills until the boy was able to go to school again.

The vehicle jerked forward, eliciting an elated yelp from Leo and loosing a flock of butterflies in Eve's stomach.

Then as the vehicle turned into the street and made its way through town she settled into the experience. Most of the folks they passed seemed to take the vehicle in stride as a familiar sight. A couple of dogs gave chase with excited barking. But by the time they reached the edge of town, the animals had given up.

Like Leo, Eve found the ride exhilarating. She closed her eyes and lifted her face, thrilling at the feel of the wind rushing by and the sensation of moving with such speed. It was something like riding in a small train with no sides or roof.

She was almost sad to see the ride come to an end when they finally reached their destination.

"So, how did you like it?" Chance asked as he handed her down.

"It was quite invigorating," she admitted. "I can see why you enjoy it so much."

Her answer drew an approving grin. Then he reached down and pulled three small sacks from under the seat. "I thought while we were here we'd pick pecans." He winked at Leo. "It's late in the season, but if we find enough, perhaps we can talk Miss Pickering into making some more of her candies."

Leo turned to her with a pleading expression. "Would you?"

Eve grinned at them both. "I can probably be persuaded."

As they moved across the meadow to the pecan trees, Chance made them a dare that he could pick the most in thirty minutes' time and Leo eagerly took up the challenge. Even Eve found herself getting into the competitive spirit.

Sure enough, thirty minutes later when they stopped for lunch, Chance was the clear winner. The outcome surprised Eve since he seemed to be doing as much chatting and posturing for their benefit as working.

But as they settled down on the blanket for their picnic, she had to admit he was an entertaining and charming companion. He amused them by pointing out cloud pictures, teaching Leo how to make stars and other figures from sticks and string, and trying to show them both how to whistle, though Leo was a more adept pupil than she was.

When there was a lull in the conversation, Eve turned to Leo, deciding it was time to ease him into thinking about family and belonging. "Tell me a little about your parents."

The boy got a look on his face that was a bittersweet mix of pain and longing. "Pa was a farmer and he could make just about anything grow. He was always teaching me things—how to ride a horse, or milk a cow or start a fire. He said it was never too early for a boy to learn things a man ought to know. But we had fun, too, 'cause he said it was okay to be a kid while I was going about learning to be a man."

"Sounds like he was a great father," Chance said.

There was a note in his voice that Eve didn't quite understand, but now was not the time to figure it out. "What about your mother?"

"Ma was the best cook in the world and pretty, too. Pa always said she was prettier than a springtime meadow. And she liked to pick fresh flowers to put on our Sunday dinner table. She sang when she cooked or sewed. And Christmas was her favorite time of year."

The boy's parents had obviously surrounded him with love.

Leo gave the two of them a look that dared them to disagree. "This year I'm finally going to have a real Christmas again."

"What do you mean by a *real* Christmas?" Chance asked.

The boy didn't hesitate. "One where I can really celebrate. I know it won't be like the ones I remember from when my ma and pa were around, but at least I won't be locked up in the shed by myself."

Eve couldn't stop the sound of her indrawn breath. How could that horrible man have treated Leo so harshly? A quick glance toward Chance showed he felt the same.

But right now they needed to focus on the happy times. "Tell me about the Christmases you remember," she said. "What are your favorite memories?"

That brought Leo's smile back. "Ma always went all out to decorate the house for Christmas. Pa used to tease her about it. There would be sprigs of evergreen and holly tied up with red ribbons on the mantel and around the doors. Then there was a Nativity set that Pa made. Ma always set it next to the fireplace—she said it was to keep the holy family warm."

What a lovely thought. Eve thought she would have liked Leo's mother very much if they'd ever met.

"And we would make decorations to put on the tree—like angels out of cornhusks and cloth, and paper stars and popcorn garland. Then, when Pa brought the tree home on Christmas Eve, we had everything ready. And we would sing Christmas songs while we decorated it."

"Those all sound like nice traditions, Leo."

Leo nodded. "And Ma had a special cloth angel with shiny tin wings to put on top of the tree. Pa used to lift me up so I could put it on myself."

"Well, those are all wonderful memories. I can see why you cherish them." Eve gave him an affectionate smile. "Perhaps this year you can start making pleasant new memories to add to those."

Was this the right time for her to bring up the subject of his finding a new family? Before she could say anything, Leo popped up and ran across the meadow. When he stopped, he excitedly called them over. Eve looked around but could see nothing but trees. "What do you suppose he wants us to see?" she asked Chance.

He stood and held out a hand to help her rise. "There's only one way to find out."

They crossed over to Leo, but Eve was as clueless when they reached him as she had been before. "What is it?" she asked.

"Will you look at that tree?" There was a touch of awe in his tone.

Eve studied the tree in question. It was a cedar, well

formed and about seven feet tall. But there was nothing to mark it as anything special. Still, Leo was slowly walking around it, studying it appreciatively from every angle.

Eve glanced at Chance, seeing if he had any idea what was going on. But Chance merely shrugged.

"Is something wrong?" she asked the boy as he reappeared from behind the tree.

He turned to her, his expression hopeful. "I was just thinking, wouldn't this make the perfect Christmas tree?"

Luckily, Leo didn't wait for a response. "It's a good height and it's full all the way around. It would look great inside the front room."

Chance studied the tree critically. "It's a fine specimen, all right."

"It reminds me of the last one my pa cut down for us," Leo said wistfully. "Mr. Belcher never bothered with decorating or anything. He never had visitors and he spent Christmas day in town."

Eve's grandmother had never bothered with a tree, either. But if having a tree would make Leo happy, then he should have one. The problem was, she wasn't certain where he would be come Christmas, so it would be hard to promise him that he would be decorating this particular cedar.

"This year will be different," Leo said with absolute confidence. "I can go to church if I want to and celebrate proper."

"It most assuredly will." It warmed her heart that he considered church service a part of the celebration, especially after all he'd been through. And Christmas was still four weeks away. Surely they could find him a good home before then.

They moved back toward the picnic blanket to begin

packing things up and Leo gave her a dazzling smile. "So can we have a tree like that one and decorate it?"

Eve hesitated. She didn't want to disappoint him, but she couldn't make promises she couldn't keep, either. It was time to have that talk. "Let's put everything back in the vehicle then there's something Mr. Dawson and I need to discuss with you."

The boy's happy expression vanished like snow in fire. "Did I do something wrong?"

"Oh, no, sweetheart. It's nothing like that."

He didn't seem reassured. "Then what? You both look so serious all of a sudden."

Chance hefted the picnic basket and led the way back to the motor carriage. "Sheriff Gleason paid us a visit while you were out with Jack and Mr. Peavy."

Eve touched Leo's shoulder briefly. "He heard back on that telegram he sent to Bent Oak."

Leo stiffened, and that braced-for-a-blow look that had all but disappeared the past couple of days was back in full force. "What did he find out?"

"He heard from a Reverend Ferris, who supported your story."

"He did?"

"Yes, of course."

"So I'm not going to jail?"

Is that what he'd been afraid of? "Of course not. The sheriff now has enough information to confirm that Mr. Belcher has no legal claim to you and you don't have to go back there ever again."

Leo's expression immediately lightened. "Then I can stay here with you if I want to."

Eve mentally winced. Is that what the boy thought, that they would continue the current arrangement indefinitely? How would he take the news that it wasn't going to happen?

Chance covered her lack of response by reaching into his pocket and pulling out the pocket watch. "Mr. Belcher is no longer laying claim to this." He held it out to Leo. "It's now yours, free and clear."

Eve noticed that Chance didn't make any reference to his having paid for the heirloom.

Leo clutched the timepiece as if he'd never let it go. "So that means now I can do what I want?"

Eve took a deep breath. It was time to explain the situation to him. "Not entirely."

"What do you mean?"

She rested her hand on his shoulder. "Leo, you must know that you're too young to be left to your own devices. You need an adult to look out for you."

His expression turned defensive.

"I'm not a little kid. I can take care of myself just fine."

"Don't worry, we'll make very certain you aren't put into the care of someone like Mr. Belcher again. We'll find you a good home with a loving family."

That answer didn't elicit the hoped-for smile. Instead, Leo met her gaze with a pleading one. "Why can't I live with you and Mr. Dawson? Don't y'all want me?"

"Oh, Leo, it's not that at all. Of course I care for you very much, and if there was any way I could offer you a home, I wouldn't hesitate. But it's just not possible."

"Why not?"

"Well, for one thing, I'm not going to be here much longer."

Leo blinked and then his eyes widened in disbelief. "You're leaving?"

"Of course. You *know* I have a job waiting for me in Tyler—that hasn't changed. I made promises to be there."

"But can't you get out of it? I mean, don't you like it here?"

"Of *course* I like it here. And as I said, I care about you, a lot. But I can't continue to live off of Mr. Dawson's charity. And there's no work for me here, no way for me to earn my keep. If there was—"

"But there is," Leo interrupted eagerly. "You could open a candy store. Everyone likes your candy—I heard them say so."

"Oh, Leo, that's a nice thought, but that's all it is. I couldn't—"

"Why not?"

Startled by Chance's question, Eve turned to him with a frown. He definitely wasn't helping any. "You know good and well why not. And I'll thank you not to give Leo any false notions."

"No, I'm serious. Think about it. Leo's right, folks really like your candies. You've already gotten an order without trying. And this is a great time of year to try out a venture like this."

Why was he doing this? They'd agreed to present a united front when they had this talk with Leo. "That may be so. But there are practical matters to consider, like acquiring a storefront with a proper kitchen, buying supplies, getting the word out. And all of those things require money, which I don't have."

"There are other solutions. In fact, you could use my kitchen and some of the floor space in my shop. As you've seen for yourself, there's more than enough of it going unused."

Was he serious? "Even if I *could* accept such generosity, it takes more than floor space to open a business."

He spread his hands. "Of course it does. But all of that can be worked out. *If* you're interested in making the attempt." He folded his arms across his chest. "So the question is are you?"

She looked from him to Leo and back again. This was ridiculous. Impossible. Oh, so enticing. "But Mrs. O'Connell and my grandmother expect—"

Chance cut off her words with a chopping motion. "This is your life, not theirs. I asked you what *you* wanted to do."

Eve felt a tiny stirring of excitement. To make a clean break from her past, to be able to work at a job that she would actually enjoy and look forward to, to stay among her newfound friends—how could she not be tempted? But she had responsibilities, an obligation to meet. Besides which, agreeing to his scheme would put her in deep debt to Chance—something she wasn't certain she was ready for. "A decision like this has consequences. If I were to do this and the shop failed, I'd have nothing to fall back on."

"You won't fail." Leo's tone held absolute conviction.

Eve would have been flattered under other circumstances.

Chance held her gaze. "I agree with Leo. But this is a decision you have to make. We can't make it for you."

That gave her pause. All her life her grandmother had made the major decisions without ever asking how Eve felt about them. Sure, she'd made a few impulsive, reactive decisions—and those often landed her in trouble. Not a good indicator of how she would do on the big things.

"Will you at least agree to give it careful consideration?" Chance asked. "After all, you have until Monday to decide."

She supposed these two deserved that much from her. "I can agree to that. And even more, I will pray about it."

She smiled down at Leo. "But for now, you are still in my care and we are both staying put at Mr. Dawson's place. Regardless of what happens come Monday, I plan to enjoy the next few days while we're still together. What do you say—no droopy expressions or moping?"

Leo kicked at a rock on the ground but nodded. "I guess so."

"Excellent." She turned to Chance. "And you?"

Chance grinned. "You know me. I'm not one to worry about tomorrow."

He said that as if he were to be commended on it. But maybe he was just doing his part to lighten the mood. "Good. Then what do you two gentlemen say we head back and see what Dotty has been up to?"

On the drive back to town, Chance mulled over the idea of Eve sticking around and opening a candy store in The Blue Bottle. And the more he thought about it, the more he liked it. Over the past few days he'd gotten used to having people around, in fact had even come to enjoy it. And this would give him the best of both worlds—a family of sorts without any of the weighty responsibilities.

Then he frowned. If she and Leo stayed on, that meant they'd still be here when his father arrived in town. He had no illusions that his father would look on the arrangement as anything but a bad decision on Chance's part—especially since he received no gain from it.

Not that his father's opinion would keep Chance from following through with his offer. His main concern would be to make certain his father didn't do anything to make Eve feel uncomfortable or unwelcome.

Perhaps he should warn her before his father actually showed up on his doorstep.

Then he gave himself a mental shake. He was getting ahead of himself. She hadn't even agreed to stay yet. He was getting as impatient—and as eager for a yes answer—as Leo. Which couldn't be a good thing.

* * *

When they had parked Tizzie back in the shed, Chance handed Leo the picnic hamper and he hefted the sacks of pecans. As he handed Eve down he noted how mussed her hair was and how flushed her cheeks were from the ride. She was smiling at something Leo had just said and for a moment she was that carefree, vibrant young woman he'd held in his arms at the dance. The urge to take her and twirl her around to the strains of an imaginary fiddler was strong. Then she met his gaze and her eyes widened in question.

He gave her one of those light, flirtatious smiles that were so good at masking his true emotions, then released her hand and nodded for her to precede him.

Why in the world did this one girl keep tripping him up on his own feelings?

When they stepped inside, they found Abigail there, chatting with Dotty. As soon as Everett's sister saw Eve, she held up a small basket. "Here are the pumpkinseeds for the brittle, along with the other ingredients Daisy figured you'd need."

"See," Leo said, "everyone wants more of your candies."

Eve winced. "We'll discuss that later, Leo." Then she turned to Abigail. "I'll get on it right after breakfast tomorrow, if that's okay."

"Of course. Whatever timing works best for you. I'm just so grateful you're willing to do this for me. Miss Teel, my friend back in Boston, is going to love these."

"Miss Pickering is thinking about opening a candy store here," Leo blurted out.

Though he knew Eve would feel differently, Chance wanted to applaud the boy's impulsive announcement. The more folks who knew about the idea, the more likely Eve was to see it in a positive light. And just as he expected, Abigail and Dotty both reacted positively.

Abigail clasped her hands in delight. "Oh, how wonderful."

"An excellent idea," Dotty agreed.

Eve lifted a hand, palm out. "Leo is being a bit premature. I haven't agreed to the plan yet—I merely agreed to think about it."

Abigail gave her a persuasive smile. "Oh, but I think having a candy store here in Turnabout is a *marvelous* idea. There was one near the school I attended in Boston and I visited it often. I miss it. And their treats were not as good as yours."

Eve held her ground. "That's very kind of you to say, but there are other matters I need to take into consideration."

Abigail sighed. "You must do what you feel you must. But, if you decide to go through with it, which I sincerely hope you will, know that I'll be a regular customer." She stood. "Now, I need to get back and help Daisy with the supper preparations." She'd barely taken two steps toward the door when she swung around again. "Oh, Chance, I almost forgot. Daisy wanted me to make sure you invited your guests to join us for our Sunday gathering."

"Of course." It seemed everyone was expecting Eve to stay at least through the weekend.

Once Abigail had made her exit, Eve turned to him. "Sunday gathering?"

"It's a tradition of sorts—after the church service a group of us take our noonday meal together."

"A specific group?"

"Very specific. I told you there were four of us who traveled here together from Philadelphia about a year and a half ago. You've met all of them—Adam, Everett and Mitch. We all had ties to Reggie through her grandfather, who also lives in Philadelphia, so she was one of the first people we connected with when we arrived."

He refrained from getting into the *real* purpose of that journey here—it wasn't entirely his story to tell. "Anyway, Reggie insisted we all take our meals together. It was her way of making us feel welcome." Among other things. "Even after she married Adam we continued the practice, though it evolved into a Sunday-only gathering. When Everett's sister came to live with him and Daisy came to town the circle expanded to include them, and eventually Daisy's father."

"What a lovely tradition. But you must be quite a large group now."

"We are. That's why we've moved from Reggie's house to Daisy's. We use her restaurant as our dining room. But there's always room for a few more."

"Enough of that," Dotty said. "Tell me more about this plan to open a candy store."

Chapter Fifteen

"So what's holding you back?"

Eve kept her gaze focused on the potatoes she was peeling. She'd left Chance and Leo to explain the situation to Dotty, stating that she needed to get started on supper, but she should have known the older woman would follow her.

"As I've explained to Leo and Chance, I have obligations to fulfill and a job waiting for me in Tyler."

Dotty tsked. "I've heard you talk of obligations and responsibilities, of what your grandmother expects and has planned for you. But I haven't once heard you say this is what *you* want to do. So I'll ask you outright. If none of that were in the mix, is being a milliner something you really long to do?"

Why did people keep asking her that? "It doesn't matter. Don't you understand? What I want or don't want doesn't relieve me of my duty. I can't show disrespect to my grandmother by going against her wishes."

Dotty frowned. "But surely, she wouldn't see it that way. I mean, given the choice, wouldn't she want you to pursue something you enjoy doing as opposed to something you don't?"

Would she? "My grandmother has always done her best

to provide for my well-being, both physical and spiritual."
That was true, even if it wasn't a direct answer.

"I see," Dotty said slowly.

Eve did her best not to squirm under her knowing look.
"Besides," she said, wanting to fill the silence, "I'm sure
you're eager to get back to your own life. I know when
you agreed to come here to serve as chaperone you didn't
expect it to last more than a few days."

Dotty waved that argument aside. "If that's your only
reason, then you're in luck. I'm actually enjoying myself
here and am in no hurry to return to the boardinghouse.
It feels good to be in the midst of all these young people
with so much going on in their lives."

Eve's first thought was that she could use a little less
going on in her life. Then she realized that wasn't true.
As difficult as some of these decisions were to make, she
didn't want to go back to having someone else make them
for her.

"But even if I decided to do this, there's no guarantee
I could make a candy store work. What if I try and the
shop fails? Then where would I be? Mrs. O'Connell won't
hold that job for me past Monday so that would leave me
with nowhere to go. Chance has been very kind to let me
and Leo stay here, but I can't live off of his charity indefinitely."

"Oh, my dear, there are no guarantees in any of the
paths we choose in life. The ones that seem the most secure
can have hidden pitfalls. And often the ones that frighten
us the most lead to undreamed of opportunities. All we can
do is pray about our decisions and then step out in faith,
knowing that the Good Lord will catch us should we fall."

Eve wondered if she truly had that kind of faith.

But Dotty wasn't finished. "And it's not true that you'd

have nowhere to go. You have friends here who would help you."

Eve wondered if they would do so if they knew the truth about her.

Dotty smiled. "You mentioned earlier you were worried Leo had formed too strong an attachment to you. I think that goes both ways in this case. Are you really ready to walk away from him?"

Eve sighed. "I am very fond of Leo, and I won't deny that I'd truly enjoy watching him grow and thrive in a loving household. But if you're hinting that I should adopt him myself, I don't think that would be wise."

"Why ever not?"

"First, because Leo should grow up in a home that has both a mother and a father. And second, I don't think I would be a suitable mother."

Dotty laughed. "No woman alive ever feels she is truly prepared to become a proper mother. But we all manage as best we can."

"You mentioned that you have a daughter I believe."

"Yes. Judith, my daughter, is married with two children of her own. She lives over in Jefferson." Her expression took on a bittersweet cast. "I had a son, as well. Freddie caught a fever just before his fifth birthday and never recovered."

"Oh, Dotty, I'm so sorry."

"It happened over twenty years ago and I've made my peace with it." She straightened. "But the point I wanted to make is that, from my observations the past few days, I would say you are doing quite well with Leo, and would make an excellent mother to him."

"Thank you for saying that. But there are things about me…" She took a deep breath. She wanted to tell Dotty the truth, but perhaps now was not the time. "I'm just not cut out to be a mother is all."

Dotty patted her arm. "I don't believe that for a moment. But I won't press you any further." She reached for her apron. "Now, how can I help to get supper ready?"

As they worked together, Eve found herself admiring this woman beside her and feeling truly blessed to have her to lean on for advice and counsel. Dotty had suffered so much loss in her life—her son, her husband, her home—yet she remained full of cheer and generosity and faith. It was an example worth emulating.

Later that evening, as they were enjoying supper, Dotty turned to Leo. "And how did you enjoy your ride in Tizzie?"

"It was great!"

Eve was glad the conversation hadn't turned to the candy shop idea again. "I enjoyed it, as well."

"And Mr. Dawson showed me how to drive it," Leo added with relish.

"That doesn't mean you're ready to do it yourself," Chance said quickly.

Eve was relieved to see him nip that idea in the bud.

"I know that," Leo said matter-of-factly. But then he added more hopefully. "But maybe someday?"

Chance flashed that little-boy grin of his again. "Maybe."

"And did y'all have a nice picnic?" Dotty asked, reclaiming the boy's attention.

"Yes, ma'am." Then Leo's eyes brightened. "And I found the perfect tree to decorate for Christmas. It would look great out there by the front window."

Dotty's face lit up in delight. "A Christmas tree—what a perfectly lovely idea."

"Leo, we discussed this," Eve said quickly. "We probably won't be living here when Christmas comes."

He jutted his chin up stubbornly. "You promised you'd think about it."

That was a fair rebuke. "You're right. I just don't want you to get your hopes up."

"On the contrary, Christmas is an excellent time to get one's hopes up," Chance said. "Hope is what Christmas is all about."

"I remember the Christmas trees we used to put up when my mother was still alive," Leo said. "She made them look so beautiful."

"I had a collection of ornaments before my house burned down," Dotty said. "They were mostly homemade, but I cherished them. The ones Judith and I made together when she was a little girl were my favorite." She sighed. "I'll have to start a new collection this year I suppose."

Then Dotty turned to Eve. "You're being mighty quiet. Do you have memories of a Christmas ornament or decoration you particularly like?"

Eve traced her fork through the peas on her plate. "We didn't put up Christmas trees at our house. Or any other holiday decoration for that matter. Grandmother always thought they were too frivolous."

"So how *did* you celebrate Christmas?" Chance asked, studying her as if trying to read her secrets.

Eve shrugged, not really wanting to share that part of her life, but unable to get out of it. "We got up on Christmas morning and read the Christmas Story from the Bible. In honor of the occasion we would have something special for our noonday meal—usually a nice ham. Then, near supper time, my two aunts and their families would join us for the evening meal."

"Didn't you exchange gifts?" Leo asked.

Eve hesitated. "My grandmother always said the best gifts we could give each other were honesty and respect."

"Oh." Leo thought about that a moment, then looked up and met her gaze. "Is it okay if I give you a present that you can unwrap this year?"

Eve's heart squeezed a bit at the concern she saw in the boy's eyes. "Of course you may, Leo." She decided not to warn him again that they might not be together for Christmas.

"As important as it is to remember the spiritual aspect of the day," Dotty said gently, "one should never be afraid to celebrate joyfully and generously. After all it *is* a day to remember our Savior's birth."

Eve did her best to ignore the speculative way Chance was watching her. What was he thinking? She imagined he celebrated Christmas the way he did everything else—with great abandon. Did her story sound sad and restrictive to him?

She certainly hoped he wasn't feeling pity, as that was the last thing she wanted from him. What she did want from him, however, was something she refused to think about.

That night, as Eve bent down to tuck Leo in, he looked up at her with wide, hopeful eyes. "Have you made up your mind yet?"

She shook her head. "Not yet. I'm sorry if this is difficult for you to understand, but I have to make certain, whatever I decide, it's best for everyone." Most especially for him. "And I want so much for you to have a real family, one who'll give you all the love and security you deserve."

She brushed the hair from his brow. "You want that too, don't you?"

He didn't give her a direct answer. Instead, he slid his

arm under his head and stared up at her. "The past few days, it was almost like being part of a family again, you know? I thought maybe you felt that way, too."

"Oh, Leo, sweetheart, this is not just about how we feel. The world doesn't work that way. Sometimes we must do things we'd rather not, simply because they are the right things to do."

"Is it okay if I say a prayer that you'll stay and that we can have a real family Christmas together?"

A real family Christmas. Those words tugged at her, set up a yearning inside her that echoed Leo's. "Of course it is." She hoped Leo hadn't heard that little catch in her voice.

Listening to him pour his heart out to God, asking Him for just one Christmas like those he'd had with his parents was almost her undoing. Could she really walk away from something that clearly meant so much to him?

Then there was the town itself. These people were all so open and friendly—what would it be like to be truly a part of their circle rather than just a guest? She might never know. Unless she did as Leo wanted and stayed here.

But could she really step out in faith, knowing she would be burning her bridges and if she failed, there would be no net to catch her when she fell?

A little voice from deep inside her whispered, *That's why they call it faith.*

Eve stepped out into the hall, then glanced down from the landing at the room below. Dotty had already retired to her own room but there was a soft yellow pool of light shining from a lamp near one of the worktables. So Chance was still up.

Taking a deep breath, she started down the stairs.

Chance had been just about to put his things away when he heard Eve on the stairs. She headed directly toward him, purpose in her steps. What was up? Was something wrong with Leo?

"May I speak to you for a moment?"

"Of course." He cleaned off a chair next to his bench. "Have a seat."

She sat absently, almost without glancing at the chair. "I've been giving this matter of staying in Turnabout a lot of thought and prayer."

He came on full alert. Had she made her decision? "And?"

"And I think I want to stay."

Now, why did his pulse leap at her words? "Good. I've already told you that's what I hoped you'd decide. So what convinced you?"

"Mostly it was Leo's desire to have us all together for Christmas. I couldn't bear to have him feel abandoned again, especially this time of year."

"Mostly? Was there something else?" Had he not played even a small part in her decision?

"I've also been thinking about what you and Dotty said about my needing to stop blindly following my grandmother's dictates and start thinking about what *I* want to do with my life. And for now, this is it."

That was definitely a start. "So what happens after you've given Leo the Christmas he's dreaming of?"

"After *we've* given that to him, you mean. I haven't entirely figured that out yet. I'm hoping the candy store will do at least enough business to support me. But if not, I suppose I'll try to find some other position here."

"So you're planning to stay in Turnabout." Yet *another* step in the right direction.

"I like the town and especially the people here. Whatever comes of this change in plans, I'll have no regrets about not going to Tyler to become a milliner's apprentice."

She smiled softly. "And perhaps, if I can establish myself, I could manage a more permanent relationship with Leo."

"Adopt him, you mean."

"I'd like to at least leave that option open for now."

He wasn't sure how he felt about the idea of Eve adopting Leo and the two of them moving out of The Blue Bottle.

"But," she continued, "I certainly don't want you to think that I intend to take advantage of your generosity indefinitely."

He shrugged. "I don't have a problem with the current arrangement. You're welcome to stay as long as you like."

"That's very kind. However, as soon as I have enough money saved up, I will try to secure accomodations at the boardinghouse. At the very least, by the turn of the year I intend to start paying you rent."

Didn't the woman know how to accept a gift? "Eve, that's quite commendable of you. But I figure the cooking and other chores you've been doing around here are payment enough. This place hasn't looked so good, or smelled so good, since I moved in a year and a half ago. And having more folks come around has been a welcome change."

"I'm glad you feel I haven't been an imposition." She didn't say anything else for a long moment but he could see some sort of inner turmoil playing out on her face.

Finally she seemed to make a decision. "Before you decide to let me stay, there is something I need to tell you."

Now this sounded interesting. Was he going to finally learn a bit more about what made the uncompromising Miss Pickering tick?

She remained silent a moment longer, as if gathering her thoughts, then took a deep breath. "I haven't been completely forthcoming about myself, and you deserve to know the whole truth."

"I'm listening."

"I told you I was raised by my grandmother. The truth is I never knew either one of my parents."

"You were orphaned young?" Where was this shame he sensed in her coming from? Being an orphan was not an unusual thing.

"Not exactly, at least not that I know of."

Not that she knew of. What exactly did that mean?

She took another deep breath and stared down at her hands. "You see, my mother was never married. She succumbed to…to the charms of a young man who was in town for a couple of months and then left her. Apparently he promised to take my mother with him but that didn't happen."

Her cheeks were flaming now and her distress was obvious. His heart went out to her and he would have called a halt to her confession, but it was obviously something she felt she had to say. So he maintained his silence, trying to be as supportive as possible.

"According to my grandmother he was a smooth-talking man full of lies, for whom all the girls in town set their caps. Of course, Grandmother tried to keep him and my mother apart but my mother snuck out one evening and went to the town dance. That's where they met."

He straightened. The town dance? Is that why she'd never attended one until the festival? Did that have anything to do with her abrupt change as soon as the dance had ended?

But Eve seemed unaware of his epiphany. "The courtship was clandestine and when Grandmother found out she boarded up my mother's windows and made sure she didn't leave the house. But the damage had already been done."

So Eve had been conceived and born out of wedlock. That explained a lot.

Eve toyed with the button at her throat. "I never knew my father's name. Grandmother just called him the devil-tongued deceiver. And as you can imagine, my mother was ostracized because of my very existence. Two months after I was born, she left, as well. Just slipped out one night without a word to anyone. No one in Iron Bluff has heard from either of them since."

Eve waved a hand weakly. "So whether or not I'm an orphan is unclear. For all I know, both my mother and father could be out there somewhere living full lives, together or apart. The only certainty is that neither of them wanted me."

He reached forward and touched one of her hands. "I'm so sorry. That must have been very difficult for you growing up. But, Eve, none of this is your fault."

"That's not the way it feels. My very existence brought shame not only to my mother, but to my entire family. My grandmother says I was named Eve after the world's first sinner."

Everything in Chance recoiled at the thought that anyone, let alone a close relation, would say something so cruel to a child.

"My grandmother is a good, God-fearing woman and she has done everything she can to raise me properly, to make certain I don't follow in my mother's footsteps. Yet I have been a constant disappointment to her. No matter how I try, my thoughtless, careless unseemly nature keeps coming through."

"Unseemly nature? Eve, you are the most proper person I know." What Eve's grandmother had actually accomplished, either through design or ignorance, was stifling all the joy and confidence in her granddaughter's life. His whole being was thrumming with outrage over what had been done to the innocent child Eve had been.

But Eve was shaking her head. "No. I *try* to be correct and seemly, but that's not the real me. And sooner or later my true nature comes out."

"If by 'true nature,' you mean the lady who knows how to smile, who jumps in to help without hesitation when folks are in trouble, who finds delight in music, then I say, let her free."

And he was now more determined than ever to help that happen.

Chapter Sixteen

Chance's words made her smile for a moment. But then reality set in once more. "Don't you see, even my own mother didn't want me?"

"Perhaps it wasn't so much that she didn't want you as that she didn't want her tarnished reputation to affect you. And regardless of all that, it sounds to me that leaving Iron Bluff was the best thing you ever did. It took a lot of courage to strike out on your own that way, and you should be proud of yourself for doing so."

She gave him a crooked smile. "But I didn't decide to leave on my own. I was sent away. So you see, I can't even claim to have that bit of bravery." Then she grimaced. "And it wasn't really striking out on my own. My grandmother made sure Mrs. O'Connell knew all about my past so she could keep an eye on me."

Her grandmother sounded like an extremely bitter woman. "But it was you, and only you, who decided to step off that train and help a lone boy who had no one on his side. That kind of fearlessness, the kind that risks all for others, is admirable."

She stared at him uncertainly. "Do you really think so? I mean it was reckless and impulsive and I gave no thought for the proprieties when I acted. It was just that sort of thing that shamed me in front of the whole congregation and forced my grandmother to send me away."

"I would not have said it if I didn't mean it. Now tell me about this so-called shameful act so I can disabuse you of that, as well."

That cocky comment earned him a small grin. But she quickly sobered and gave a small nod. "I suppose you deserve to know the full truth. There was a baptism service down at the lake a few Sundays ago and afterward the congregation had a picnic. The Dabney boy saw some of the older kids playing with an old homemade raft and tried it out himself when no one was looking. First thing I knew he fell off in water over his head. I was there on the edge of the pond when I heard him screaming. I went in after him without even thinking."

That was it? "Surely you couldn't be faulted for that."

She squirmed a bit, looking miserable. "There were a couple of men nearby, as well. They got to him almost as quickly as I did. I could have left it to them."

"Still—"

Her face was flaming now and she wouldn't meet his gaze. "When I came out of the pond, my clothing was soaked through and..." She swallowed loudly. "It was clinging to me in a most unseemly manner. The bodice was worn in places and rather thin. I shamed myself, and I shamed my family, before the entire congregation."

How could her actions be viewed that way? And by a church congregation no less. "There is no shame in what you did. In fact, as when you went to Leo's rescue, you should be commended for your courage."

"That is kind of you to say, but acting without thinking is one of my biggest faults."

The urge to draw her to him and hug away her pain was suddenly so strong he had to fight to control it. The way she was feeling right now, it would be taking almost criminal advantage. Instead he settled for brushing some hair from her forehead and gently stroking her cheek before leaning back.

"Never, *ever* be ashamed of the impulse to help another human being. It is what the Bible commands us to do."

She met his gaze and held it. The gratitude shining there seemed to be afire, seemed to be sucking the oxygen from the air around them. And he was trying very hard not to picture the images her words had conjured up. If they didn't break this off soon he was going to do more than hug her, he was going to give her a taste of what almost assuredly would be her first kiss.

No! Not this way. By sheer force of will he broke the connection. But it left him feeling shaken inside.

She blinked as if coming out of a trance and looked slightly confused. Then she gave him a shy smile. "Thank you for saying that. You've definitely shown me a new perspective and given me something to think about."

He took a deep breath, focusing again on the reassurances she needed right now. "Eve, believe me when I say your leaving that place is their loss. And good riddance to them. You are now with people who appreciate you for the good person you are and many of whom would be truly sorry to see you go."

She smiled with a little more confidence. "I would be sorry to leave, as well. I feel very much at home here."

"Then it's a good thing you're staying." He raised a brow. "Does Leo know yet?"

"No, I wanted to tell you first, to make certain, once you heard my story, you would still want us here."

"I hope I've made it clear that I do." He liked the idea that she'd come to him first. And that she'd trusted him enough to share such a personal bit of her life with him.

She smiled again. "You have." The she turned more businesslike. "So we are agreed that we will give Leo the special family Christmas he wants so desperately?"

"Of course." He raised a brow. "You know, you'll have to do some actual merrymaking."

"Naturally. The poor boy has had few enough opportunities to celebrate the past few years. We want to make this one extra happy for him."

"That's the spirit. So you are agreed that we will make it gay and festive."

"As long as we also give time to focus on the spiritual aspects."

Chance nodded in satisfaction. "I wouldn't have it any other way."

As Eve climbed into bed a few minutes later, she was still pondering that earlier conversation. Could Chance possibly be right? It was so tempting to believe him, to absolve herself of fault. But it was also true that he viewed her industriousness and sense of purpose as too strict, a view with which she did not agree. So could she accept one portion of his perspective and not another? It was difficult to judge.

Of course, the one part of the evening she was trying to avoid thinking about was that moment when their gazes had locked. She had thought for just a heartbeat that he might actually lean in and kiss her. And she didn't know whether to feel relief or disappointment when she'd been proved wrong.

No, that wasn't true. It was very definitely disappointment.

* * *

Over breakfast the next morning, Eve informed Leo and Dotty of her decision.

Leo jumped up from the table and gave her neck a tight squeeze, something that surprised her.

"This is going to be a *really* great Christmas," he said excitedly. "And I've already gotten my first present."

Dotty, while less physical, seemed equally pleased. "I'm so glad you're staying. We're going to have such a good time working together and getting to know each other better."

Eve returned her smile. "How do you feel about helping me design my candy shop?"

"I think that sounds like a lot of fun."

So once the kitchen was cleaned up after breakfast, the two ladies went to work. First Eve cooked up a batch of the pumpkinseed brittle, so it would be ready for Abigail whenever she came by to pick it up. Then they took an inventory to figure out what additional supplies would be needed.

Then they discussed work schedules and how much time Eve could allot to her candy-making efforts each day and how much she estimated she could make during that time.

Then Dotty suggested they tackle the storefront itself.

Eve looked around, then realized she and Chance hadn't discussed the actual space allocations yet. She glanced his direction and spotted him watching her.

"You ladies need help with something?" he asked.

"I was wondering what part of this space you had in mind for me to use as the candy shop."

Chance stood and joined them. "You're welcome to any part of it you need, as long as it doesn't include any of my work area."

"But surely you want to reserve some space for relaxing—a parlor of sorts."

Chance grinned. "In the four and a half days you've been here, have you ever seen me use any part of this as a parlor? Except perhaps to play checkers with Leo and that's after business hours."

"What about Sundays?"

Chance rubbed his jaw. "I hadn't thought about that. Tomorrow will be the first Sunday I'm not here alone." Then he shrugged. "But the candy store will be closed on Sunday so I still don't see a problem. Use whatever you need."

Eve looked around. "Well, it isn't as if this will be a restaurant, so I really don't expect anyone to eat here." Assuming she had any customers at all. "So I guess I just need a place to display my candies and interact with the customers."

"Then I'd say the bar counter is your best bet. I think there are a few stools over in the storeroom—I can pull them out and pick out the best of the lot. Maybe set one behind the counter for you and a couple in front, just in case they're needed."

He seemed to have a good head for thinking these things through. "That would be lovely."

"You'll want a menu board of some sort and some display trays—I can take care of that for you, as well. They won't be fancy but they'll do the job."

"Oh, but I don't want to take you from your own work."

He waved a hand dismissively. "It won't take me long. I have most of the materials I'll need on hand already."

"What about the tables?" Dotty asked.

Eve gave a little start. She'd all but forgotten Dotty was there. "What do you mean?"

"Well, I know you're not expecting your customers to

eat there, but I thought it might be nice to pretty them up a bit so the place looks more inviting when they walk in."

Chance grinned. "Dotty, my love, what are you trying to say?"

"I'm trying to say that you are as messy as a magpie, Chance Dawson. You collect shiny objects and build your nest of a workshop with them. We need something a bit more decorous for Eve's candy store."

"Did you have something particular in mind?" Eve asked.

"Some pretty cloths to cover the tops with for starters. And maybe some sort of small centerpieces for the tables."

Chance raised his hands. "All of that is outside the scope of my talents. You're on your own."

Dotty, however, disagreed. "Those chairs, while sturdy enough, are eyesores. I think a new coat of paint would do wonders for them."

"Now, that I can do. You ladies just tell me what color you want."

Dotty turned to Eve. "What do you think?"

"I've always been partial to blue."

"Blue it is. I'll do half of them today and the other half on Monday—we don't want to find ourselves sitting on the floor tonight."

Dotty straightened. "Well then, while you two finish all this business talk, I'm off to find some table coverings." And with that, she went upstairs for her wrap and purse, the headed out the door.

Chance turned back to Eve. "How much thought have you put into what you plan to offer and what you'll charge for it? And you probably ought to come up with both a per-piece price and a by-the-dozen price."

Eve shook her head. Why hadn't she already thought of these things? "As far as what I'll offer," she said slowly, "to start with I think I'll keep the selection small—the same things I made for the Thanksgiving celebration, which were pumpkinseed brittle, sugared pecans and fudge. And then add chocolate drops, caramels and nougats." The more she thought about it the more she wanted to add. But she forced herself to rein in her enthusiasm.

"As for what to charge, I'm afraid I have no idea where to start on figuring that out." It still seemed a bit fantastical to think folks would actually pay for her candies.

"Well, it's definitely time to think about it." Chance rubbed the back of his neck thoughtfully. "You'll want to get back the cost of your supplies, of course, and make a profit, as well. After all, you have expenses to pay. And you're familiar with the candy counter at the mercantile, so that will give you a gauge to measure with."

She nodded, trying to appear confident. But apparently she wasn't quite successful.

He gave her a slightly amused look. "How good are you at mathematics?"

"It wasn't my favorite subject in school but I managed."

"Well then, let's keep it simple. Sit down and figure out what it costs you in supplies to make a batch of each kind of candy. Then figure out how many pieces are in a batch and divide it out to get the production cost per piece. Then you want to add in your profit. Once you have that figured out, you can figure out how to price it."

It seemed so simple the way he explained it. Which reminded her...

"I have something I've been meaning to talk to you about on another topic."

He leaned against the bar. "I'm listening."

"Now that we've decided Leo and I are staying right here, at least through the end of the year, I think we need to get Leo enrolled in school."

"Of course. I should have thought of that myself. Let's see, he's ten, so he'd be in Miss Whitman's class. We'll see her in church tomorrow."

"Good. But there's something else."

He raised a brow. "And that is?"

"Leo hasn't been in school for nearly two years. He's going to be behind the other kids his age."

"He's a smart kid—it won't take him long to catch up."

"I hope so. But it would be better for him if he received some extra help at home."

"You want to teach him yourself?"

"Actually, I've noticed how good you are at giving instruction and I thought perhaps you'd agree to do it. I just want to make certain he has the best help possible."

Chance's face went blank for a moment. What was wrong—didn't he *want* to help Leo? Had she crossed some sort of boundary without realizing it?

Then he seemed to recover. "I have an even better idea. Did you know that Dotty used to be the town's schoolteacher?"

"She was?"

Chance nodded. "She's only been retired about six years now. If you want to give Leo the best help possible, Dotty's the person you need."

"I'll ask her as soon as she returns."

Before Eve could say more, Abigail arrived to pick up her pumpkinseed brittle. "Hi there," she said by way of greeting. "If I'm too early just send me on my way and I'll come back later."

"Not at all. Give me just a moment to fetch it for you."

As Eve disappeared into the kitchen, Chance did his best to pay attention to Abigail's bubbly chatter. But his mind was on the earlier interchange with Eve. Should he have told her the truth, that he could never teach Leo to read because he didn't know how himself? But the memory of how she told Leo that people who can read are more respected and knowledgeable had held him back. Did that make him a coward? He was afraid he knew the answer to that question, and it didn't paint him in a very flattering light.

He was almost relieved when Eve returned so he could gracefully take his leave of Abigail and head out to his work shed behind the building.

He definitely needed some time alone to think.

Chapter Seventeen

An hour later Eve went out behind The Blue Bottle, looking for Chance. She found him in the work shed, laboring over a piece of equipment that looked very much like a washing machine with something attached to it by a series of belts.

"Hello," she said, holding out a cup of coffee.

He glanced up, surprised by the gesture. "Thanks."

She smiled. "I hope you don't mind the interruption, but I thought you might be ready for a break."

"I don't mind at all. And you're right. A short break with a hot cup of coffee sounds very good right now."

She studied the equipment up close. "Pardon my curiosity, but do you mind if I ask what it is you're working on?"

He smiled. "Not at all. I'm attempting to motorize a washing machine."

"Motorize? You mean like your motor carriage?"

He laughed. "It's the same principle, yes. I'm hoping that, by connecting this steam engine to this washing machine in just the right fashion, I can take a lot of the hard work out of this chore."

Eve was impressed. "You'll have the gratitude of many

a homemaker when you have this ready. Doing laundry has always been my least favorite chore."

"It's my hope that this will make laundry no more of a chore than any other housecleaning task."

"How did you come up with this idea?"

"It came from a casual conversation I had with Selma Winters, the lady who takes in laundry for some of the folks around here, including me. She was telling me how most men don't realize what hard, backbreaking work it is. And that there's no end to it. I watched her at work and realized she was right. And I also realized that there had to be a better way."

"So just like that you decided to find that better way."

He shrugged. "I like solving puzzles. And that's what this is to me, one big, tantalizing puzzle."

"And do you feel as if you're close to solving it?"

"It's hard to tell. I have to fashion a series of interconnected gears that can be turned by a belt from the motor to power the washing machine paddles and the wringer device separately. It's proving more difficult than I had imagined."

She smiled. "I have faith that you'll work it out." Could she get away with another personal question? She decided to try. "I notice you sometimes do some whittling at your worktable. Did you by any chance make those nutcrackers I saw stuck on a shelf on the back wall?"

He nodded. "Whittling and carving are hobbies of mine. Working with wood helps me to think. So I often spend time doing that when I'm trying to work out a problem with something like this."

The man continued to amaze her with his talents. She'd been so wrong to think of him as lackadaisical. "But those nutcrackers are beautiful. You should have them displayed in a place of honor, not stuck in a dark corner."

He shrugged again. "There's not many folk who'd come by to see them anyway."

She crossed the room to pick one of them up. "Do you mind if I find a better place for them, so *I* can see them?"

"Help yourself."

"What else do you make besides nutcrackers?"

"Nothing special—just whatnots and trinkets, really."

He didn't seem to want to talk about it, but she was still curious. "Like what?"

"Oh, tops, toy soldiers, animals, that sort of thing."

Chance wasn't certain what to make of Eve anymore. Bringing him that cup of coffee had been unexpected. And her interest in his work seemed genuine enough. Was she just trying to be pleasant, to repay him for the use of his building, or could there perhaps be something more there?

And just how ready was he for that something more?

Instead of answering that question he remembered he had something to tell her, which would give him an excuse to change the subject. Taking another sip of coffee to fortify himself, he glanced up at her. "Now that you've decided to stay, there's something I need to let you know."

Her expression immediately turned wary. What was she afraid of? "My father is planning a visit here for Christmas."

Her face lit up. "Oh, how wonderful for you." Then her face puckered in dismay. "But we've taken up all of your spare rooms. Perhaps Leo and I can double up while he's here." How would Leo feel about that?

Chance, however, had other ideas. "That won't be necessary. My father can take a room at the hotel."

"I wouldn't dream of letting you do that. If he's traveling all this way to see you—"

Was she picturing a joyful father-son reunion? She'd learn different soon enough. "Believe me, he'll be more comfortable staying at the hotel than he would here. And *I'll* be more comfortable with that arrangement, as well."

This time her brows drew down in question.

He ignored it. "I'm only telling you this because I didn't want his visit to take you by surprise. I also wanted to prepare you—my father is very outspoken and not always the most tactful. I want to apologize in advance if he should do or say anything to make you uncomfortable."

"I see."

There was a long pause and he wondered what she was thinking.

Finally she asked, "When do you expect him?"

"In about two weeks. He's planning to stay through Christmas."

"Then we'll plan our Christmas celebration accordingly. Are there some particular family traditions you'd like us to include? Special meal items perhaps."

"There's no need to go to any particular trouble. Father will be equally happy with whatever is provided." Or, rather, equally *un*happy.

Eve wondered at the strange tone in Chance's voice when he spoke of his father. Did the two have a falling out of some sort? Is that why Chance had moved so far away?

No matter what the situation between the two men, it didn't seem right to not find room for Chance's father to spend his visit in his son's home. Especially since he was traveling so far to be with him at this special time of year.

She'd have to come up with a plan to take care of that in the next two weeks. With or without Chance's help.

She held out her hand for his now-empty coffee cup.

"I'll let you get back to your project. Dotty and I have some more work to do ourselves toward getting the candy shop ready."

Sunday morning the four of them strolled to church together. Chance had offered to transport them in Tizzie since the church building was on the other side of town. There was a nip in the air for this first day of December, but Eve and Dotty both declared they were up for a walk.

After the service, Eve made a point of having Chance introduce her to the schoolteacher.

Once the introductions were complete she got right to the point. "I understand you teach those students younger than eleven."

"That's right. And Mr. Parker works with the older children."

"I'd like to enroll Leo. He's ten years old so he would fall into your class."

"Leo's a good boy," Chance added. "You won't have any trouble with him."

Eve hid a smile. He sounded just like a proud father.

"Of course," Miss Whitman replied. "He'll be more than welcome to join us." She gave Eve a warm smile. "May I take this to mean you and Leo are planning to extend your stay here in Turnabout?"

"Yes, we are. Though I'm not exactly certain for how long yet."

"I'm so glad. You're going to like it here. I moved here five years ago to take this teaching position and I have never regretted it."

"I can understand why. The folks are all so friendly." It seemed as though there were as many transplants as people born and raised in Turnabout. "I also wanted to let you know that Leo hasn't attended school or had any kind of teaching for more than two years now."

Miss Whitman's expression sobered. "I see. That means he'll be behind the other children his age." Then she smiled reassuringly. "But don't worry, that's not an insurmountable problem. He'll just need a little individual attention to catch up. I'll be glad to work with him after school if you like."

"Thank you. And Dotty has started working with him at home already and should be able to continue to do so, at least for the next few weeks."

"Excellent." She smiled. "With Dotty's help, Leo will be caught up in no time. Tell Leo I look forward to seeing him in class tomorrow."

With a wave she left them, and was almost immediately replaced by Sheriff Gleason.

Eve tensed. Had he found a family willing to take Leo? Why hadn't she thought to tell him about the change in plans yesterday?

"Just wanted to let you know I haven't had any luck in finding a permanent home for Leo yet, though a few folks have offered to take him in for the holidays if that's needed."

Eve felt guilty about the immediate rush of relief his words brought. She quickly shook her head. "Thank you but that won't be necessary. Mr. Dawson and I have decided to keep to the current arrangement, at least until after Christmas."

He nodded. "I heard about your plans for a candy store and thought that might be the case. Do you want me to continue making inquiries, or do you plan to make *this* a more permanent arrangement?"

Eve wasn't ready to commit to anything at this point.

"My situation continues to be uncertain, so I'm not prepared to say I can care for Leo permanently."

The sheriff seemed surprised by her answer. "I see."

"On the other hand," Chance said quickly, "since Christmas is coming up, and Miss Pickering plans to give this business a try until then, perhaps we can just leave things as they are and reassess at the New Year."

Sheriff Gleason nodded. "In the meantime, if I happen to hear of any family who would be willing to adopt him, I'll let you know."

"Thank you, Sheriff. I appreciate all you're doing on Leo's behalf."

Eve glanced across the churchyard to where Leo and Jack were deep in conversation. More and more she was thinking of Leo, if not as her son, at least as her personal responsibility. She'd grown to love him dearly. Could she give him up to another if a willing couple were found?

"He looks on you as a mom you know."

Chance's words, softly spoken from right beside her, took her by surprise. She turned and saw him watching her with sympathetic, knowing eyes. Was she so transparent to every one? Or just to him? Her mind still churning over the questions tumbling around in her mind, she sent up a silent prayer.

Dear Father above, please give me the strength to do what is best for Leo when the time comes. And the wisdom and discernment to know what that is.

Feeling somewhat steadier, she allowed Chance to escort her toward where Dotty stood talking to friends.

From there they would be going to the Sunday gathering with all of Chance's friends.

She hoped she didn't do anything to embarrass him.

Chapter Eighteen

When they arrived at the Fultons' Leo was excited to discover Daisy had a very unusual dog. With a shaggy black-and-white coat and several jagged, faded scars, he should have looked fierce. But in actuality, the wagging tail and different-colored eyes made him look endearing.

"His name's Kip," Daisy told Leo. "You and Jack can go out in the back lot with him until lunch is on the table if you like."

The two boys didn't need any further encouragement.

Then Daisy turned to the others. "I'm so glad you and Dotty agreed to join us," she told Eve. "It's a real blessing to see how our circle is continuing to grow."

Eve moved with her toward the kitchen. "I appreciate the invitation. Now tell me what I can do to help."

"Don't be silly. You all are my guests." She swept a hand to include Reggie and Dotty. "If you ladies want to have a seat over there in Abigail's reading corner while the men push the tables together, I'll get everything ready to serve."

"Don't be silly," Reggie echoed. She handed Patricia over to Abigail. "We can help you in the kitchen."

Daisy grimaced. "Now you sound like Everett. I'm still

quite capable of preparing a meal, even if I *am* starting to waddle when I walk."

Dotty laughed. "I can't think of a better reason to pamper a woman, can you?"

Eve found the atmosphere in Daisy's kitchen to be far different from the one in which she'd grown up. Daisy was urged to get off her feet while Mrs. Peavy took over her post at the stove. There was actually very little to be done—apparently Daisy had prepared most of the meal ahead of time. These women shared laughter, stories, compliments and worked with an attitude of joy. They took an obvious pleasure in each other's company, a camaraderie that Eve had never experienced before. And all the while they were getting the job done.

Food and dishes were carried out of the kitchen and into the dining area. Here too the camaraderie was evident. And none of the men seemed averse to helping get the table set or the food on the table.

Once everything was ready, the boys were called in and Ira supervised their washing up before they took their seats at the table.

Daisy's husband, Everett, said the blessing and then the bowls and platters were passed around. The meal was informal with conversation, teasing and laughter flowing freely. Eve answered when someone spoke to her, but did not try to interject herself into the mix.

Then, during a lull in the conversation, Abigail turned to her. "Did you decide about the candy store yet?"

Eve suddenly felt herself to be the center of attention. She gave a self-conscious nod. "Yes. I've decided to give it a go."

There was an immediate chorus of congratulations and pleased comments from those who knew of her plans, and a clamor for explanations from those who didn't. Uncomfortable, Eve was relieved when Chance and Dotty shared in explaining the news.

The meal was wonderful and the fellowship was even better. When it was over, everyone pitched in to set the restaurant and kitchen back to rights.

Eve took a moment to talk to Daisy before they made their departure. "Thank you so much for inviting me."

"It was my pleasure. And I'm so glad you've decided to stay in Turnabout. I hope you'll continue to join us here on Sundays."

Her husband appeared at her side and wrapped an arm possessively around her shoulder, while focusing on Eve. "Best wishes for the success of your new venture. Please allow me to print a free advertisement in Tuesday's paper."

"Oh, that's most kind, but I could never—"

Daisy held up a hand. "It costs him practically nothing to do this and makes him feel all magnanimous." She glanced fondly at her husband. "Did I get that word right?"

He grinned. "You know quite well you did."

"But I like to hear you say it."

Eve enjoyed their playful banter and hoped wistfully that she might one day experience something similar herself.

She went outside to fetch Leo. As they were walking around to join the others on the sidewalk, he glanced up at her with an earnest expression. "I'm glad you decided to stay. And not just because you're going to open a candy store."

Eve smiled, charmed by the way his mind worked. "Me, too."

He jammed his hands in his pockets. "It almost feels like we're a real family, you know—with a ma, and a pa, and even a grandmother."

Luckily, he didn't wait for a response, because she

wasn't certain what she would have said. Without warning, he sprinted ahead to join Chance and Dotty.

She made her way more slowly as she digested his words. A real family. It was a wonderful dream. Too bad it wasn't true.

And what would she do come the new year when it was time for this little "family" to disband? She pushed that thought aside. She would take Dotty's advice and enjoy this moment and not dwell on things that couldn't be changed.

Or at least she would try very hard to do that.

Eve glanced up as Leo stepped into the kitchen the next morning. "Are you all ready for your first day of school?" She resisted the urge to adjust the collar of his shirt.

"I suppose."

The words were uttered in an indifferent tone but Eve could sense the boy's nervousness. Her arms itched with the urge to hug him, but she refrained.

"Don't worry," Chance assured him, "you'll do great."

"Yes, you will." Eve began dishing up the eggs. "And to get you started off right, I picked up some strawberry jam at the mercantile to go on your biscuits for breakfast."

That seemed to cheer Leo up more than their assurances had.

Eve made quick work of serving their plates. Later, just as they were finishing, Jack Barr and two other children stopped in to see if Leo wanted to walk to school with them.

Leo turned to Eve expectantly. "Can I?"

Eve was pleased that Leo had sought her permission, but she had planned to walk him to school herself. However, he seemed so eager to join his friends that she swallowed her disappointment and simply nodded.

After the children had gone, she turned to find Chance

watching her, an understanding look in his eye. "You handled that well. You're going to make him a fine mother."

She smiled, trying not to let him see how jarred she was by his words. Is that what everyone was thinking, that her becoming Leo's mother was the ultimate outcome of this arrangement? More and more it was what she hoped, but it was by no means certain in her mind. Because she was also plagued by the thought that she might fail him.

Not knowing exactly how to respond to Chance, she held her peace.

If he noticed he didn't say anything. Instead, he asked, "So what are your plans for today?"

"I wrote a letter to Mrs. O'Connell last night informing her of my decision, so I'll need to post it first thing. Then I'll get to work making candy. I have several orders to fill already today."

"I can take care of posting that letter for you. I have to check on something at the depot anyway."

"Thank you, that would be very helpful."

"As for your candy business, do you mind if I make a suggestion?"

She eyed him suspiciously. "Such as?"

"Before you fill the orders you already have, make a batch or two of something to set out on the counter to sell. Since this is your first day, you'll probably have a few folks come in just out of curiosity. It would be good to have something available for them to purchase should the impulse hit them."

That made sense. "I suppose I could make something simple, like chocolate drops."

Chance gave her an approving nod. "And maybe a batch of something else as well, to show you plan to stock a variety."

"I don't want to make too many unordered items—what if it doesn't sell?"

"Have faith in yourself. And if you insist on worrying about such things, make something that keeps well. Because it *will* sell, if not today, then tomorrow or the next day. Word of mouth will be your biggest selling tool."

She rubbed her cheek. "And I suppose, when I make the additional batches of pumpkinseed brittle Abigail ordered I can make a little extra to put in the counter display."

He nodded approvingly. "Now you're thinking like a businesswoman."

That compliment cheered her immensely. She made shooing motions. "Now leave me to my work."

When she entered the kitchen she found Dotty waiting for her. "I'm ready."

"Ready for what?"

"I want to help you with your candy business. I figure I can make myself useful doing some of the simpler tasks if you just give me directions."

Eve eyed her friend with a dismayed frown. "Please don't feel obligated."

"I don't. In fact, I'm hoping to learn a few of your tricks while I'm helping."

Eve started to protest again, then remembered how she had felt the first time Miss Trosclair allowed her to make candy with her. Could Dotty actually *want* to help? "All right. I normally go from memory and the way things look when I'm making candy. But I'd like to get some of these recipes down on paper, especially the ones I don't fix too often, or new ones I'm trying out. So you can start by helping me write some of these recipes down as I go. That way, we'll both have a guide later on."

By the time the first batch had cooled enough to set out

and the second batch was cooling on the table, Eve's first customer had arrived.

"Hello," the woman said. "We met at the Thanksgiving Festival. I'm Maryann Pratt."

Eve placed her immediately—the doctor's wife.

"I heard so many good things about your candies, but they were all gone before I could get a taste at the Thanksgiving Festival. I had to come by and see for myself if everyone was right."

Eve smiled. "Of course. Try one of these chocolate drops. And I've got some pumpkinseed brittle in the kitchen that's just about ready to set out. I'll let you taste a piece of that, as well."

The woman shook her head. "Oh, I couldn't accept all of that without paying you."

"Of course you can. I wouldn't want you to purchase something you're not going to like."

That earned Eve another smile from the doctor's wife. "What a wonderful philosophy."

Eve waved toward the trays on the counter. "You just go ahead and try a piece of fudge while I fetch the brittle."

When Eve came back, Mrs. Pratt was beaming. "This is delicious, my dear. My quilting circle is meeting at my home tomorrow and I'd love to have a dozen pieces of each if that's not too big an order for you."

Her first in-store order. It was suddenly beginning to feel real. "Not at all. I have a couple of orders ahead of you, but I can have it ready for you by three o'clock this afternoon if that is acceptable."

Several other people stopped in after that, all of them placing orders of various sizes. Then, just before lunchtime, Everett Fulton stopped by.

"How's the candy business going?" he asked.

"It's going fine."

"Don't let her fool you." Chance had stood up from his workbench and was crossing the room toward them. "She's had a number of orders from folks passing in the street since word got out."

Mr. Fulton glanced at the candies displayed on the counter. "I can see why. These look mighty tempting."

"Help yourself to a piece," she offered. "I'm giving out free samples today."

"Trying to get folks hooked, are you? Good strategy."

Chance eyed his friend. "So did you just come by to check out the candies, or did you have something else in mind?"

"A little of both. I need to get some information for that advertisement I promised you for tomorrow's newspaper."

So he was really going to run an advertisement. But it seemed as if everyone already knew.

"And if you don't mind, I'd actually like to turn it into an interview so local folks can get to know a little more about you."

"An interview! But there's really nothing to tell." Eve felt panicked. What if questions came up about her parents? She couldn't let herself lie. But the truth could destroy her newfound friendships.

Chance gave her an understanding look. "Don't worry, Everett won't ask you anything you're not comfortable sharing."

"Of course not. I promise to make this very quick and painless. A few questions about where you're from, what you enjoy doing, why you came here and we'll be all done."

Eve gathered up her courage and nodded. "Of course. But rather than you asking me questions, can I just give you that information?"

Everett smiled. "Of course."

So for the next five minutes, Eve talked about how she

got interested in candy making, her work as backup piano player in her church, the way she looked forward to the first dogwood blooms in spring and how her favorite chore on her grandmother's small farm was feeding the chickens. She told him about traveling to Tyler to begin work as a milliner's apprentice but then ending up in Turnabout instead when she had to get off the train to help a friend, and how happy she was that that had happened. When she finally stopped talking, Everett gave her another smile.

"Easiest interview I ever did," he said as he closed his notebook.

She felt some of her tension ease. She'd managed to give him what he wanted without betraying any secrets or having to tell him no.

Chance had listened to her interview with equal parts amusement and admiration. He'd never seen anyone get around Everett with such ease before. And she'd done it while still giving him the information he needed. Not only had she not betrayed any of her own secrets, but she hadn't betrayed any of Leo's, either. And she'd done it without giving Everett any openings to get in one of his sometimes too astute questions.

It was quite an accomplishment.

When she turned to look at him, there was a hint of guilt in her eyes.

"Well done," he said reassuringly. "That was fast thinking on your part."

She fiddled nervously with a button at her throat. "I hope he's not upset with me."

"Don't worry, I could tell he was quite happy. You gave him more than enough material for his article." He quickly turned the subject, giving her something else to think about. "You've had my mouth drooling all morning with that sweet stuff you've been setting out on the counter."

She relaxed and waved toward the trays. "Feel free to help yourself. Consider it part of my rent."

"I may take a nibble here and there, but as I said before, there's no need for you to feel in any way obligated. You're more than pulling your weight around here and I'm enjoying all the company you're bringing in."

"And you aren't distracted by that?"

"I like having people around." He deliberately gave her his cockiest grin. "And speaking of people, I won't say I told you so, but based on the folks who have been through here today, it looks like your business is off to a good start."

Eve laughed. "A lot of that can be put down to curiosity and friends coming in to show support. I'm not expecting this to be a regular occurrence."

Chance shook his head. "It puzzles me why you always look at the negative side of things. It's just as easy and so much more pleasant to look at the positive side."

She gave him a wistful smile. "Your perspective is based on your previous experience."

Chance found that statement particularly poignant. It was high time she started adding to the positive side of her experiences.

And he might just consider making that his own personal mission.

When the school bell sounded that afternoon, Eve paused in her work to wait for Leo's return. He had several friends with him when he walked in the door. She treated each of them to one piece of candy of their choosing.

When they had all gone, she smiled down at Leo. "So how did it go today?"

Leo lifted a shoulder. "It was okay. Miss Whitman is nice and I already knew a lot of the other kids from the festival." He grinned. "Knowing you run a candy store has actually made me popular with the other kids."

"Is that so?"

"Yes, ma'am." Then he gave her an uncertain look. "You don't mind, do you?"

"No, but make sure you do your part to earn that friendship, don't just trade on what people can get from you."

He nodded solemnly.

"Now, Dotty will be ready to help you with your studies in a little while, but first I think Mr. Dawson has some chores for you to do." She and Chance had discussed that it was important for Leo to carry his share of responsibilities while he was here. "You'll find him out back."

Almost as soon as Leo disappeared out the door, Miss Whitman stopped in. "I wanted to let you know that Leo is fitting in quite well," the schoolteacher said. "He seems to be a bright boy."

"Thank you for letting me know."

"In fact, I'm certain that if he works hard, by the New Year he will be nearly back on track with the other students his age."

"I'm so relieved to hear that." Eve was sure catching up with his peers would give Leo's confidence a boost.

"I also had another reason for stopping by," the schoolteacher added. "I heard about this candy shop of yours and I'm here to place an order. I'm looking for some special treats to give my students on the last day of class before Christmas."

"What a wonderful idea. I insist you allow me to provide them at no cost. It's the least I can do to repay you for the special attention you're giving Leo."

"Oh, that's very kind of you to offer, but this is to be a gift from me to the children."

In the end, they agreed to split the cost between them.

After the schoolteacher left, Chance, who'd walked in in time to hear this last exchange, gave her a pointed look. "You'll never make a profit if you keep giving away your candies."

Eve gave him a raised brow look in return. "So says the man who has opened his home to two strangers without charge."

"That's different."

"Is it?"

"Yes, it is. For one thing, you are no longer strangers. And for another, the way I see it, I'm getting home-cooked meals and a more orderly establishment out of the deal. I consider that more than adequate payment for your use of this extra space that I wasn't using anyway."

The man refused to admit that he was just plain generous. The word *modesty* didn't seem to fit Chance on the outside, but it sure worked for who he was inside.

Eve happily settled into the day-to-day routine of her new life. First thing in the morning when she came downstairs she would find Chance already seated at his workbench. They'd chat for a few moments about the events of the prior day, or their plans for this one, and then she would head to the kitchen to prepare breakfast. Once the morning meal was done, they would scatter—Leo would head out to school, Chance would tinker at one of his worktables or head out back to work on his washing machine, and Eve and Dotty would plan the midday meal and then get to work on the candy making.

The three of them ate lunch together and once more attended to their various chores.

After school was out for the day, Leo returned, usually with a number of friends in tow, and Eve always made sure there were some "discard pieces" of candy available to serve them.

In the evenings, after supper, Dotty would spend time helping Leo with his schoolwork while Eve cleaned the kitchen. Then she would play the piano while Dotty knitted and Chance and Leo played checkers or Leo watched Chance carve some new figure.

Eve began experimenting with new recipes, some of which became hits with her customers while others failed. But she found the defeats did not bother her as much as they once would have.

And the number of customers she had continued to surprise her. Not only did some folks walk in to buy a few pieces for themselves or to share, but she had a number of orders trickle in for parties and gifts. By Wednesday morning she had to purchase new supplies and was delighted to find she had the funds to do so.

Midmorning on Wednesday, Eve stepped out into her shop in response to the bell to find Daisy standing at the counter.

"Hi there," she said with a big smile. "I was headed out to do a little shopping this morning. But Abigail and several of my regulars have been raving about your shop so I decided to take a little detour to see for myself." She gave Eve a sly look. "Besides, I hardly ever see Chance anymore."

Eve hadn't thought about the fact that by cooking for Chance she was taking business away from Daisy. "I'm so sorry. I didn't mean to take away one of your customers. I only—"

Daisy held up a hand. "Oh, goodness, don't think anything of it. I certainly wasn't fussing. In fact I'm plum tickled that Chance has such a pleasant reason to spend more time at home."

What did she mean by that?

Daisy fanned her face with her hand. "Oh, my. I feel flushed of a sudden. Do you mind if I have a seat?"

"Of course not." Eve immediately rushed to one of the tables and pulled out a chair. "Here, let me take your shawl and you just sit yourself right here. Can I get you anything?"

Daisy gave Eve a reassuring smile as she took her seat. "I'm okay." She put her hand over her stomach. "But there are days when I'm not certain this little one is going to wait until the New Year to put in an appearance." Then she grinned. "And just between us girls, I'm getting just as impatient myself."

Eve wasn't certain how to respond to that. "I was getting ready to boil some water for tea. Why don't you let me fix you a cup, as well?"

"That sounds lovely."

Eve returned to the counter and picked up one of the trays. "And while you're waiting, I'd like to get your opinion on this new candy I prepared today."

Daisy grinned. "You talked me into it." She let her hand hover over the tray while she studied the pieces. "But there's no need for you to serve me tea out here—I can join you and Dotty in the kitchen."

"Nonsense. You just stay right there. I'm ready to get out of the kitchen for a while and I'm sure Dotty is, too."

With a grateful nod, Daisy took a piece of candy from the tray and leaned back in her seat.

Fifteen minutes later Daisy took a sip from her cup then smiled in delight. "This tea has a wonderful flavor. Tangy but with a hint of something fruity. Is it peach?"

Eve nodded. "I like to experiment with tea flavors as

well as candies. I hope you don't mind. I added a pinch of cinnamon and then sweetened it with some syrupy peach juice left over from last night's cobbler."

"What a clever idea. How did you ever think to do that?"

Eve grinned. "Quite by accident—literally. Years ago I accidentally spilled a little vanilla in my tea and discovered I liked it. Since then I've occasionally experimented with other flavorings, like mint, herbs, juice from berries and such." It was not something her grandmother approved of so she hadn't had many opportunities to indulge herself in this. But since she'd arrived here, she'd let her imagination run free.

"You ought to add your flavored teas to the offerings on your board there. You might be surprised the number of folks who'll stay long enough to drink a cup when they come in for something else."

Dotty leaned forward eagerly. "A tea shop—what a lovely idea. And I could help take care of the customers for you, Eve."

Expand her business already? But seeing the eager gleam in Dotty's eyes she couldn't say no. "I suppose we could try it out and see what happens."

"Absolutely." Daisy raised her cup. "If you don't I will."

"Oh, if you want to offer it at your restaurant—"

Daisy waved a hand dismissively. "Eve, don't be a goose. I only meant to say that it's too good an idea not to pursue. And it would fit so much better here than at my place. Besides," she said, patting her stomach, "I have too many other things happening in my life right now to even think about starting a new venture."

Chance walked in, wiping his hands on a rag, just in time to hear the end of the conversation. "What new venture?"

Daisy grinned up at him. "Hi, stranger. Eve is going to expand her candy store to include a tea shop."

"Is she now?" Apparently Eve was really enjoying her new role of businesswoman.

"Actually, Dotty and I are," Eve clarified. "If it's okay with you, that is."

"This space up front is yours to do with as you wish." Chance couldn't stop a wry grin from forming. Who would have dreamed that this former saloon would now be housing a candy store and tea shop as well as his workroom? And it looked like there was going to be a whole lot more of a lady's touch in The Blue Bottle in the near future.

Dotty patted her hair as she beamed in pleasure. "Oh, this is going to be such fun. I already have some ideas how to arrange things out here to entice people to sit a spell."

Eve smiled. "Then I shall leave that aspect to you."

Dotty nodded her acceptance. "And I shall leave the tea selections and preparations to you."

Daisy pushed back from the table. "Well, it looks like you ladies have some planning to do. You can count on me to help spread the word. Maybe I can even get Everett to slip a little notice in Friday's newspaper." She stood. "Thanks for the tea and the candy, but I need to do my shopping and get back to the restaurant."

"Are you sure you're up to it?" Eve asked.

"Yep. As long as I don't have to run any races I'll be fine." The she snapped her fingers. "Oh, I almost forgot the other reason I stopped by today. If you'd like to set a tray of your candies out on the counter at my restaurant I'll be glad to sell them for you."

"Only if you promise to take a portion of the profits."

Once she and Daisy has worked out their arrangements and Daisy left, Eve broached the subject of the tea shop with Chance, who gave her his blessing.

"Are you sure you don't mind?" she asked.

"As long as you and your customers don't mind my messy workshop over on the other end of the room."

"I haven't heard any of my customers complain so far."

Still, as Chance stared at the half of the room dedicated to his workshop he felt a stirring of dissatisfaction. And slowly an idea began to take shape. Perhaps a trip to the lumber mill was in order.

"If this goes well, I could even bake some shortbread or cookies to go with the tea."

Eve smiled as she passed the bowl of greens to Chance at the lunch table. Dotty hadn't stopped talking about the tea shop since Daisy left earlier that morning. The woman seemed as excited by the tea shop as she herself had been about the candy store.

"Since you are obviously very enthused about the idea, I'll be happy to let you run the tea shop and of course collect the profits. I seem to have my hands full with the candy store."

Dotty smiled but shook her head. "That's very generous of you, but this will be a shared enterprise. The recipes are yours, as are the blending skills. But I will have fun being involved."

Just as they were finishing up with lunch, Chance received a delivery from the lumber mill. He introduced Eve to Hank Chandler, the owner of the mill, and the two men unloaded the boards in the back of the workshop.

Eve watched them stack the lumber. She counted a dozen evenly sized planks about four feet tall and two feet wide. The warm-hued wood was ready for whatever project he had in mind. Another carving project perhaps?

But when she asked him outright, he refused to enlighten her, telling her instead that she'd have to wait and see.

When Leo came in from school, the boy wandered over to see what Chance was busy with and to Eve's surprise, Chance put him to work.

When Eve stepped out of the kitchen to call them in to supper, she got her first look at his project. Across the room, in front of the area that contained his workbenches, Chance had erected four accordion screens of three panels each. She liked that it was only chest high, and that there were gaps between the screens. It managed to mask his work area without completely hiding it. If she looked across the room from her counter, for example, she could still see him sitting at his workbench.

"Do you like it?" Leo asked. "I helped. And Mr. Dawson says it'll make your shop more professional-looking."

He'd done this for her? Eve approached the dividers, admiring the simple flower engraving he'd carved on the top of the center panel of each screen. He really was quite talented. "Chance, this is beautiful."

He shrugged off her compliment and for a heartbeat actually looked uncomfortable with her praise. "I figured since you were going to hang around here for now that we ought to do what we could to make this look like a real shop."

"Thank you so much. I think it's wonderful."

He began putting his tools away. "You're welcome. Leo and I can paint them if you like. Just let me know what color."

"I rather like it unpainted with the wood grain showing."

Chance nodded as if he approved her choice. "I'll apply a stain to them then. I already have a can of some that ought to work." Then he straightened. "But that can wait until later. I think you were calling us in to supper."

"Of course. If you menfolk will get cleaned up, Dotty and I will get the table set."

Eve was so touched by his gesture that for a moment it was all she could do not to cry. No one had ever done anything like this for her before. And the fact that the screens were something she'd never have thought to ask for, yet were so perfectly right, made them all the more special.

No matter what happed after Christmas, no one could ever take away what she felt right now.

Chapter Nineteen

Eve hurried into The Blue Bottle the next morning. "Mr. Blakely had some Christmas decorations for sale at the mercantile today."

Chance looked up, surprised by how flushed and excited she looked. "Oh. Did you want to purchase any?" If that's what had set her eyes aglow he'd definitely see that she had some.

But she shook her head. "No, but I was thinking, the main reason I stayed was to make certain Leo had the family Christmas he wanted so much."

Chance nodded, wishing she'd list her other reasons. Did he figure anywhere in there?

"It got me thinking that maybe we should start decorating around here. Not with store-bought things, but with things we can make ourselves. That's what his memories were all about—crafting ornaments with his mother, selecting a tree with his father."

"What a lovely idea." Dotty folded up the paper she'd been reading. "And since tomorrow is Saturday, it'll be the perfect time."

Chance's mind started playing with possibilities. "What did you have in mind?"

"I think the main thing will be to have lots of greenery to hang. I splurged and purchased some red ribbon that we can add to it. Then we can craft decorations with whatever scraps of fabric and paper we can find. Oh, and when I was a child, my Sunday school teacher taught the class how to make angels from corn husks. I think I still remember."

"Something I did with my own daughter," Dotty said, "was to fashion stars, wreaths and animals from straw. And you can even add a little touch of paint to them if you like."

Chance was thinking along the lines of toy soldiers he could carve as a gift for Leo and what bits of metal and tin he had lying around that might be useful for decorating. But the decorating items they were describing would need components he didn't have on hand. "Sounds like we need to head outdoors and collect some raw materials."

"Excellent idea," Dotty said with a nod. "There are some holly bushes on my property and some evergreens out behind the place. You two ought to go ahead and collect what you can today, and then we can spend tomorrow on the fun stuff." She leaned back in her chair. "I'll stay here and keep an eye on the candy store and tea shop."

Chance turned to Eve with a raised brow. "You heard the lady. What do you say?"

She stood. "I say I'm ready to go. Lead the way."

A couple of hours later and she and Chance had amassed quite a collection. Tizzie's backseat was overflowing with greenery and lots of other little treasures they'd collected for possible use in tomorrow's decorating activities.

Right now they were headed back to the vehicle from one last trip along the wooded trails behind the burned remains of Dotty's home.

"Slow down," Chance grumbled good-naturedly. "My arms are full and these branches are heavy."

Eve laughed over her shoulder at him. "You just want to make certain I don't get to the picnic lunch Dotty packed for us before you do."

"Can you blame me?" he said. "Dotty included a slab of her buttermilk pie."

Eve started to respond when she suddenly stumbled on the uneven ground and landed on her knees and hands in a most undignified manner. Before she could so much as gather her wits, Chance had dropped his armload of greenery and was kneeling beside her, a hand on her shoulder and a worried frown on his face.

"Are you okay?" He helped her up to a squatting-on-her-heels position. "No, don't try to get all the way up just yet. Take a minute to catch your breath."

"I need to get off this knee," she said.

"Of course." In a moment he somehow had her sitting flat on the ground. "How's that?"

"Better." He still had an arm around her shoulder and it was difficult to concentrate on anything but the warmth of his touch and the beating of his heart at her back. Trying to focus her thoughts elsewhere she took a deep breath. "I'm sorry to be so clumsy."

"Don't apologize. I should have had hold of your arm."

She could tell by his tone he was berating himself. "I'm a big girl. I should have been watching where I was going." She stared at her skirt. "Oh, no."

"What is it?"

"I've got a tear in my dress."

"That can be mended. How bad is your knee?"

She felt her leg right above the left knee. "I don't think it's anything worse than a bad scrape. It'll probably be sore for a few days but, like the dress, it'll mend."

"Still, we should have Dr. Pratt have a look at it just to be sure it's nothing worse." His eyes searched her face. "Are you hurt anywhere else?"

Eve ignored the throbbing of her right palm and shook her head. No point in his worrying over another minor hurt.

"Can you stand if I help you up?"

"Of course."

Once she was on her feet, he didn't release her immediately. "Steady now. Don't put too much weight on that left leg."

She nodded, knowing she was going to have to hobble back to the car. Which, her treacherous mind whispered, was a good excuse to lean on him. Despite his caution not to, she tested her weight on her left leg and grimaced involuntarily.

"That does it." In one quick, fluid motion he had swept her up in his arms.

Startled, she wrapped an arm around his neck to steady herself. "What are you doing?" If her voice was a bit breathless, he could put it down to her pain.

He raised a brow, a purposeful set to his jaw. "Can't you tell? I'm going to carry you back to Tizzie."

"But this is silly. Put me down at once. I'm perfectly capable of walk—"

Before she could finish her protest, he hefted her to settle her more securely in his arms and headed in the direction of the vehicle. Realizing it would be useless to argue further, she settled back against his chest. She was amazed at how effortlessly he held her, as if her weight was nothing more than the armload of small branches he'd carried earlier.

The rhythm of his heartbeat played in her ear, echoing the beat of her own betraying pulse.

When they arrived at the motor carriage, rather than setting her on the ground to let her climb in as she'd expected, he leaned forward to set her directly inside. When he did, it brought his face within inches of her own. Her gaze flew to his and what she saw there left her unable to move, almost unable to breathe. There was an intensity there, a depth of emotion that touched off something deep inside her—something warm and tingling and altogether unfamiliar. He was so close she could feel his breath on her face, could see the flecks of gray in his blue eyes, could smell the scent of wood and soap and something faintly metallic that was uniquely him. There was a flicker of something in his eyes, and suddenly she knew he felt it, too. And that he was going to kiss her.

Or was that just wishful thinking?

Not letting herself second-guess the moment, she closed her eyes and lifted her face, giving him the permission she hoped he was seeking.

She heard his sharp intake of breath just a heartbeat before his lips pressed against hers. And then his hand, the one that was still around her shoulder, tightened and drew her closer.

Everything else receded. There were no other sounds, no other scents, no other sensations but those in the circle of his arms. The gentle warmth of his lips was so sweet, so dizzying, she hoped it would never end.

But abruptly it did. He suddenly released her and stepped back, his breathing labored and a small pulse point fluttering near the corner of his mouth.

"I'll be right back," he said in a tight voice. "Don't move from that seat." And with that, he spun on his heel and headed back down the trail.

What was wrong? Had she been too forward? Or perhaps too inexperienced? Whatever had happened, the joy she'd felt just seconds ago suddenly disappeared, replaced by insecurity and confusion.

Chance marched down the trail, mentally calling himself all sorts of despicable names. He needed to put some space between himself and Eve to clear his head. He shouldn't have let himself take advantage of her vulnerable state to steal that kiss. He certainly hadn't planned it. But carrying her as he had, holding her close against his chest, feeling how fragile and vulnerable she was, had stirred up all his protective and possessive urges.

Then, when she'd locked her gaze with his, had looked at him with such awakening warmth, it had stirred something more. Still, he'd used his tenuous control to hold himself back. But when she'd so innocently and sweetly offered her lips to him, it had been his undoing.

No, he shouldn't have let himself kiss her, but God help him, he couldn't find it in his heart to regret it. He'd finally found the real Eve beneath that prim, no-time-for-frivolous-fun exterior. And she'd been worth waiting for.

But as long as he kept his secret from her, he couldn't pursue her. It wasn't fair to her. Or to him.

But knowing all that he had to lose, could he risk letting her learn of his problem?

Chance returned with the branches that had been his excuse for leaving her with no more idea of what he should do than when he'd left.

As they drove back through town, Chance noticed Eve had withdrawn into herself. Was she regretting that kiss already?

Unable to stand the silence, he tried for a neutral topic. "How is your knee feeling?"

She gave him a polite smile. "Better. In fact, I don't think it's anything we need to bother Dr. Pratt."

"Better to be safe than sorry." Was he reduced to reciting platitudes now?

Chance stopped the car in front of the doctor's house, where he also had his clinic, a few minutes later. He quickly jumped out and went around to help her from the vehicle.

Eve held a hand up as he approached. "I can walk if you'll just lend me your arm."

Figuring that was the safest option—for both of them—he nodded and took her elbow as she climbed out. Then he instructed her to put her hand on his shoulder while he put his arm around her waist. Slowly she hobbled alongside him up the walk. When they reached the front steps, however, he ignored her sensibilities and swept her up, then set her down on the porch.

Dr. Pratt's examination didn't take long. "Her knee is banged up a bit. It appears she landed on something hard like a rock or branch. And she has a few other cuts and scrapes. She can expect to be plenty sore for the next couple of days but it's nothing serious. It'll heal faster if she stays off of her feet as much as possible."

Eve entered the room just then and the doctor handed her a piece of paper. "Give this to Obed Flaherty down at the apothecary shop and he'll fix you up an ointment to put on that scrape."

"Thank you." She turned to Chance. "See, it was nothing."

Before Chance could say anything, Dr. Pratt spoke up. "It's always best in these situations to get an injury looked at. Better to be safe than sorry."

Chance caught the quick glance she shot his way, her expression reflecting that she remembered his saying almost the exact same thing.

They shared a quick smile over it, but her expression quickly shadowed over and she dropped her gaze again.

Was this the way it would be from now on? Had he destroyed the warm friendship they shared by his impulsive act?

Dear Lord, let that not be true.

Eve did her best not to wince as they slowly walked from the motor carriage to the back door of The Blue Bottle. At least there were no steps as there'd been at the doctor's house—that had been torture.

She'd insisted they not use the front door—she didn't want to make a spectacle of herself with her undignified hobble, disheveled appearance and unladylike clutching at Chance's arm for support.

It was bad enough that she couldn't get the thought of that kiss out of her mind, she didn't need an audience to see her discomfiture.

They entered to find the candy shop empty. Good, no customers to explain her condition to. They'd barely entered the workroom, though, when Dotty stepped out of the kitchen, a welcoming smile on her face. "Good, you're back—" Her smile abruptly changed into an expression of concern as she hurried forward. "Gracious me! What happened? Are you all right?"

"Just a bit of injured dignity is all," Eve said reassuringly. "Like a goose, I tripped over a bit of uneven ground."

"She banged up her knee," Chance said firmly. "Dr. Pratt wants her to stay off of that leg as much as possible."

"Oh, you poor dear. Come over here and have a seat."

As Chance helped her cross the room, Eve halted at the foot of the stairs. "I think I'll go up to my room for a bit instead." She wanted to be alone, to wallow in her misery for a bit with no one to watch.

But Chance's jaw set in a stubborn line. "You're not going up there unless you let me carry you."

"Don't be silly. You are *not* going to carry me up those stairs." Just the thought of how she might betray herself again if he held her close was too mortifying to bear.

"Then you're not going." His tone brooked no argument.

"For goodness' sake, Chance, I can use your arm or the banister and make it up without being carried."

"And have you take another, even worse tumble? I think not."

"There now, you two." Dotty looked from one to the other with an expression that reminded Eve the woman had been a schoolmarm at one time. "Why don't I serve you some refreshment out here? Once you have a little food in you I'm sure you'll be able to work this out without raising your voices. Whatever *this* is."

Eve felt her cheeks warm. Had they been raising their voices?

Chance finished helping her to her seat, then stepped back. "I'm going to go unload our findings from Tizzie." He met her gaze. "And you stay put. No heading to the kitchen to help Dotty." His tone was polite but firm.

"Perfectly right," Dotty said. "Let me hang up the closed sign so we can have a bit of privacy and I'll have the table set in just a few moments."

Eve watched Chance and Dotty head off in opposite directions. She was finally alone, though not for long she was sure. Every bit of control in her released and she slumped forward, propping her elbows on the table and her head in her hands. She admitted to herself that she'd been rude to Chance just now when he offered to carry her up the stairs. It certainly wasn't that she didn't want him to hold her again. Quite the opposite—she longed to experience that feeling of being protected and cherished again, to test whether it would be as achingly sweet as before or if that had just been a fluke.

And that very longing scared her.

Just as in the past, her impulsiveness had done her in. But this time the price had been steep—Chance's respect.

Would she ever be able to regain it?

The meal was light and blessedly brief. Dotty kept the conversation going by asking about the materials they'd found for use in crafting decorations and speculating on how much Leo would enjoy using them.

As soon as the meal was over, Chance excused himself, saying he had errands to run. "I'll stop by the apothecary while I'm out and pick up that ointment for you."

"Thank you." She finally found the courage to meet his gaze directly and searched for some sign that she hadn't completely burned her bridges with him.

To her surprise, the look he gave her was softer, less confrontational than earlier. "Will you give me your word that you won't attempt the stairs until I get back?"

When he looked at her like that, with that mix of concern and protectiveness, she couldn't remain aloof. "I promise."

With a satisfied nod, he turned and crossed the room. But instead of heading out immediately, he disappeared into the storeroom. A moment later he popped back out with a short stool. He placed it in front of her chair. "If you want to prop your leg up use this." He raked his hand through his hair. "And I'd like you to keep the candy shop closed until I get back." His gaze held hers, demanding an answer.

She found herself nodding agreement almost without conscious thought.

With that, he left.

Dotty rose and picked up a platter. "He's just worried about you."

"I know."

"And that makes you unhappy?"

"No. It's just—" Eve closed her mouth before she said something she shouldn't. She raised her chin and changed topics. "Chance is a kind, generous man—I, more than anyone, know that."

"Ah, so you think it's just his generous nature at work here."

"Of course. I mean, what else could it be?"

Dotty gave her a knowing smile. "What else indeed."

Eve traced a circle on the table with her finger. "He's got a kind word and ready smile for all the ladies, so it doesn't mean anything special if he should show me kindness, as well." She straightened, deciding it was time to change the subject. "I feel like a sluggard just sitting here while you're working. Surely there's something I can do to help."

Dotty laughed. "Chance would have my head if I put you to work. But there is something you can do to make the time pass more pleasantly."

"What's that?"

"I'd enjoy having a bit of music. And you don't need your legs to play the piano."

Eve smiled. "Of course. But that hardly seems like help."

"'A joyful heart lightens the load' is what my grandmother used to say. And music always gladdens my heart."

Eve was still at the piano an hour later when Chance finally returned. When he came inside he had an odd assortment of pieces of wood. From what she could see from where she sat, there was a tall piece as big around as her wrist, several irregularly shaped discs that still had bark on them and were roughly ten inches in diameter and a handful of other miscellaneous pieces. Did he have a new project in the works? Or were these for their Christmas decorating project?

He set all the pieces on his workbench and then crossed over to her, reaching inside his jacket.

"Here you go," he said, handing her the jar of what she supposed was the ointment Dr. Pratt had prescribed. "Obed said to spread it on your knee twice a day."

She accepted the jar from him, then wondered how in the world she was supposed to apply it if she couldn't go up to her room.

As if reading her mind, Chance began closing all the window shades, then locked the front door.

He came back to stand in front of her. "I'll be working in the shed out back for about thirty minutes, so you'll have the privacy you need to do what you must. Would you like me to call Dotty for you before I leave?"

His continued kindness toward her after the earlier incident made her want to cry even more. Not trusting herself to speak, she shook her head.

With a nod, he left.

She applied the ointment to her knee, feeling her wilted resolve strengthen with every moment. He hadn't completely rejected her—his actions of a few moments ago proved that. She was certain she'd seen real concern in his gaze, not just polite attention. The two of them could be friends, even if the door had likely closed on anything more.

Don't think about that, she told herself. *That possibility had been remote at best so you haven't really lost it.*

So why did that thought hurt so very much?

Chance returned almost exactly thirty minutes later. And he even called out before coming all the way inside to make certain it was okay. When he stepped in, Eve noticed he was carrying something he'd apparently made with that long slender piece of wood she'd spotted earlier.

She recognized it for what it was before he made it halfway across the room—a crutch.

"Since I know it's probably pointless to tell you to stay off your feet the next couple of days," he said, "I made you this."

She studied the crutch. It was simply made—an upright topped by a braced crosspiece in a *T* formation—but it looked quite sturdy. And he'd found some cloths that he'd rolled up and tied securely to the top of the crosspiece to form a cushion.

"You made this?" Dotty asked. "Well now, isn't that just something?" She caught Eve's eye. "But then again, I imagine this is a kindness he'd show most anyone."

Eve gave her a warning look, but Dotty merely sat back with a satisfied smile.

Eve cut a quick glance Chance's way to see what he thought of Dotty's not so subtle point, but he merely looked puzzled as he glanced from one to the other.

Time to change the subject. "Thank you so much for this gift. It will definitely make life easier until my knee gets better."

"Try it out," he said. "I'd like to make certain it's the correct height."

By the time Chance had the crutch adjusted to his very finicky satisfaction, Leo walked in with some of his friends. As soon as he saw Eve using a crutch he halted in his tracks. "What happened?"

"Nothing to be worried about," she reassured her friend. "I tripped this morning and hurt my knee, but it'll be fine in a few days." She smiled. "I'm afraid I didn't get much candy making done today, but I think there are a few pieces of taffy left from yesterday."

Dotty took care of the children and tactfully ushered them out quickly.

As soon as they'd gone, Chance turned to Leo. "I think it's about time I empty the storeroom," he said casually. "You want to help me?"

"Sure."

For the next hour, Eve watched as Chance and Leo pulled every bit of furniture and miscellany out of the room. Chance carefully examined each piece and decided whether it should go into his shed out back or into the trash pile. He was certainly serious about cleaning it out!

When he was finally done, he grabbed the broom and swept it out.

Then he returned to stand in front of Eve. "I have a compromise solution for you on the issue of the stairs. I know it's not ideal, but I want you to use the storeroom as your bedchamber for the next couple of days."

Again, he'd gone to considerable trouble for her.

"I've made arrangements with Edgar down at the hotel to borrow one of his spare cots, and we can fetch whatever personal items you need from upstairs. What do you think?"

She thought he was the noblest, most giving man she'd ever met. "I think it is an excellent compromise. And I'm sure I'll be quite comfortable in there."

He seemed relieved at her response. Was he expecting her to argue with him?

She caught a knowing look from Dotty and shook her head in response. She would not overstep again.

He deserved so much more.

Chapter Twenty

After supper, while Dotty and Leo cleaned the dishes, Chance gathered up all of the items he and Eve had collected before her accident. The evergreen branches he set aside—everything else he spread out on the far end of the counter, away from Eve's candy trays. He also collected the paint and brushes he had on hand and some twine.

When Dotty and Leo joined them from the kitchen, Dotty hurried upstairs to get her contributions of ribbon, paper and yarn along with Eve's sewing box that contained ribbon, needles, thread and scissors.

Leo looked at the abundance of materials, his eyes gleaming with excitement. "Oh, boy. Not even Ma used all of this."

Eve laughed. "We may not use all of it, either. But Chance and I figured it was better to have more than we needed." She looked at the mounds of items spread before them. "So, where shall we start?"

Leo picked up one of the round discs Chance had collected from the sawmill.

"When I was down at the mill picking up the wood for Eve's crutch, I saw a large twisted branch on the discard pile." He always checked the scrap pile when he was at the mill. Pieces that were no good for Hank's purposes sometimes were just right for his. "It gave me an idea and I had Hank cut these for me."

"What will you use them for?" Leo asked.

"I figured we could paint Christmas scenes on them. I've already bored a hole at the top. When we're done, we can insert some string and hang them up with the decorations."

"What a splendid idea," Dotty said.

"There's eight of them, so we can each do two. Here are the paints—do whatever comes to mind. I figure the more variety we have the better."

Eve painted a simple manger and babe with a star shining above on the first. On the other she did a candle with a sprig of holly beside it.

Leo painted a decorated tree and a candy cane.

Dotty did a pair of praying hands and a large star.

Chance did a snowman and a sled.

Eve glanced at them and then gave him a smile. "I take it you have fond memories of snow."

He grinned in return. "It's one of the few things I miss about Philadelphia. But I understand you do get the occasional snow flurry here."

Dotty nodded. "I even remember getting nearly a foot one year. It was quite a sight to behold."

They set the discs aside to dry and then began work on other items. By the time they were done, they had quite an assortment.

When it was time to send Leo up to bed, Eve realized with a pang that she wouldn't be able to tuck him in tonight. Chance must have realized what she was thinking because he gave her a sympathetic nod. Then he clapped the boy on the shoulder. "Go on up and get ready for bed. I'll come by and check on you in a few minutes."

Strange how that nightly ritual had become such a part of her in so short a time. It brought home to her how very hard it was going to be to let Leo go when a new family was found for him.

Strange, too, how her impressions of Chance had changed. She no longer saw him as a happy-go-lucky charmer, but as a man with deep feelings and a strong sense of responsibility.

Later, when she slipped into her own bed, she didn't mind so much that both the room and bed were smaller and that she had no window. Instead she was warmed by the thought that Chance had spent nearly the entire afternoon preparing this place especially for her. That thought kept her content and comfortable all through the night.

When Eve stepped out of her room—or rather hobbled out—the next morning, Chance was just heading down the stairs.

"Good morning," he said with a raised brow. "You're up earlier than normal. Did the new room not agree with you?"

"Not at all. I was quite cozy. But without a window, I had no idea what time it was when I awoke. So I just went ahead and got up."

He frowned. "Sorry, I hadn't thought about the window."

Eve laughed. "Chance, you're very talented and can fix a lot of things, but you can't put a window in a room that's bordered on all sides by other rooms." She gave him a reassuring smile. "I promise you, I'm quite happy there."

"How's your knee?"

"Much better, thank you." She raised a hand, palm out. "But don't worry, I intend to use this crutch when I'm moving about and not attempt the stairs today."

He nodded approval.

"But I won't promise about tomorrow."

His brows drew down. "Eve—"

She didn't let him finish. "I apologize if I appeared ungrateful yesterday. You were very kind to be so concerned about me, and to do all of this." She swept her arm, indicating the crutch and the makeshift bedchamber. "This really was going above and beyond. And in return I was undeniably snappish."

He smiled. "You were hurt—that no doubt affected your temper."

Happy to let him believe that was the reason, Eve nodded. "At any rate, thank you so much for going to all that trouble to set up the temporary bedchamber."

He shrugged. "I've been meaning to clean out that storeroom for months. This just gave me the excuse to get it done."

The man really wasn't comfortable with accepting compliments. "If you give me a few minutes I'll get the coffee brewing."

"I'll help."

They walked toward the kitchen in comfortable silence, as he adjusted his steps to match hers.

"I tell you what," Chance said as they stepped into the kitchen. "I never got around to looking at yesterday's paper. Why don't you read it to me while I stoke the stove and get the coffee on."

"Oh, but—"

"I may not be much of a cook, but I do know how to make coffee." He gave her a boyish grin. "And I do like to listen to you read."

Pleased to see that he was comfortable teasing her again, she smiled. "Very well. But don't think I'm going to let you get away with keeping me in a chair all day."

He placed a hand over his heart. "I wouldn't dream of it."

Dotty walked in about the time Chance had the coffee ready and Eve refused to meet her gaze. The widow had far too much fun pointing out the undercurrents in her and Chance's interactions for Eve's comfort. Dotty offered to cook breakfast if Eve would continue to read out loud. Eve knew it must be a ploy to keep her in her seat, but decided to play along.

Right after breakfast they began decorating the shop. Some of the evergreen was formed into a garland and generously garnished with the pinecones, seeds, pods and other interesting bits that they'd selected from the pile last night, some of which had been painted a bright red. This they draped on the dividers.

Eve sat on a stool near the counter and gave directions as well as handled the occasional customer who came by. She also took pieces of the greenery and formed a wreath adorned with a large red bow and some sprigs of holly.

To her delight, Chance pulled out some small wooden toys he'd carved in times past and offered them up as added decoration. He'd also fashioned several shiny stars out of tin. Eve took some twine and tied these ornaments onto the wreath, too, and then Chance hung it on the wall behind the counter.

After much discussion on the best place to hang the wooden discs they'd painted last night—some of it downright silly—it was decided to put them across the front of the counter.

When they were done hanging the greenery and the painted discs, Eve looked around with a critical eye. "Hmm, I think it needs something else. What do you think, Leo?"

He nodded. "We definitely need more."

"We have more evergreen sprigs," Chance offered.

"Why don't we make some paper chains?" Leo asked.

Dotty snapped her fingers. "I have an even better idea—paper doll chains."

Dotty taught them how to fold the paper, draw the half outline of a girl or boy, then carefully cut the figures so that when you unfolded it you ended up with the desired chain. They draped these across the front of the counter between the discs connecting them with strings of red and green yarn. Eve figured out how to alter the design to create chains of angels.

"It appears Eve and I got a bit carried away while we were out yesterday," Chance said innocently. "There's quite a bit of greenery left over."

She felt a childish urge to stick her tongue out at him. He knew good and well he was the one who had insisted they collect so much. Then she saw the gleam in his eyes as he watched her and knew he'd deliberately been teasing her.

"We could hang some over on your side of the room," Dotty said, apparently missing that bit of by-play.

Chance shook his head. "There's almost too much in here as it is."

"I know," Eve said, "why don't we put some out front around the doorway and windows?"

"I like that," Leo said enthusiastically.

Fifteen minutes later, Chance found himself outside on a ladder waiting for Leo to hand him a wreath Eve and Dotty had just fashioned. Today had been a good day. Not only had the decorating been surprisingly fun, but he'd seen Leo happier than he'd been since he arrived in Turnabout. And some of the warmth and teasing seemed to be finding their way back into his relationship with Eve.

It seemed there might be hope for them yet.

The subject of his thoughts appeared and he frowned down at her from the ladder. "Where's your crutch?"

She waved a hand dismissively. "Just inside the doorway. Honestly, my knee is much better and I don't aim to do much walking, just directing."

He shook his head. The woman was too stubborn for her own good. "Pride goeth before a fall," he warned.

Eve grimaced. "Please don't talk about falls while you're up there on that ladder."

The thought that she worried about him made him feel more magnanimous. "Don't think I'm not aware that you just changed the subject," he said sternly. Then he smiled. "But I will give in with my usual good grace."

He saw her choke back a laugh at that, and with a satisfied smile, turned to Leo. "Now, hand me up that wreath so Eve can tell me where to place it."

Chapter Twenty-One

By Sunday afternoon Chance was ready to admit Eve's walking had improved and she could safely handle the stairs again. All of her things were returned to her room and life went back to normal—or what had become normal for the four of them.

The weather turned much colder on Monday and Dotty decided they should add hot cocoa to the tea shop offerings, which proved to be quite popular, especially when Eve put in some drops of peppermint flavoring.

On Tuesday Leo slid into his seat at the supper table and announced, "I must be the luckiest boy in town. Not only do I have a great new family, but I get to live in a candy store." Chance caught Eve's reaction—a bittersweet mix of pride, tenderness and fear. It seemed she still hadn't made up her mind to adopt the boy. It was obvious she wanted to. What was she so afraid of?

Wednesday morning, Chance stepped past the dividers, headed for the kitchen. It was cold out back in his work shed and he was ready for a cup of Eve's coffee. And maybe he'd snag a piece of candy while he was at it.

Or two.

He hadn't quite reached the kitchen door when he heard

someone come in from the street. Turning to greet Eve's latest customer, he stiffened as he recognized the impeccably dressed gentleman standing ramrod straight in the doorway.

"So this is your place," his father said by way of greeting. From his tone it was obvious he wasn't impressed.

Chance decided to ignore both the comment and the tone. "Hello, Father. You arrived a few days earlier than expected." Typical of him—a way to stay in control.

"I don't believe I specified a particular date in my letter to you."

Eve stepped out of the kitchen just then carrying a tray of candies. She paused a moment when she saw they had a visitor. "Hello. I hope I'm not interrupting anything."

Before Chance could say anything, his father stepped forward.

"How do you do?" he said. "I'm Woodrow Dawson, Chauncey's father."

"Chauncey?" Then she glanced Chance's way as understanding dawned. "Of course. So nice to meet you, Mr. Dawson. I'm Eve Pickering."

"And do you work for my son? His cook perhaps?"

Eve's face reddened and Chance jumped in to correct his father's assumption. "Eve does *not* work for me. She runs a candy shop here in this building and is also a houseguest."

His father frowned. "Candy store? Houseguest?"

Dotty stepped out of the kitchen, wiping her hands on her apron. "I thought I heard voices out here." Then she paused when she spotted the new arrival. "Hello there, I don't think we've met. I'm Dotty Epps."

Chance spoke up before his father this time. "Dotty, this is my father, Woodrow Dawson. Father, Dotty is also a houseguest of mine, and she also helps around the candy shop." He relished the confused expression on his father's face. Now if he could just get the man out of here before he said something truly insulting.

His father gave him an exasperated look. "And are there other houseguests I should know about?"

"Actually there is one more. A ten-year-old boy you'll meet once school lets out for the day."

"I see." He tugged on his lapels. "So have you expanded your business endeavors to include a candy store and a boardinghouse?"

Did the man realize how cutting his words and tone were to Eve and Dotty? "The candy store belongs to Eve, not me. And I said they were *houseguests,* not boarders."

Eve stepped forward, as if to intervene. "Can I offer you some refreshment, Mr. Dawson? I'm afraid lunch isn't ready yet, but perhaps you'd enjoy a glass of lemonade. Or if you prefer something warm, I can fix you a cup of coffee or tea." She waved a hand to the trays set out on the counter. "And please help yourself to any of these that might tempt you."

"I'm sure Father wouldn't want you to go to any trouble," Chance said quickly. "I'll escort him to—"

"Nonsense," Eve said. "It's no trouble at all. And he must be tired after such a long trip."

"A cup of coffee would be welcome," his father said with a condescending nod.

"That settles it. One cup of coffee coming up." She smiled at the visitor, though Chance could have told her it was a wasted effort.

As soon as Eve and Dotty disappeared into the kitchen, his father pinned him with one of his formidable looks. "So what's *really* going on here?"

"Quite frankly, sir, I don't see where that is any of your concern."

"Anything that affects one of my sons *is* my concern. We're family." Then he followed up that touching sentiment with, "Just what kind of mess have you gotten yourself into this time? Do these people have some hold over you? Or are they just taking advantage of your easygoing nature?"

Why did his father immediately focus on the negative possibilities? "It's nothing like that. In fact, it was my idea for them to move in here and I'm enjoying both their company and the visitors their shop is bringing into my place. Their business is thriving. In fact," he said defiantly, "I've told them they're welcome to stay for as long as they like."

His father shook his head. "You were always too softhearted."

In his father's world, being compassionate was a weakness, not a virtue. "This is my home and I will invite whomever I choose to share it with me. The subject is closed."

But his father was not one to let a subject drop until he'd had his say. "A manipulative woman can make you think the things she wants were your ideas all along. And you always have been susceptible to the charms of a pretty woman."

Chance's temper rose several notches, despite his intention not to let his father rile him. "Father, you know nothing about these people. They're good, decent folk. Dotty is a dear friend who has helped me almost since my arrival. Eve interrupted her own travel plans to take responsibility for a young orphan boy in need, even though she in effect stranded herself here."

Did his father understand what a sacrifice that had been? "No one took advantage of me or forced me into anything. This whole plan *was* my idea. And I expect you to be civil to my guests while you are in my home. If you can't do that, then I will ask that you not come here."

His father stared at him a moment, his expression unreadable. But Chance returned his look without blinking, and eventually his father nodded. Had he really just won this exchange?

"Of course. Civility is always in order, no matter the circumstances." Then his father looked around. "But a candy store of all things." He turned back to Chance. "Tell me they are at least paying you rent for the space this business is taking up."

"They're not."

"I knew it. They *are* taking advantage of you. Chance, how in the world do you expect to ever make a profit at anything if you aren't a good steward of your own resources?"

Could Eve and Dotty hear this discussion? If so, what were they thinking? "I make enough to get by on comfortably. If that's enough for me, who are you to say otherwise?"

"*Enough to get by on.* Thunderation, son, is that the extent of your ambition?"

They were down to the same old arguments. But this time Chance would not be cowed. He straightened and gave his father a measured look. "I'll thank you to remember that you are in my home. And that the woman you describe as taking advantage of me is trying very hard to convince me to let you stay here. But I will not allow you to talk to me or my friends this way while you are a guest here. If you can't show me, and them, some respect, then it might be best if you take a room at the hotel."

His father drew himself up stiffly. "If you feel so strongly about it, then perhaps I shall."

Why didn't that feel like a victory? "And another thing.

I've told you before that I prefer to be called Chance. That's how the people around here know me and I would appreciate it if you would honor my wishes."

"Chauncey is a perfectly fine name. It was your mother's father's name."

"Yes, yes, I know all that. And Grandfather was a fine man. But as I said, I prefer to go by Chance."

Eve stepped out of the kitchen with two cups of coffee, along with a creamer and sugar bowl, balanced on a tray. "Here you go, gentlemen. Chance, I thought you might like to have a cup as well while you and your father catch up." She smiled a thank you as Chance took the tray from her and set it on one of the tables.

The idea of him and his father having a cozy chat over coffee was almost laughable. But he didn't feel like laughing.

She beamed at them as if they were prize students. "I'll just be back in the kitchen working on another batch of candy if you should need anything else."

"Thank you. But I'll be escorting my father to the hotel as soon as we've had our coffee."

Her expression immediately changed to one of dismay. "Please don't do that."

Chance knew her distress was genuine, but she had no idea what she would be letting herself in for if he complied.

Before he could set his foot down on the matter, though, she continued, "I wouldn't be able to sleep well at night if I thought my staying here caused you to relegate your father to a hotel rather than have him stay in your home. You haven't sent that cot back to the hotel yet, so we have an extra room."

Was she about to suggest his father move into the storeroom? He couldn't wait to see the dignified man's reaction to *that* suggestion.

But he had underestimated Eve once again. "I can have my things moved down there again in no time."

"That's *really* not necessary," Chance said quickly. "I'm sure Father wouldn't want to put you out of your room. And besides, he really will be more comfortable at the Rose Palace."

"The Rose Palace?"

Chance nodded. "That's the name of our hotel."

"I see." The older gentleman turned to Eve. "That's a very generous offer, Miss Pickering, but as my son mentioned, I wouldn't want to put you out of your room."

Thank goodness his father's good manners had kicked in. "Quite right," Chance agreed. "The Rose Palace it is."

"I won't hear of it," Eve insisted. "Chance, your father didn't travel all this way to stay at some hotel, he came to spend the holiday with *you*. And I truly don't mind moving downstairs—I got used to the place when I stayed there last week. The room is really very cozy and it's closer to the kitchen." She gave Chance a smile that was almost pleading. "Besides, being down here will allow me to get started in the kitchen early without disturbing anyone."

His father spoke up before he could. "Well, if you're certain this won't discomfit you unduly, then I will accept your most generous offer."

"Wonderful!" Eve appeared quite pleased with herself.

Chance managed to swallow his groan. This was not going at all as he'd planned. But he hadn't counted on Eve's interference.

If his father did even one thing to make Eve, or his other houseguests for that matter, feel uncomfortable, he would kick the man out, even if he had to do it over Eve's protests.

Eve turned to Chance. "If you don't mind helping me move my things, we can have the room ready for your father in no time at all."

Chance raised a brow, feeling out of sorts with her. "Surely we don't need to do that now."

"The sooner tackled the sooner done. Besides, I'm sure your father would like to settle in and perhaps get freshened up after his long trip."

She turned to his father. "Dotty will be out in just a minute with something to tide you over until lunch, and to keep you company." Then, with a smile Chance's way, she headed for the stairs.

As they climbed to the second floor, Chance tried one more time to dissuade her. "This really isn't necessary. To be honest, my father is used to more sophisticated accommodations than I can offer him here. He'd undoubtedly be much more comfortable at the Rose Palace."

"I don't think his visit is about physical comfort or silk bed coverings. I think it is about spending time with you."

Chance grimaced. She wasn't going to believe him until she saw the truth for herself. And if things ran true to course, it wouldn't take long.

Twenty minutes later, the storage room had once again been turned into Eve's bedchamber and his father had been ensconced in the upstairs room.

"I know you mean well," Chance told Eve as he moved toward his worktable, "but I hope you don't live to regret this kindness."

"I won't."

He shook his head at her confidence. She was always seeing the best in others—too bad she couldn't do that for herself.

When Eve stepped out of the kitchen to announce lunch was ready, she found Chance's father downstairs talking to Dotty. Or rather Dotty was talking to him, in her usual animated, cheery fashion.

Chance was at one of his worktables, head down, point-edly ignoring them. But something in his demeanor made her believe he was aware of everything going on.

As the three rose, Mr. Dawson glanced Chance's way with a frown. "You take your meals in the kitchen?"

Chance spread his hands to indicate their surroundings. "As you can see, there's no formal dining room here. Besides, it's the warmest room in the place, so it's quite comfortable."

Dotty touched Mr. Dawson's arm lightly for a second. "I always find food tastes much brighter when you eat it in the place it was prepared. I'll be interested to hear what you think."

Chance's father gave her a considering glance and then nodded. "Of course."

Eve smiled at the deft way Dotty was able to deflect Mr. Dawson's focus. Bright taste indeed—what did that even mean? But perhaps the man wasn't as intractable as Chance had tried to suggest.

When they sat down to the meal, Chance deferred to his father to say the blessing, which Eve saw as another positive sign, despite Chance's stiff demeanor.

As the plates were being passed, however, she noticed that Chance was focusing on his food and not his father. Determined to keep the silence from getting awkward, she smiled at the older gentleman. "How was your trip, Mr. Dawson? That's quite a distance you had to travel."

"It went as well as any trip of that length can. I had the use of a private train car for most of the trip, so that made it bearable."

"Father likes to travel in style," Chance said dryly.

Mr. Dawson gave him an irritated look. "There's nothing wrong with taking advantage of the things money can buy, if you have the funds." Then he turned to Eve. "And speaking of travel, I understand you came in on the train recently yourself. If I may be so forward as to ask, where do you hail from?"

"A little town up in Arkansas called Iron Bluff. I doubt you would have heard of it." Why was Chance keeping so quiet? It wasn't like him.

"You're right, I haven't. And you were traveling alone?"

"Why, yes." She tried not to squirm under his scrutiny. "I'd accepted employment offered by a friend of my grandmother's who lives in Tyler, Texas. I was traveling there to begin work."

"And yet you are here."

To Eve's relief, Chance spoke up before she could. "Eve's plans changed when she found out Leo needed her help. It was quite a selfless act on her part."

This time Eve wanted to squirm for an entirely different reason.

Thank goodness Dotty stepped in to change the subject. "And what exactly is it that you do, Mr. Dawson?"

"I'm a retired congressman. I also have interests in several land holdings and financial institutions that keep me busy."

Dotty's eyes widened, though Eve wasn't certain the emotion in them was altogether genuine.

"That sounds quite impressive," the widow said.

"Yes," Eve agreed, trying to do her part to keep the conversation on a positive note. "It was good of you to take time out of what sounds like a busy schedule to come all the way here to spend Christmas with your son."

Mr. Dawson cast a disapproving glance at his son. "Yes, well, it was becoming increasingly obvious that Chance wouldn't be returning home for a visit anytime soon. I decided to take matters into my own hands."

Chance finally spoke up. "*This* is my home now," he said tightly. Then he turned to Eve. "The soup is delicious."

She knew a cue when she heard one. "Thank you. Mr. Macgregor had some fine soup bones in his butcher shop this morning and it sounded like just the thing for a cold day." Then she smiled Dotty's way. "But wait until you taste the pecan pie Dotty baked for us. I've been fighting the urge to steal a bite all morning."

"I'm sure it will be quite delicious." Mr. Dawson turned back to Dotty. "And what about you? Are you from Arkansas, as well?"

"Oh, dear me, no. I was born and raised right here in Turnabout. In fact, I've never traveled very far from home. Other than to visit my daughter and her family over in Jefferson, that is." She sighed. "But I've always dreamed about seeing more of the country before I pass on."

"Perhaps some day you shall."

Dotty nodded. Then she gave him an arch look. "I suppose you're wondering, if I'm from around here, how I ended up living here in your son's place."

He smiled indulgently. "I do admit to a bit of curiosity."

"My own home burned down a couple of months ago and I ended up in the boardinghouse. Then your son very generously invited me to stay here when Leo and Eve arrived."

"I'm sorry to hear about your home."

"I do miss it. But God had a plan. If that hadn't happened I likely wouldn't have ended up here in the midst of these young people and all their wonderful goings-on."

"Goings-on?"

Dotty nodded and waved her hand expressively. "Oh, yes. The candy shop, and opening our new tea shop, and making a special Christmas for Leo—all wonderful things for an old woman with time on her hands."

"I find you have a unique perspective on life, Mrs. Epps."

Eve agreed.

But her friend merely laughed and waved away the sentiment. "Oh, please call me Dotty. The only people allowed to call me Mrs. Epps are children and strangers." She gave him a smile. "Neither of us is in the first group and you are no longer the second."

"I would be honored. But only if you call me Woodrow."

Well, well. Eve leaned back in her seat, a secret smile playing on her lips. Had Dotty managed to charm Chance's father? The disapproving gentleman seemed so much less stern when he spoke to her. Friendly even.

Was she just doing this for the sake of keeping things from getting too tense between father and son? Or was there another, more genuine something brewing here?

She glanced Chance's way, but he still wore that scowl that hadn't been far from his expression since his father arrived. If she shared her current line of thought with him, would it deepen his frown or lighten it?

Chance sat through most of the meal keeping a tight lid on his emotions. As soon as his father had walked in the door, all those old feeling of inadequacy and resentment had come flooding back. But by the time the meal was over, he'd managed to get past that. He wasn't the same kid he'd been back in Philadelphia—a lot had changed since he'd come to Turnabout. And as far as he was concerned, he'd changed for the better.

He was never going to be the kind of man his father wanted him to be. And he was fine with that. The people here in Turnabout saw worth in him—he glanced across the table—even Eve. And he was beginning to realize that mattered to him.

Mattered a great deal.

As they rose from the table, his father turned to him. "I thought I'd walk down to this bank I now have a partnership in and look it over. Care to accompany me?"

Chance was tempted to say no, but instead he nodded. "Of course."

Almost as soon as they stepped out on the sidewalk, his father started in with his questions. "So how did this Pickering woman come to be stranded here—something about helping a child?"

"Leo, a ten-year-old boy, got in a spot of trouble and was booted from the train. When Eve saw he was alone and in need, she came to his rescue." He met his father's gaze without blinking. "That's the kind of woman she is."

"And you're sure they weren't traveling together?"

Did his father think the two of them had pulled an elaborate hoax on him? "I'm quite sure. And the sheriff has since verified Leo's story."

"So now you think these strays are your responsibility?"

Chance gritted his teeth, then forcibly relaxed his jaw. "That is the last time I want to hear you refer to Leo and Eve that way. They're good people. And I feel privileged to have them in my life."

"Good grief, son, you sound as if these two are lifelong friends. You only just met them a few weeks ago."

"Let's just say that for as long as they are living in my home, they are under my protection."

"And how long might that be?"

"For as long as they need a place to stay. I'm in no hurry to see them go. Now, why don't we change the subject before one of us crosses a line he shouldn't."

His father gave him one of those authoritarian looks, but this time Chance maintained a controlled expression and waited him out.

Finally his father nodded. "Very well. Tell me about this Adam Barr fellow we're going to meet. He's one of the men Judge Madison recruited to travel here with you a year and a half ago, isn't he?"

"He is. Adam is a friend. As you undoubtedly already know, he's not actually your new partner—his adopted son, Jack, is. Adam is just managing the business until Jack comes of age."

"I did some research into the men who accompanied you here."

Of course he had.

"Do you know Adam Barr spent time in prison for embezzlement?"

"I do." His father looked surprised at that. "I also know he was innocent of the charges."

"How do you know that?"

"Because he told me."

"As simple as that?"

"Yes. As simple as that. Because I know Adam. He's an honorable, responsible man who values truth and justice. He would no more steal than he would cut his own throat."

"And are you familiar with all of the clauses he put into your loan agreement?"

"Of course."

"So you know that your loan is due, payable in full plus interest, at the end of this year."

Chance stiffened as he realized what direction this discussion might be taking. He'd known about the due date of course. When he'd first approached Adam about getting the loan, they'd discussed the project and how long it might take to complete. Adam had suggested they make it a one-year loan but Chance had been certain he could finish up much sooner than that. "Adam and I discussed the availability of an extension on this loan should I need one."

"And did you get that in writing?" His father was wearing that I-have-you-now look.

"There was no need. Adam's word is enough for me."

"But Adam isn't the only decision maker involved here, is he?"

He had been when the loan was signed. Eileen Pierce had always been more or less a silent partner. "So, are you saying there will be no extension?"

His father grasped his lapels. "I'm not in the habit of throwing good money after bad. One should always be a good steward of his money."

No matter who got hurt in the process.

"To extend such a loan, I'd have to first be convinced there was a good chance of seeing a return in a reasonable amount of time." His father seemed mighty pleased with himself. "Or have something else I want in exchange."

There it was. "And what might that be?" But he already knew.

"For you to come back to Philadelphia, where you belong. Hang it all, Chance, this provincial backwater is not for you. You belong in Philadelphia where you would have access to the finer things in life. And where your family is."

"I disagree." Chance was pleased that his voice was calm and measured. "I think I fit in much better here in Turnabout than I ever did in Philadelphia."

"You can't possibly believe that."

"I do. I have my own business here, which I enjoy and am actually good at. And more important, I have the respect of my friends and neighbors because of who *I* am, not what family I come from or how much money I have access to."

His father drew himself up. "These so-called friends, have you shared with them your...your problem?"

So his father was finally ready to confront him on this issue. "Say it, Father—my *shame*—the fact that I can't read. For once just call it what it is."

His father gave him an annoyed look. "There's no need for these melodramatics." He glanced around. "Thank goodness there's no one close enough to overhear."

Chance swallowed the retort sitting on his tongue and took a breath. "To answer your question, the only person here who knows about my *problem* is Dotty."

"Ah, yes, your friend Dotty. Interesting woman."

"Dotty has been a good friend to me this past year and a half. And she understands my inability to read because she had a brother who suffered the same condition."

That seemed to take his father aback and he was silent for a few moments.

Finally, Chance broke the silence. "This matter of the loan—I'd prefer we keep that between you and me for the moment. There's no need to bring Adam into this." When his father raised a brow, he added an argument he knew would carry the most weight with him. "It is, after all, a family matter."

His father thought a moment, then nodded. "Very well. For now."

Chance fired off a question of his own. "Tell me, why are you in Turnabout? I mean, why did you *really* come here?"

"You're my son and I wanted to see you. Isn't that reason enough?"

"You wanted to see me, or you wanted to check up on me? It seems you're more concerned with finding fault with my home and houseguests than with understanding my new life."

Predictably, his father had to explain why he was right and Chance was wrong. "I come here and find you've surrounded yourself with hangers-on who are living in your place rent free and have turned half of your workspace into their own business—from which you get no recompense. Of course I'm concerned that you've allowed yourself to be taken advantage of. What father wouldn't want to protect his son from such a thing?"

It was no use. His father would never be able to come to terms with the fact that Chance was happy in Texas.

Or did that even matter to him?

"So what did you think of Chance's father?" Dotty asked.

Eve put away the last of the dishes as she tried to choose just the right word. "He seems a very self-assured man."

"It was generous of you to give up your room to him. Though I'm not certain Chance sees it in the same light."

"There's some tension between them, that much is obvious. But that's more reason to keep them together as much as possible, don't you think? It will give them a better opportunity to work things out."

"I agree. I know Chance thinks he has valid reasons to feel as he does, but the Bible teaches that we should honor our mothers and our fathers. There are no conditions placed on that command. It will bless Chance as much as his father if he can find it in his heart to do that."

That brought Eve up short. The teaching applied to her as well, of course. True, her parents had never been a part of her life physically. But that didn't excuse her from the obligation to show them honor. Truth to tell, in her heart she'd only ever felt hurt and betrayal when she thought of them.

But how could she feel otherwise? Given the circumstances of her life, surely no one could expect her to—

Dotty's words, *There are no conditions placed on that command,* left her with no room for excuses.

But Dotty had moved on to another topic. "And I do think Woodrow, down deep, is a good man with his son's best interests at heart."

Eve gave her friend a grin. "Are you perhaps a bit taken with Mr. Dawson?"

Dotty returned her grin. "Let's just say I find him an interesting man. I can see where Chance gets some of his charm."

She thought Mr. Dawson had charm?

Then Dotty laughed. "But don't worry. I'm a mature woman, set in my ways. I'm just enjoying his company, nothing more."

The shop bell sounded just then and they both headed to the outer room. To Eve's surprise, it was Eunice Ortolon, the boardinghouse proprietress. This was her first visit to the candy store.

"Hello there," she greeted them. "I've heard such good things about these candies that I thought it was high time I come check them out for myself."

"Well, we're very happy you did," Eve responded. "Do you already know what you'd like or would you like to sample a few things to help you decide?"

"Sample? Oh my, yes, that would be most helpful."

As the woman took a piece from the first tray, she eyed Eve with a cat-at-the-cream-pitcher smile. "I hear Chance's father is in town for a visit."

"Why, yes, he arrived on the morning train."

The woman plucked a piece from the second tray. "Does he plan to stay long?"

"Through Christmas I believe."

"How nice. One should spend Christmas with family if one can, don't you think?"

This time Dotty answered. "Of course. And is your daughter, Susan, coming to spend the holidays with you?"

Eunice's face lit up in pleasure. "Naturally. Susan wouldn't dream of spending Christmas anywhere else." For the next several minutes, the woman chatted nonstop about her daughter and all her wonderful attributes. At one point, Dotty actually glanced Eve's way and winked, forcing Eve to stifle a giggle.

Then Eunice turned to Dotty. "But speaking of daughters, I suppose you are going to Jefferson to spend Christmas with Judith and her family."

Eve blinked. She'd just assumed that Dotty would be part of their Christmas here at The Blue Bottle. She should have realized that her friend would want to spend the holiday with her own family. Did Chance know? How would Leo take it?

But Dotty was shaking her head. "Not this year, I'm afraid. Her husband's grandmother is getting on in years and the entire family wants to make this Christmas special for her. All of them are traveling to Kansas City to spend time with her."

Eunice touched Dotty's sleeve in a gesture of sympathy. "Oh, I'm so sorry, Dotty dear. I thought they would have invited you to come along."

"They did. But this is their time." She smiled at Eve. "And I have some good friends to spend the holidays with right here." Then Dotty changed the subject. "Now, you've tasted every variety of candy Eve has. Have you decided which ones you'd like to purchase?"

"Oh dear, they were all so very good, it's hard to decide. And I find I'm no longer in the mood for anything quite so sweet at the moment. Perhaps I'll think on it and return another time."

"You're always welcome," Eve said.

Once the woman had left, Dotty grimaced. "You should never have offered her samples. Then she would have had to buy something."

"Whatever do you mean?"

"Eunice only came in here to see what she could find out about Woodrow. She would have made a purchase just to have an excuse to stand here and chat."

Eve laughed. "I don't mind. It's a slow day today anyway." Then she sobered. "I'm sorry you won't get to spend time with your family for Christmas."

Dotty gave her hand a squeeze. "This Christmas, you all will be my family. Besides, my birthday is in February and we are already planning a nice get together to celebrate."

The talk of family brought Eve's thoughts back around to Chance and his father. Was the walk through town drawing them any closer together?

Or driving them further apart?

Chapter Twenty-Two

"You're Mr. Dawson's pa?" Leo had gotten home from school a few minutes earlier and been introduced to the visitor. Chance was keeping a close eye on them, ready to intervene at a moment's notice if his father went too far.

"I am," his father said with considerable satisfaction. Chance recognized it for what it was—the pride of ownership, not pride in the man he had become.

Leo, who was as direct as any ten-year-old boy, frowned. "How come you two don't live closer by? Don't y'all like each other?"

The man didn't hesitate. "Because Chance decided to set out on his own and come here."

He supposed he couldn't fault the man for that answer—it was 100 percent true. He also noticed his father completely avoided answering the second part of Leo's question.

But apparently Eve wasn't ready to leave it at that.

"Keep in mind," she said, "if Chance hadn't moved here, you and I would never have met him."

"Oh." Leo took a moment to mull that over, then gave a nod. "Then I guess I'm glad you did." He grinned. "Did you know he has a motor carriage?"

"Does he now?"

"Yes, sir. And I'm sure he'd give you a ride if you wanted one."

Now, there was a picture to expand the imagination— his father riding in a motor car.

But Leo was already off on another subject. "Do you like our decorations? We made them ourselves."

His father eyed them critically. "They are certainly unique."

Leo scrunched his nose. "What does *unique* mean?"

While Chance's father and Leo carried on their conversation, Eve caught his eye and gestured toward the kitchen. "Would you help me with something?" she asked.

He straightened. "Of course."

Once they were inside the kitchen, he looked around. "What do you need help with?"

She smiled and pointed to a platter on the top shelf of the cupboard. "Would you hand that down to me please?"

He gave her a puzzled look. Her short stature, of course, made it difficult for her to reach high objects, but it seemed like a strange request all the same. He turned and did as she asked while he tried to hear what was going on in the other room. "Anything else?"

"Yes. Sit here and talk to me while I peel some carrots."

This time she had his complete attention. "What?"

"You heard me. Sit and talk to me."

"All right—what's this really about?"

She grinned. "I guess I can't fool you. I just think your father needs a little dose of Leo without you hovering around ready to pounce the minute he says something wrong."

Is that what he'd been doing? "You don't understand. My father—"

"Your father is a forceful individual. But I think Leo

can hold his own. Besides, Dotty is there. She'll watch out for Leo. And she's armed with her knitting needles."

He smiled at her joke, marveling that it wasn't so long ago when she wouldn't have dared say such a thing. He slowly took a seat at the table, studying her face. Was it possible she was on his father's side?

Eve took the chair next to his. "Chance, it's obvious there is something causing tension between you and your father. Perhaps his visit here is an opportunity for the two of you to work things out and reach a more tolerant understanding of each other."

"*Tolerant understanding.* Do you know why he came here? To force me to return to Philadelphia with him—something I'm prepared to fight with all I'm worth."

She placed a hand on his. "If he's come all this way in order to convince you to return, it must mean he cares for you a great deal."

She gave him a smile that she probably thought was encouraging. "Besides, he can't really make you go back if you don't want to go."

"You'd be surprised. He can make it very uncomfortable for me to stay."

"What do you mean?"

Should he tell her? Suddenly he wanted very much to share his concerns with her. He placed his elbows on the table and leaned forward. "Through a bit of scheming and manipulation, he now holds an interest in the note to this place. If I don't pay up by the first of the year, he can take The Blue Bottle from me."

He heard her sharp intake of breath as he watched her eyes widen in dismay. "Oh, Chance, I'm so sorry. I know how much this place means to you."

There was such genuine caring, such tenderness, reflected in her eyes—it was a balm to his very soul. He was almost afraid to move for fear it would dissolve away, but he gently took her hand, sandwiching her delicate appendage between his two larger, work-roughened ones. The memory of that kiss, a memory he'd been working very hard to repress, came flooding inexorably back. He ached to taste her lips again, to pull her so close he could feel the beat of her heart keeping time with his, to thread his fingers through her hair and finally see what it looked like when it was free of those confining pins.

But he couldn't do any of those things. Not here with three people on the other side of that door.

And not until he'd been completely honest with her. He had to tell her everything, reveal his secret shame. Only then could he begin to trust this sweet something he felt growing between them.

But at times like this it was so difficult to remember....

She blinked and at last the spell was broken. In truth it had probably lasted only a few seconds. But it had felt so much longer.

Eve leaned back with a smile, but he thought he saw the slightest trembling in her lips. Was that regret in her eyes? Or relief?

"We must have faith that it will all work out as it should," she said bracingly, and it took him a moment to remember she was talking about his father holding his note. "I think in the end your father cares too much about you to do such a thing. And if I'm wrong, well, that still doesn't mean you have to go back to Philadelphia. You started over once, didn't you? Surely you can do it again if you must."

The last time he'd had a safety net of sorts—this time there would be none. Could he do it? Perhaps, with the right person by his side.

"Let's hope it doesn't come to that," he said as he stood.

"If I can get my project working, perhaps I can pay off the loan and the whole question will be moot." He moved toward the door. "Now, delightful as this little interlude has been, I really do think I should get back out there and see how things are going."

Eve watched him leave the kitchen and slowly began peeling the carrots. Had he also felt that connection when they touched? It had been like that day in the woods when they'd kissed and for the barest moment in time she thought perhaps it would happen again, had thought he wanted it, too. But she'd felt the exact moment when he'd pulled back, had sensed his withdrawal as truly as if he'd removed a physical touch.

What she didn't understand was why.

Chapter Twenty-Three

The next morning Chance was at his workbench when Eve stepped out of her bedchamber. Truth to tell, he'd been waiting for her to appear.

Her smile as they exchanged greetings definitely brightened his morning. "I'm sorry you had to give up your room."

She waved a hand. "I volunteered it. And it's really not a hardship."

"But you don't have a window." He remembered that had bothered her last week.

"True, but that means there is no place for the cold air to seep in."

He shook his head in mock dismay. "Always looking for the silver lining."

She put a hand on her hip. "If one is going to look, then one should look for something good, don't you think?"

He grinned at her teasing. She'd definitely come a long way from the prim, too-busy-to-have-fun miss who'd arrived here a few short weeks ago.

"Did you and your father have time to catch up with each other's news yet?"

He shrugged, feeling some of his good mood slip away.

"As much as I expected. Sharing the day-to-day minutiae is not something we indulge in very much."

"Perhaps you should try it. You might be surprised by the results."

He declined to respond to that, and apparently she took that as a sign to press harder.

"I'm sure he'd like to see your work. Why don't you show him your washing machine project?"

"It's not the sort of thing my father would be interested in."

"What isn't?"

They both turned at the sound of his father's voice. He was at the top of the stairs, heading down.

"You're up mighty early," Chance said by way of greeting.

"And still you two are up ahead of me."

Eve smiled. "I'm just going into the kitchen to prepare breakfast. I'll have the coffee ready shortly if you gentlemen want to join me in a few minutes."

Once she'd left the room, his father turned back to him. "What isn't the sort of thing I'd be interested in?" he repeated.

"Eve suggested I show you my current project."

"That sounds like an excellent idea."

"It's out back in the work shed."

"Then we'll wait for the sun to come up. How does right after breakfast sound?"

Was his father really interested, or was he just trying to prove something? "Very well."

Chance went back to examining the insides of the mechanical toy he'd just taken apart. To his surprise, his father began wandering around the workshop, examining various items as he went. He paused when he got to the shelf that held the nutcrackers.

"I see you collect these just as your mother did."

"Actually, I made them."

That definitely got his father's attention. "You mean you painted them?"

"Yes. And carved them."

His father picked one up and ran his thumb absently over the back. "I had no idea you were interested in becoming an artisan."

"It's just a hobby."

His father examined the one he held more closely. "They're a bit crude of course—not the style you'd find in your mother's collection—but they do show promise."

Leave it to his father to look for the black cloud rather than Eve's silver lining. "As I said it's just a hobby, not something I plan to build a business around." He stood. "I think I'll check to see if the coffee's ready."

A few minutes later they were both sitting at the table, sipping cups of coffee while the kitchen filled with the enticing scent of biscuits in the oven.

"So tell me about this project of yours," his father prompted. "It must be something big if you were willing to mortgage everything you have for it."

"Not *big* in the way you would define that term."

"Chance is being too modest," Eve said from her position at the stove. "It's a wonderful idea, something that's going to help many, many people."

"I'm intrigued. Tell me more."

Chance wondered what his father was up to. As meticulous as the man was, he'd no doubt already researched everything to do with this project.

"Why don't you go ahead and show him now?" Eve said. "It's getting light outside and breakfast is still several minutes off."

Her attempts to push him and his father together, while well meant, were getting tiresome.

But to his surprise, his father stood. "Lead the way."

As soon as Chance pointed out the equipment he used to his father, he could see the doubt in his eyes. He looked around the entire work area, as if trying to find something worth praising.

Then Chance swept a hand toward the washing machine and engine. "Here it is."

His father frowned. "It's a washing machine."

Had he really not known? "It is. What I'm doing is making improvements to it."

"What kind of improvements?"

Chance patted the machine fondly. "I'm attempting to motorize it."

His father grimaced. "What in the world made you decide to focus on *this* of all things?"

"Have you ever seen a washerwoman at work? It's endless, exhausting labor. If I can work the kinks out of this, it will make people's lives easier."

"You've sunk a lot of money into this. Where did it all go?"

"That engine over there that I hope to make power this thing is the third one I had to buy. There were issues with the first two that made them unsuitable. And I've had to purchase an additional washing machine to obtain the extra parts and modify others to create the proper gear attachments."

"Son, you need to think of your customer when you create a product. Do you honestly think a washerwoman would be able to afford such a costly device?"

"Of course not. But I've been in talks with a Mr. Clarence Braxton, who owns several large hotels, both here in Texas and up in Kansas. His business generates large loads of laundry every day. He's very interested in something that will make his staff more efficient."

His father rubbed his jaw. "I see. Perhaps you did inherit a bit of the Dawson business sense after all." He crossed his arms over his chest as a cold gust of wind swooshed by. "Are you close to getting this thing working properly?"

"I believe I am. There are still one or two issues to address, though." Was his father actually seeing value in the project? Would that be enough to dissuade him from calling in the loan?

"And you're trying to tackle the whole thing yourself."

"It's my project, and I enjoy trying to work it all out."

"The smart businessman hires out the manual and expert labor part of the job. You could come back to Philadelphia and have access to some of the finest engineers and mechanics in the country. Under your direction they could solve your design problems in no time."

So much for his father's interest and support. He just saw it as another way to convince his son to return to Philadelphia. He'd almost let Eve convince him his father had changed. But the man still didn't understand him. He probably never would.

Chance turned and headed back. "Eve will have breakfast on the table by now."

He didn't bother looking back to see if his father was following.

Eve took one look at Chance's face when they returned and knew it hadn't gone well. Leo and Dotty were in the kitchen with her now, however, so there was no time to ask questions.

A few minutes later Chance's father returned as well and they sat down to breakfast. As they began passing the platters around, Chance's father spoke up. "You know, I've been looking around this place of yours, and with just a bit of planning, I believe you could carve out a nice set of living quarters here."

Eve quickly glanced Chance's way. Did he realize that this meant his father was perhaps thinking of Chance being here long term? But she saw only anger in his face.

"I'm quite comfortable with the place as it is now," he said flatly.

His father's lips pinched tight for a moment, then he focused on his food.

Eve caught Chance's gaze and frowned meaningfully. He grimaced, then cleared his throat. "So tell me, Father, how are my brothers faring? I understand Miles and Rebecca are expecting a new addition to the family."

His father's expression lightened. "That's true. My new grandchild should be here sometime in March."

"Grandchildren are such a blessing," Dotty said with a smile. "Will this be your first?"

"My third. Charles has one boy and my second son, Thomas, has a little girl."

So, in addition to brothers, Chance had a niece and a nephew. Did he miss being a part of their lives?

Dotty and Mr. Dawson continued to carry most of the conversation, and for the rest of the meal they managed to avoid sensitive topics.

After breakfast, Leo headed off to school and Dotty turned to Chance's father. "I have some shopping to do this morning. You're welcome to join me and let me show you some of the town."

Mr. Dawson gave a short bow. "It would be my pleasure."

Once Eve and Chance were alone, she turned to him. "Do you mind if I ask you a personal question?"

She saw a slight tensing of his features. Should she leave it alone?

But he gave a short nod. "Of course not."

"Don't you miss being with your family? I mean, I understand that you've built a new life here and that you're happy with it. But don't you ever want to go back just for a visit?"

He shrugged. "Someday."

Perhaps he wasn't any closer to his brothers than he was to his father. Which seemed such a shame.

He took the chair beside her and leaned back. "My family and I have a rather unusual relationship."

"In what way?" Was he going to trust her with his story?

"I told you once I have three older brothers. Miles, Thomas and Kevin are actually my half brothers—the sons of Father and his first wife. There's roughly two years between each of them. My mother was Father's second wife and I'm six years younger than my youngest half brother."

"And did your brothers hold this against you?"

"Not at all. Other than treating me like the baby of the family, my brothers and I get along just fine."

"There doesn't seem to be anything unusual in that."

"As boys my brothers were greatly admired—they were competitive, talented and ambitious. And when they grew up, they all lived up to their potential."

She was still confused. "And haven't you? I mean, there are so many things you're good at—carving, mechanics, inventing."

He gave her a you-don't-understand look. "Miles, the oldest, is now a prominent physician. Thomas is a well-respected lawyer. And Kevin is a lieutenant in the army. The two oldest are married to wonderful women and, as my father mentioned at breakfast, have children of their own."

She didn't detect any resentment or jealousy in his tone. "It sounds like a family to be proud of."

"Oh, yes. The Dawsons are a family that seems to have it all. With the very notable exception of the youngest son."

"That's not true." She was outraged on his behalf.

He shrugged. "I've never been the ambitious sort. I like to take each day as it comes. I prefer to tinker with things and see what makes them work, and to seek out adventure rather than sit in an office and direct others."

"But that doesn't make you a lesser man. You're a business owner, a skilled artisan and a person who is well liked by his neighbors and friends. There's nothing to be ashamed of in that."

He gave a crooked smile. "I totally agree. But I'm giving you my father's perspective so you'll understand why things are the way they are between us. Most of my life he's been after me to stop all my dillydallying, as he calls it, and pursue some career that would allow me to live up to the family name, the way my brothers did."

She slowly nodded. "That must have been difficult for you."

Again he shrugged.

She tried to give his father the benefit of the doubt. "Some folks just don't understand that a person can't become something he isn't just by wishing it to be so. That which makes a person feel happy and fulfilled is not the same for everyone."

Chance leaned forward and took her hand. "Well said. Only I didn't tell you all of this to gain your sympathy. I've accepted that Father is never going to understand me or even accept that he can't change me. I made peace with that a long time ago. I merely wanted you to understand so you would stop trying so hard. It's a waste of time."

He might believe he meant what he just said, but she

knew that deep down he hadn't made peace with any such thing. There was something in his eyes whenever he looked at his father, some hint of loss that made her ache for him. "I don't believe in giving up on people. Perhaps, while he's here, you can help him to see how much better this life is for you, that this is what makes you happy."

"Eve, don't—"

She didn't let him finish. "But you won't accomplish that if you keep shutting him out."

That straightened his spine and slapped a frown on his face. "He's the one who—"

Again she interrupted. "Look at this from his perspective. Ever since he arrived you've been examining everything he says, waiting for him to do or say something you can get your back up over. How do you think that makes him feel?"

Chance wasn't quite certain what to say. Had he been guilty of doing as she said? Even if he had, his father had given him every reason to be on guard. Hadn't he?

"Regardless of what your relationship was in Philadelphia," she continued, "you have an opportunity to start fresh here. Give him the same grace you want from him. View the things he says as coming from a caring father, not an enemy. Really listen to the things he's saying and try to understand why they are important to him."

She withdrew her hand from beneath his and he immediately missed the warmth of her touch.

"Now, I have a batch of pecan chocolate drops to make for Henrietta Strickland's eighth birthday party tomorrow."

He sat where he was for several minutes after she'd returned to the stove. Was she right? Was he part of the reason he and his father couldn't get past this constant locking of horns?

If that were true, what could he do about it? Did he even want to bother? Then he remembered the I-believe-in-you look on Eve's face, and he was suddenly very certain that he did.

Chapter Twenty-Four

The next morning as Leo left for school, a young man showed up carrying a telegram. "It's for Mr. Dawson," he announced.

"Which Mr. Dawson?" Chance's father asked.

"Mr. Chance Dawson."

Chance was busy at his worktable, so Eve, who was closest to the door, accepted it on his behalf. When she carried it over and attempted to hand it to him, however, he shook his head.

"I'm right in the middle of this and don't want to stop. Why don't you read it to me?"

Apparently he wasn't concerned that it might be something of a personal nature. She opened the slip of paper and read it aloud.

"It's from a Clarence Braxton." She saw Chance's head come up at that. "He says 'I will be passing through Turnabout on the eighteenth of this month. Would be very interested in a demonstration of your motorized washing machine at that time. Sincerely, C. Braxton.'"

Chapter Twenty-Five

The eighteenth arrived all too quickly.

Chance woke feeling ready. He'd worked tirelessly since the telegram arrived a week earlier to make certain everything was the absolute best he knew how to make it. He'd run test after test until finally last night he'd met with success—a complete run through of the entire process. If things went today as they had last night, Mr. Braxton should be quite impressed.

The only thing that had him worried was the sputtering that had started up at the very end of the wash load last night. When he'd shut down the machine and checked it out in minute detail, he hadn't identified a likely culprit. And when he started it up again the noise had disappeared.

He was praying it had been just a fluke, and would not repeat today. The only thing he could do at this point was make one more pass through his checklist and then hope for the best.

All during the past week, Eve had been quietly supporting him, bringing him food when he was too busy to eat with the family, providing cups of coffee and hot cocoa when the chilly temperatures had numbed him from the inside out, holding a lamp for him when he worked past sunset. She never complained, never questioned his total focus on the project, always knew what he needed before he did.

She'd also served as his test subject, standing in for the typical lady of the house who washed clothes on a regular basis. Right now, she could run the machine almost as well as he could.

Chance took a deep breath. If he was going to pursue any kind of future with Eve, she had to know the truth. "You once asked me why I traveled all the way from Philadelphia to Texas and I never answered your question."

She smiled. "It really wasn't any of my business."

"No, but I want to tell you now."

"But you're supposed to be—"

"It'll wait."

She folded her hands in her lap trustingly. "Very well. I'm listening."

"Most of my life I've been what my father refers to as an irresponsible scapegrace, drifting from one mess to another."

"Surely that's an exaggeration."

He took encouragement from her ready defense of him. "Not by much. Some of it was just exuberance or curiosity, but some of it was pure mischief." He paused a moment, then continued. "Then I crossed the line. I borrowed a motor bicycle without permission, and it turned out badly. There was an accident. Luckily no one was hurt, but it could have been a whole lot worse."

"Oh, how awful it must have been for you."

"No more than I deserved. I was reckless and irresponsible."

She touched his arm in a comforting gesture. "It was wrong to take the motor bicycle, but you were young and adventurous. And I'm sure you were sorry."

"I was brought before Judge Arthur Madison, who just

happens to be Reggie's grandfather. I didn't know him, but for some reason he thought I deserved a second chance. Judge Madison knew of this trip the other three men were taking to start new lives here in Turnabout. He offered me a choice of serving jail time or coming out here with them to try to make it on my own." Which was true as far as it went. But again, those were not his secrets to tell. Getting his own out would be difficult enough.

"This Judge Madison sounds like a wise and forgiving man."

"He is. Oh, there were some strings tied to the deal, but it was still a very fair, more than generous offer."

"Well, from what I've seen, it appears his faith in you was justified."

"I try to live my life here so that he never has cause to regret his decision. But more than that, the thought of what could have happened that day still haunts me."

"Thank you for sharing your story with me."

"I'm afraid there's more."

"Oh?"

Would she still thank him when he was done explaining? "There's a secret I've been carrying around for most of my life. In some ways, it defines me and why I got into so many difficulties in my youth."

Her eyes had widened and there was a touch of wariness there now. But she remained silent, waiting for him to continue.

Suddenly at a loss for words, he blurted out the bare fact. "I can't read."

Her brow furrowed in confusion. "What? You mean you never learned? Surely—"

"No, I mean I *can't*. I've gone to some of the best schools, had special tutors, have tried until my eyes burned beyond bearing. I just can't read and will never be able to."

"But how have you managed all these years?"

Was that a slight withdrawal he felt? He willed himself to keep calm, to give her time to adjust to the notion. "I've found ways to avoid revealing my problem by deflecting notice or pretending."

"How can you *pretend* to read?" Her tone was almost accusatory.

This wasn't going at all the way he'd hoped. "I've been blessed with a strong memory so, as a student, if the teacher went over something in class I normally retained the information. But it wasn't a real substitute for reading. I was turned out of three different schools before my father gave in and got me a series of private tutors."

"And you've managed to keep it a secret all this time? From everyone?"

"A few people know—Dotty for instance. She's the one who reads things like important documents and letters. My father knows, of course, but he doesn't dig deep enough to find out the extent of my problem. It would be too dark a stain on the Dawson family name if he found out the truth—that his son was illiterate."

"You can't read at all?" There was a definite chilliness to her tone that was worrying him.

"Some days, if I focus very hard and there's no pressure for me to do so, I can make out some words. But that's a rare happenstance."

"I see." Her expression had closed off now.

"Eve, I'm the same man I was ten minutes ago. Does my ability—or rather inability—to read matter so much to you?"

"No."

Her answer was quick and sure and exactly what he'd hoped to hear. Yet there was something in her demeanor, a wall going up, that told him all was not well. "Then what is it?"

"You deceived me."

He stiffened. "I never once lied."

"You did though. You did your best to make me believe you actually could read. You found ways to have me read your newspapers and telegram, you sidestepped my suggestion that you teach Leo, you talked about some of your favorite books, all in ways designed to make me think you could read. Do you deny it was deliberate?"

The temptation to lie was almost overwhelming. But he couldn't do it, especially not to her, not ever again. "No."

She flinched as if he'd dealt her a physical blow. "And you did this knowing how I felt about one's ability to read. And how—" her voice cracked, but she quickly got herself back under control "—how I was beginning to feel about you."

God help him, he wanted to take her in his arms and hug away the pain he saw in her eyes. But how could he when he was the one who'd put it there? "Yes." It was hard to get the word past the lump of regret in his throat.

She nodded, a gesture that felt to him like an acknowledgment of his betrayal. "Just like my father."

"No!" The word exploded from him and she flinched again but didn't back down. Chance realized now what was going through her mind and tried desperately to find the right words. "Eve, what you say about my deceiving you is true, but it was just in this one area and it wasn't aimed at you. It was a habit I developed long before I ever met you to get me through life."

He could tell his words weren't sinking in. "I love you, don't you understand? I would never deliberately hurt you. Whatever else you choose to believe, please, you have to believe that. If I had wanted to deceive you in that manner, for such despicable purposes, why would I be confessing the truth now?"

He saw a flicker of something in her eyes just then and he felt a tiny spark of hope jump to life.

But then she shook her head as if to clear it and rubbed her brow wearily. "I need time to think this through," she finally said, her voice raspy and barely under control.

"Eve, I'm so—"

"Please, just go." She attempted a smile. "You have a demonstration to get ready for, remember?"

If he could somehow fix this by staying, he'd ignore the demonstration, hang the consequences. But she was dismissing him, putting distance between them, asking for time to think.

He turned and slowly made his way to the door, regret weighing him down like a millstone. He'd been arrogantly intent on trying to get Eve to open herself up to what life could offer, and yet he'd continued to hide behind his charade from fear of public ridicule. And because of that he'd not only lost the respect of the woman he loved, he'd hurt her.

Eve watched Chance walk away, her heart shattering into bleeding shards.

The whole time her grandmother's voice kept whispering in her ear, telling her how absurd she'd been to trust her heart, that Chance was no better than that devil-tongued deceiver who'd fathered her, that she was foolish to believe anyone could truly love her.

But for just a short, magical point in time, she had believed.

Chapter Twenty-Six

Dotty entered the room, eyeing Eve with extreme disappointment. "What did you do?" Her question came out more as a demand.

"I—" Eve shook her head, unable to gather her thoughts enough to say what was spinning through her mind.

Dotty studied her for a moment, then her shoulders slumped. "He told you his secret, didn't he?"

Eve nodded.

"And you sent him away."

"No! I mean, yes, but not because of his problem with reading."

Some of the tension in Dotty eased. "Then why?"

Eve felt the trembling in her hands make its way to her legs and sat down before she fell. "Because of the deception surrounding it."

Dotty eyed her with an unreadable expression for a long moment. "I see."

Eve sighed. "No, you don't. You see, my mother was deceived by a young man who came through town and sweet talked her with honeyed lies and half truths, until she gave herself to him. Then the young man slipped away and I was born nine months later."

Dotty reached out and squeezed her hand. "Oh, my dear, I'm so very sorry."

Eve appreciated Dotty's sentiment, but she wasn't looking for pity. "I've tried to live my life in such a way as to prove I was not my mother, that such a thing could never happen to me." And now it seemed she had stumbled along the same path.

"And is that truly what you think is going on here? That Chance deceived you in order to seduce and then abandon you?"

"I…" When it was put like that, Eve was no longer so certain.

"And if Chance truly wanted to deceive you, for whatever reason, why would he come to you now with the truth? A truth, I might add, that painted him in a light he had reason to believe you would find very unflattering."

Eve was beginning to believe she had made a terrible mistake.

But Dotty wasn't through yet. "I appreciate that you told me your own closely guarded secret, but I assume you don't offer up that information to anyone who discusses family with you."

"I've never lied about it."

"Of course not. And neither has Chance. He just goes to great lengths not to have to share it."

Eve remembered that interview with Everett and felt the heat climb in her cheeks. Had she been guilty of looking at the mote in Chance's eye?

Dotty eyed her sympathetically. "He loves you, you know. Are you ready to throw that out over a matter of pride? More important, what does your heart tell you?" She patted Eve's knee and then stood. "There, I've said my piece. I'm going back out there to watch Chance's demonstration and leave you to think on this for a spell." And with that, Dotty left her alone.

As Eve watched Dotty leave, she felt her mind begin to clear. Something inside her fell into place, something that felt solid and true and right. With all her heart, she believed that no matter what he'd done, Chance was a good and honorable man, a man who would never knowingly hurt her, and would in fact do his utmost to keep her safe and happy. He was the man she loved, the man who brought joy and excitement to her life.

She suddenly sat up straighter. He'd told her he loved her. And she'd totally ignored his declaration. Was it too late? Could he still feel that way after the way she'd reacted to his laying his heart bare for her?

If only he would give her the opportunity, she'd do everything in her power to make this up to him, to prove to him how very much she loved him.

Chance felt Eve's presence before he ever saw her. His back was to her as he did a final check of his equipment, but it was as if some sort of magnet between them began to vibrate whenever they were near. At least that was how it was for him. Apparently not for her.

Finally satisfied that everything was in order, he turned to address Mr. Braxton. As he launched into an explanation of what was going to happen, and what parts of the process were still under development, he couldn't help but watch Eve from the corner of his eye. The soft, you-can-do-this expression she wore confused him. Had she decided to support his efforts out of pity? That was worse than an out-and-out rebuff.

But perhaps it was nothing more than the fact that she'd invested so much time in the project this week she wanted to see it through.

Trying to shake that distraction from his mind, he turned and started up the engine. For a moment, everything performed just as it should. The motor powered a belt, which turned the crank, which operated the paddles, which created the motion to clean the clothes. "As you can see," he said with more than a touch of pride, "this device can save your people from the more difficult part of washing laundry."

Mr. Braxton nodded approvingly, and even his wife seemed intrigued.

"In just a minute, I'm going to make a simple, minor adjustment, and the engine will switch from powering the paddles, to powering the wringer."

Before he could put words to action, the device started making an ominous sound. A heartbeat later there was a prolonged wheezing, then a series of loud clatters and pops, and then the engine just died.

For a moment there was only shocked silence. Chance felt his excitement over his success die as explosively as had his machine. It could have been any one of a half dozen things that had caused the problem. He'd figure it out, and solve the problem eventually. But his opportunity to have Mr. Braxton back him was over. And with it went his hope of paying off his loan by the end of the year.

"That's bad luck, son," Mr. Braxton said. "For a moment there I really thought you had something good." He turned to his wife. "Shall we head for the hotel, my dear? It's mighty cold out here."

And that was it. No chance for redemption. Was his father pleased that things had gone this way?

As if he'd read Chance's thoughts, his father clamped a hand on Chance's shoulder. "That was too bad, son. I was pulling for you."

Now, wasn't this a surprise? In the same day Eve had

let him down, his father had actually shown some compassion.

Then Eve stepped forward, not to commiserate with him, but to speak to the Braxtons. "Please don't go just yet. Why don't you come inside and enjoy some chocolate bonbons or some pralines and a nice warm cup of tea?"

Mr. Braxton shook his head. "I'm sorry, but—"

"Did you say pralines?" Mrs. Braxton asked, ignoring her husband's protests.

"I did." Eve smiled proudly. "Freshly prepared this morning."

The woman turned to her husband. "Oh, let's do, Clarence. You know how much I enjoy those."

He sighed and nodded. "Very well. But we won't stay long."

Chance watched Eve happily lead the pair into the shop through the rear door. Then he turned to Dotty and his father. "Why don't you two join them? The wind's picking up and there's no point in us all catching a chill. I'll be in as soon as I make certain everything is properly shut down."

His father seemed on the point of protesting, but Dotty touched his arm and gave him a pointed look. A heartbeat later he nodded and escorted her inside.

Relieved, Chance turned back to his equipment. He needed to be alone for a few minutes. First, that gut-wrenching scene with Eve, and now this disaster. Perhaps his father was right, perhaps he should return to Philadelphia, especially if he lost The Blue Bottle. Not to his father's home, of course, but he could pursue his work on motorizing the washing machine—and any number of other ideas swimming around in his mind—with easier access to parts and to mentors.

Funny how that thought didn't give him much comfort. His thoughts returned to Eve. The brokenness he'd seen in her earlier—that he'd been the cause of—seemed over-shadowed by something else just now. Was she just putting on a good front for their visitors? She'd certainly turned them into customers for her candy shop quickly enough. Commiserating with him, on the other hand, had apparently been the furthest thing from her mind.

Well, at least someone had made a sale today.

When Chance stepped back inside fifteen minutes later, he hoped he'd given the Braxtons enough time to have their tea and leave. But to his surprise the two of them, along with Eve, were gathered around one of his worktables. What in the world was going on now?

A second later, Eve caught sight of him and her face lit up in a smile.

He blinked. He'd never thought to see that smile aimed his way again.

"There you are," she said. "Mr. and Mrs. Braxton were just admiring your creations."

They were what?

"Oh, yes," Mrs. Braxton gushed. "The nutcrackers, rocking horses and tin stars—all of these decorations are absolutely marvelous. I was just telling Clarence that we should decorate our hotel lobbies in a similar fashion."

"I'm pleased you like the decorations, ma'am. But creating those things is just a little hobby of mine."

"A hobby." Mr. Braxton gave him a stern teacher-to-student look. "Young man, I know you are dedicated to this washing-machine project of yours, and I will admit that it does have promise if you can overcome the obvious problems we witnessed today. But this is where your real talent lies. Workmanship like this is something to be valued and nurtured." He rocked back on his heels. "I should know—my father was a furniture maker who took great pride in his work."

He gestured toward Eve. "Miss Pickering here showed us the work you did on those room dividers, and she said you did it all in one afternoon. I call that more than a hobby."

Chance wasn't quite certain what to say.

But Eve didn't seem to have that problem. "Chance is too modest to brag," she said, "but he does more than carve these beautiful pieces. You've already noticed the tin stars. He makes mechanical toys, as well. Leo, the ten-year-old who lives with me, loves them, as do his friends."

Chance still wasn't certain what was up with Eve. Did she think she was coming to his rescue the way she had with Leo on the train station platform?

Mrs. Braxton sighed. "This is every child's dream—a toy store and a candy store all under one roof."

Mr. Braxton nodded sagely. "In a larger town you could make quite a go of it with such a business."

"Oh, don't be so mercenary, Clarence." Mrs. Braxton gave her husband an affectionate smile tinged with a touch of exasperation. "They seem to be *making a go of it,* as you say, right here." She turned to Chance. "It's too late for this year, but if I ordered, say fifty of these nutcrackers and several dozen of some of the other items to be delivered before next Christmas, would you be able to fulfill the order?"

Chance blinked. What had just happened?

Mr. Braxton was apparently feeling the same way. "Now, Martha, we should discuss this before you go placing orders. We haven't even discussed price yet."

Mrs. Braxton waved a hand. "Oh, I'm certain you gentlemen can get that all worked out. My question is whether or not he is willing and able to fill such an order." She turned to Chance. "So, are you?"

Chance considered the idea for a minute. Was he willing to change his whole way of looking at things, to turn his interest in designing improved machinery into a sideline and focus on his handicraft as a means of making a living? The more he thought on it, the more right it seemed. He smiled at Mrs. Braxton. "Assuming we can reach an agreement on price, I am."

Mr. Braxton shook his head with a wry smile for his wife. "Martha, my dear, your enthusiasm leaves me little negotiating room. Chance here is going to think he has me over a barrel."

Eve spoke up immediately. "Chance is a fair and honest man. You have no need to worry when it comes to negotiating a fair price."

Far from taking offense at her outspokenness, the man gave Chance an amused smile. "This little lady has been singing your praises ever since we walked in here. She's the best advertisement you have for your business."

He nodded, not bothering to look Eve's way. "Miss Pickering is a good one to have in your corner, all right," he said evenly. "She's not afraid to stand up for something she believes in."

From the corner of his eye he saw a little wrinkle form above her nose. What was wrong? He was doing his best to keep his distance. Isn't that what she wanted?

Mr. Braxton turned businesslike. "Well then, shall we sit down and discuss price?"

As the two men moved to the table that served as Chance's office, Mrs. Braxton turned to Eve. "Let's leave the men to their dickering. I'd very much like another piece of your delicious pralines."

Chance cast one quick glance at the retreating ladies before he offered Mr. Braxton a seat.

Could he continue to live under the same roof with Eve, knowing how she felt about him? Perhaps it was just as well he wasn't going to be able to pay that note. This new venture of his could be carried out from anywhere. A fresh start in a new location might be just the thing.

But he knew, deep down, that leaving here would be unimaginably more difficult than leaving Philadelphia had ever been.

Chapter Twenty-Seven

Eve kept up with Mrs. Braxton's cheerful, if somewhat flighty conversation. But her focus was on Chance. It was obvious he was trying to avoid her, but she knew that was her own fault. Was he doing it because he thought she wanted it? Or because it was what he now wanted, as well? All she could do was hope that she would have the opportunity to redeem herself somehow.

A few minutes later, Dotty and Mr. Dawson entered from the kitchen, Dotty carrying a tray with cups and a teapot, and Mr. Dawson carrying a tray of sandwiches. Eve was going to have to talk to Chance about building a tea cart.

Assuming they were all still living here after today.

"Sorry to take so long with the tea," Dotty said cheerfully. "But I thought you might care for something to eat, as well."

Mrs. Braxton laughed. "That was very thoughtful of you but I'm afraid you went to all that trouble for nothing. I've been nibbling on these delicious pralines and have no room for anything but the tea."

Eve suspected Dotty had known that but had deliberately delayed her and Mr. Dawson's return to give her time to talk to the Braxtons.

"So what was that all about?" Mr. Dawson inquired once the Braxtons departed.

"Mr. and Mrs. Braxton have just ordered fifty of my large nutcrackers, one hundred ornament-sized nutcrackers, one hundred tin stars and several dozen of other Christmas items they'd like me to produce."

His father frowned. "But what about your washing-machine project?"

Chance shrugged. "I'll continue to work on it in my spare time. But I'm beginning to believe it's time to shift my focus." Strange that, in a way, he had Eve to thank for that. Had she known that this would be the outcome of her talk with the Braxtons?

"So you meet with an obstacle and just like that you give up on the whole thing."

Chance frowned. "That's not what I said. I'm not giving up on anything. I'm simply giving something else a higher priority at the moment."

"I thought this invention of yours was something you were passionate about and I was willing to support you on it. It sounds to me as if you still don't know what you want to do with your life."

Before Chance could respond, Eve stepped in.

"Mr. Dawson, I know that deep down you love your son and think you're looking out for his best interests, but that's not how love works. True love means accepting a person for who he is, despite whatever decisions he makes." She risked a quick glance Chance's way. "And loving him imperfections and all."

She turned back to Chance's father. "Your son is a good and honorable man, with a lot to offer. He's a son to be proud of. Chance has many wonderful talents and he's choosing to use them. That's to be celebrated, not criticized."

She was defending him? Was it just her protective nature kicking in? Or dare he hope it was something more?

"Miss Pickering, I'm certain you mean well, but this is between me and my son."

"I'm sorry, sir, but I can't stand silent and let your statements go unchallenged. Because Chance deserves so much more. And besides—" she cast a sideways glance Chance's way "—I have something to say to him myself and it won't wait."

Chance had never seen his father sputter the way he was now. But his focus was all on Eve as their gazes locked. What did she want to discuss with him?

But his father finally found his tongue. "Now, see here—"

Dotty touched his arm. "Come along, Woodrow. You and I should go take a walk." Dotty pulled Chance's father from the room.

It seemed to take forever, but finally they were alone.

Chance studied her face, afraid to read too much into what she'd just said. "That was quite a feisty defense you made with my father," he said carefully.

"I meant every word of it." Then her expression twisted into a mask of regret. "I'm so sorry. I was a confused, frightened fool who was too afraid to listen to her heart."

"I'm *not* the same sort of man as your father," he said stiffly.

"I know. You are Chance Dawson, the most generous, decent, caring man I know."

Was she really trying to say she'd forgiven him? "I don't need your pity. Or some misplaced gesture of gratitude."

"Good. Because that's not what I'm offering." She took a deep breath. "Let me be clear. I love you. Very much."

The tension inside him pulled so tight he felt as if he would snap apart at any moment. "Eve don't. Don't say things you don't mean."

"I would never, ever do that. If you no longer love me, say so and I'll understand. I hurt you in a most unforgiveable way. But I can't stand by and let you go on thinking that I don't admire and respect you for the wonderful man you are."

She reached up and placed a hand on his cheek. "But more than that, I need for you to believe me when I say that I love you more than you can ever know. You taught me to trust myself and my heart. To understand that the things my grandmother taught me, about both my mother and myself, were based on her own hurts and bitterness and shouldn't be allowed to color my life."

He saw tears pool in her eyes. "And the thought that I let you down so terribly when you shared your own private pain with me is something I deeply regret."

He placed a hand over hers, trapping it there on his cheek. "I will never be able to read." His eyes searched her face, looking for a flicker of distaste or withdrawal.

But instead he saw something soft and warm and accepting. "It would give me great joy to read to you so that we can enjoy books together." She placed her free hand against his heart and he wondered if she could feel its accelerated pounding.

"I love you, Chance Dawson," she said with undeniable conviction, "just the way you are, just the way God made you."

Unable to resist further, Chance pulled her to him, giving her the kiss he'd wanted to give her since the first one they'd shared that day she fell. His hand eased around her neck, cradling it protectively, reveling in the softness of her skin and the silkiness of her hair, even as he tasted her lips.

He still loved the contradictions in this woman—the vulnerable strength of her, the shy courage, the quiet sense of adventure. What he once thought was a prim little mouse had a tiger's spirit.

He could happily explore those contradictions for the rest of his life.

When they finally separated, Chance didn't take his arm from around her waist. Her face was flushed, her hair mussed and her breathing slightly labored. And she was utterly beautiful.

She loved him! Believing that made him certain he could face anything, no matter how big, no matter how dark, that might come his way. "I love you, Eve Pickering, and want to spend the rest of my days with you, finding ways to bring joy to your life, and to your heart, if you'll have me."

She threw her arms around his neck in an exuberant embrace. "Oh, yes."

Eve pulled back slightly to look into his eyes, seeking that connection that touched her so deeply. The love shining there was all the confirmation she needed that she had finally found her way home. It was there in the tenderness of his embrace, the strength of his arms, the warmth of his hand on her waist. To know she was so loved took her breath away. It was a precious gift and one she would never treat so cavalierly again.

And it was a gift she wanted to share. Perhaps, one day, she would search for her mother, and hear her side of what had happened all those years ago.

But for now, there was Leo. And perhaps someday in the not too distant future, there would be other additions to their family, as well.

Epilogue

Eve poured five steaming cups of cocoa and added a touch of cherry syrup to each. It was Christmas morning after all, and that called for a special treat.

Then she carefully set each of the cups on her brand-new tea cart. Chance had given it to her this morning as her Christmas gift. She wasn't certain exactly how he'd known she wanted it since she'd never got around to mentioning it, but somehow he always seemed to know these things.

She smiled softly as she traced her finger over the carved border—pretty little flowers on twining stems, and right in the center, a heart. A reminder, he'd said, that she had *his* heart, now and forever. It was her very first Christmas gift, other than the one given from heaven, and she didn't think anyone had ever received a better one.

With a happy sigh, she pushed the cart to the doorway and paused a moment to view the beautiful tableau before her in the outer room.

She had to admit, Leo had been right—the tree he'd picked out was perfect for this place. They'd all pitched in to decorate it yesterday, even Chance's father. And it looked beautiful.

Dotty and Mr. Dawson sat in two of the chairs arranged in front of the tree, deep in discussion, both wearing smiles.

Leo was on the floor playing with the toy soldiers Chance had given him a few minutes earlier, and Chance was stooped down beside him.

Her breath caught in her throat at the picture they made of a loving father and son.

Chance looked up and the smile he sent her way set the dragonflies dancing in her stomach and made her pulse quicken. She would never, as long as she lived, get used to having him look at her that way, as if she was something rare and precious and desirable. The thought that in just three days' time she would become his wife filled her with overflowing joy and wonder.

Chance stood and headed toward her in long, floor-eating stride, his gaze never leaving hers. "I've been waiting for you," he said, stopping short of meeting her.

"I've only been gone a few minutes," she answered with a laugh.

"But I had something I wanted to give you."

"Something else?" She stopped the cart next to him, wishing they were alone so she could sneak a kiss. It was an activity she'd grown quite fond of in the past few days.

"Uh-huh." He glanced up, inviting her gaze to follow his.

Mistletoe? Now, when had he gotten around to hanging that?

"You must now pay the forfeit." He seemed quite pleased with himself.

She pretended affront. "So, you were actually planning to *take* something, not *give* something."

His grin broadened. "Let's just say I'm hoping for a willing exchange." With that, he leaned down to steal the kiss she was all too willing to give.

Conscious that they were not alone, they separated quickly. But he gave her hand a quick squeeze and sent her a special meant-only-for-her smile as a promise that there would be more later.

"Shall we give Leo his final gift?" Chance asked.

The night before they had decided they would immediately start the process to formally adopt the boy.

Eve nodded and grasped the handle of the cart again. Before she'd quite realized what he was about, Chance had reached around her and bookended her hands with his. As they started across the room, she felt his lips on her head and gave a quiet sigh.

"You're the perfect height," he whispered.

Then they reached the others and he moved past her to help hand out the cups.

Eve looked around with suddenly misty eyes at the group of very dear people in this room. When his father left Turnabout a few days after the wedding, they planned to join him on the trip to Philadelphia so Eve could meet Chance's family. And if things continued as they were, Dotty just might be coming along.

Her life was so blessed, so full of joy, that she wasn't sure her heart could contain it all. And she realized *this* was her true Christmas gift—a loving family to belong to. A family who loved her and willingly accepted her into their midst.

Her Christmas family.

* * * * *

Dear Reader,

Hello and thank you so much for picking up Chance and Eve's story. These were two very wounded characters who seemed destined to live their lives without a happily ever after. It was a difficult story for me to write, and it took me quite some time to get them to tell me their full story, but I hope you will agree with me that it was totally worth all the effort.

As I write this, my thoughts are already moving on to the fourth book in this series, which will tell Mitch Parker's story. Of the four grooms, Mitch has been the most enigmatic to me, so I am looking forward to having him finally give up some of his secrets, hurts and dreams to me. Please visit my website at www.winniegriggs.com to get updates on this and other books. And I love hearing from readers! Feel free to contact me at winnie@winniegriggs.com with your thoughts on this or any other of my books.

Wishing you much love and many blessings in your life,

Winnie Griggs

Questions for Discussion

1. Eve did not realize that Leo was a stowaway until the conductor accused him of such. Does that seem realistic to you?

2. Did you think Leo's actions at the opening of the book were believable for a child of ten given what he'd been through?

3. At first Chance seemed merely intrigued by Eve and the circumstances. At what point do you think this changed and why?

4. What did you think of Chance's offering Eve and Leo rooms at his home? What do you think his true motives were for doing so?

5. Was the town's open-arms acceptance of Eve and Leo believable? How do you react to strangers who are unexpectedly thrown into the midst of one of your circles—either home, work, church or social?

6. What did you think of Eve's reaction to the dancing at the Thanksgiving Festival, both before the fact and after?

7. Dotty served as a mentor to both Chance and Eve at various points throughout the book. Do you think she was effective in that role? Did she help one of them more than the other?

8. What did you think of Eve's decision not to follow through on her commitment to the milliner in Tyler?

9. What did you think of Chance's attitude about his dyslexia?

10. What did you think was really at the heart of Chance and his father's strained relationship? Did you see any similarities between the two men?

11. Do you think Chance's father truly loved him? Why or why not?

12. Did Leo's change from a skittish, almost belligerent boy at the beginning to a happy, trusting boy at the end ring true to you? Why or why not?

REQUEST YOUR FREE BOOKS!

2 FREE INSPIRATIONAL NOVELS
PLUS 2
FREE
MYSTERY GIFTS

Love Inspired

HISTORICAL

INSPIRATIONAL HISTORICAL ROMANCE

YES! Please send me 2 FREE Love Inspired® Historical novels and my 2 FREE mystery gifts (gifts are worth about $10). After receiving them, if I don't wish to receive any more books, I can return the shipping statement marked "cancel." If I don't cancel, I will receive 4 brand-new novels every month and be billed just $4.74 per book in the U.S. or $5.24 per book in Canada. That's a saving of at least 21% off the cover price. It's quite a bargain! Shipping and handling is just 50¢ per book in the U.S. and 75¢ per book in Canada.* I understand that accepting the 2 free books and gifts places me under no obligation to buy anything. I can always return a shipment and cancel at any time. Even if I never buy another book, the two free books and gifts are mine to keep forever.

102/302 IDN F5CN

Name	(PLEASE PRINT)	
Address		Apt. #
City	State/Prov.	Zip/Postal Code

Signature (if under 18, a parent or guardian must sign)

Mail to the **Harlequin® Reader Service:**
IN U.S.A.: P.O. Box 1867, Buffalo, NY 14240-1867
IN CANADA: P.O. Box 609, Fort Erie, Ontario L2A 5X3

Want to try two free books from another series?
Call 1-800-873-8635 or visit www.ReaderService.com.

* Terms and prices subject to change without notice. Prices do not include applicable taxes. Sales tax applicable in N.Y. Canadian residents will be charged applicable taxes. Offer not valid in Quebec. This offer is limited to one order per household. Not valid for current subscribers to Love Inspired Historical books. All orders subject to credit approval. Credit or debit balances in a customer's account(s) may be offset by any other outstanding balance owed by or to the customer. Please allow 4 to 6 weeks for delivery. Offer available while quantities last.

Your Privacy—The Harlequin® Reader Service is committed to protecting your privacy. Our Privacy Policy is available online at www.ReaderService.com or upon request from the Harlequin Reader Service.

We make a portion of our mailing list available to reputable third parties that offer products we believe may interest you. If you prefer that we not exchange your name with third parties, or if you wish to clarify or modify your communication preferences, please visit us at www.ReaderService.com/consumerchoice or write to us at Harlequin Reader Service Preference Service, P.O. Box 9062, Buffalo, NY 14269. Include your complete name and address.

LIH13R

Reclaiming the Runaway Bride

Seven years and two broken engagements haven't erased
Garrett Mitchell from Molly Scott's mind. Her employer insists
Molly and Garrett belong together. To appease the well-meaning
matchmaker, the pair agrees to a pretend courtship. But too late,
Molly finds herself falling for a man who might never trust her.

Garrett is a prominent Denver attorney now, not the naive
seventeen-year-old who always felt second-best. Surely the string of
suitors Molly's left behind only proves her fickleness. Does Garrett
dare believe that she has only ever been waiting for him? The third
engagement could be the charm, for his first—and only—love.

Charity
HOUSE

Finally a Bride

by

RENEE RYAN

*Available November 2013 wherever
Love Inspired Historical books are sold.*